How did she tell him she couldn't risk kissing him again?

"We're only friends. Nothing more. Haley assured me you're not engaged…Ryan is the one getting married."

Jared drew back. "You didn't believe me?"

"At the diner, Ryan said you had wedding business. Trixie said she was going to be the entertainment for a bachelor party. So I thought…"

"I can see where that might have been confusing."

He had the good sense not to laugh. She credited him with that, though believing she'd kissed an engaged man—and loved it, had sent her anxiety soaring. But that was all he had to say? "Yes. Confusing," she huffed.

"So now you know there's nothing improper about my attraction to you." His lips curved into a sexy smile. He crooked his finger, then patted a spot on the blanket beside him.

Camilla stood rigid. The man oozed with seduction. He didn't understand the war taking place inside her. If she surrendered now, it would be the same as tumbling ten thousand feet off Rendezvous Mountain and landing crumbled at the bottom. She had to leave. Had to go home. She didn't belong in Wyoming. Plus, she'd watched the agony her sister endured from a broken heart. Branna was stronger. Wiser. Had mended and bounced back.

But she wasn't Branna.

Emotions swirled like an eddy. Thoughts spun like a tornado in her mind. Love scared her more than she ever imagined. A broken heart just might kill her.

Praise for Linda Joyce

BAYOU BORN, Book One of the Fleur de Lis series, is a 2014 RONE Award Finalist.

~*~

BAYOU BOUND, Book Two of the Fleur de Lis series, won 1st Place in Romance from Southeastern Writers Association. It received 4.5-Star reviews from *InD'tale Magazine* and *Long and Short Reviews*.

~*~

"Linda Joyce delivers another compelling story of second chances that will have you heeding the Bayou's beckoning."

~Melissa Klein, author of Her Hometown Hero

~*~

"Linda Joyce is the master of emotional impact and epic storytelling."

~Kathy L Wheeler, author of Color of Betrayal

Bayou Beckons

by

Linda Joyce

Fleur de Lis Series, Book 3

This is a work of fiction. Names, characters, places, and incidents are either the product of the author's imagination or are used fictitiously, and any resemblance to actual persons living or dead, business establishments, events, or locales, is entirely coincidental.

Bayou Beckons

Contact Information: info@thewildrosepress.com

Cover Art by *Kim Mendoza*

The Wild Rose Press, Inc.
PO Box 708
Adams Basin, NY 14410-0708
Visit us at www.thewildrosepress.com

Publishing History
First Champagne Rose Edition, 2015
Print ISBN 978-1-5092-0122-8
Digital ISBN 978-1-5092-0123-5

Fleur de Lis Series, Book 3
Published in the United States of America

Dedication

This book is dedicated to the people of the Gulf Coast who lost their lives, to those who survived, and those who continue to thrive ten years after Hurricane Katrina—southerners of sturdy stock who know there's no place like home.

Acknowledgments

I fell in love with Wyoming during a family vacation to Yellowstone National Park. Afterward, my friend Kim Pentecost put me in touch with Rancher M (I'm protecting his identity). He gave generously of his time, explaining about the climate, public land, water rights, ditch riders, bears, and more. I'm grateful for the knowledge he imparted. Any information less than accurate is either my misunderstanding or poetic license. And thank you, Kim Pentecost, for sharing your friends with me.

Obtaining weather reports—easy peasy. Yet research about Hurricane Katrina and the Pearl River proved challenging. I reached out to Jeremy Pittari, Managing Editor of the *Picayune Item*. His links provided the answers I needed. Thank you, Mr. Pittari.

An on-my-hands-and-knees bowing THANK YOU to my writing group, Leigh Jones, Leah Sims, and Melissa Klein. I value your insights and dedication.

A big hug to my beta readers, Latasha Clements, Peggy O'Keefe, and Cheryl Walz. You made this a richer story. I appreciate your time and your support. And to Dr. Amy Reich for being such a wonderful listener and reading for me.

Sending love to Marilyn Baron, Yong Takahashi, and Tracey Gee for their undying support.

To Linda's Lovelies, I thank each of you for your interest and support in my writing.

And to my loving, supportive husband, Don, I thank you for sharing your life with me. True love is what knits us together on the journey of life.

Chapter 1

Country music twanged from the jukebox as leather soles from two-steppers scraped the wooden dance floor inside the warehouse dressed up like an old Western saloon. The din from the crowd at Lucky Seven fueled Camilla's excitement, putting a zip in her step. The tunes might not be Cajun Zydeco, but her feet didn't care.

"How about another dance?" the tall cowboy asked when the music ended.

Camilla brushed her long auburn hair over her shoulders, then shrugged and offered her most sheepish eyes. "Sorry, darlin', I see a game of pool calling my name."

She batted her lashes. He was nice enough. Polite. Tanned. Callused hands. Jeans that hugged his butt beautifully. But her rule since leaving home—only one dance allowed.

Occasionally, she danced between the sheets. No matter how sexy, how strong, how charming the dude. Only once. No entanglements. No dates. No future. The rule played to benefit them more than her. Soon her time in Jackson Hole would end. She would go home. No man in tow.

Sauntering toward the next room where groups of men gathered around four pool tables, she entered the noisy billiards area. Long neck bottles of half-finished beers cluttered a shelf. The yeasty aroma of spilt brews filled her senses. Heads of dead animals decorated the walls. Metal signs advertised Skoal, Copenhagen, and Redman—part of the rodeo culture in Wyoming. All the men playing pool dressed in cowboy boots and jeans. The tourists were easy to spot. They wore colorful polo shirts. In the far right corner, the winner of a game that had just ended sported a plaid shirt, dinner-plate belt buckle, and a light gray, spotless Stetson. Peacock—she dubbed him, the term her Granddaddy Lind called a man who dressed too dapper—scooped up several fifty-dollar bills. The nickname fit the cowboy as perfectly as the expensive hat on his head. Something about the square of his shoulders, his shit-eating grin, deep dimples, and overall too-proud bearing made her itch to teach him a lesson. A bad habit of hers after what happened with Steven.

"Hey, y'all," she called out in her best Louisiana drawl. "I'd like to play." She flitted further in their direction.

Snickers came from the group of men who'd just lost their wagers.

"Sure," Peacock said. "One-fifty is the buy-in. When I win, I'll take you for a steak dinner." He stepped away from the group and closer to her. Looking up, she met his gaze and held it. It would be a cold, humid-less day in Louisiana before she'd back down from a challenge.

"And what will you give me"—using her most southern coquettishness, she brought her hand to rest on her chest—"if *I* win?"

The onlookers chuckled. She imagined their minds

rolling in gutters, like on Bourbon Street on a Friday night, but if that was the case, she had them exactly where she wanted them—thinking she was an outsider, a silly female, and they had the skills to teach her a thing or two. Hubris hooked them.

Peacock took a half step closer. Leaning in, he sniffed as though trying to catch a whiff of her scent and whispered, "Anything. You. Want." His warm breath brushed her ear. With moves as smooth as his voice, he started to slip his arm around her waist, but she twirled the opposite way and grabbed a pool cue leaning against the wall. Either way, the game would begin or she'd defend herself if he tried to touch her again.

"Game on," one of the bystanders said eagerly.

"Rack'em boys," Camilla said with a saucy tilt of her head. "Mr. Stetson, how much did you win before?"

"One-fifty," another bystander called out.

"The pot is three hundred." She smiled wide, issuing the challenge. He would take it. No way a man like him would let a flea-of-a-girl like her best him. She laid three one-hundred dollar bills on the edge of the table. All of her earnings from last Friday night's pool game.

Peacock narrowed his eyes. "I've never lost to a girl before."

"And maybe you won't this time, either." She tried sounding completely innocent.

Crack. She broke and the game began. Chatter from players at the other tables drifted over, but the group surrounding Camilla remained silent.

It didn't take her long.

Peacock shifted his weight from one foot to the

other, then repositioned the Stetson with the brim sitting lower to shadow his eyes.

After she sank her last ball in a pocket, she stood with the pool cue triumphantly beside her. Her gaze locked on Peacock's. He shoved up the brim of his hat.

"You played me," he snarled. "Not ladylike behavior. I might have to teach you some manners."

"Yeah," a man growled. "Let's show her some—"

"Wait. I played fair and square. Is this how you treat a lady in the West?" she demanded.

Peacock pulled cash from his pocket and tossed it on the table as though it were yesterday's trash. "Three hundred."

When he narrowed his eyes to a tiny squint, her breath caught in her chest.

"Now, gentlemen, I'm asking you, who exactly hustled whom?" She handed fifty bucks to each of the three players, their losses from the earlier game. Their expressions of confusion satisfied her pride.

Peacock snorted, then turned his back and walked away. "Who gives money away like that?" His voice rose above the din. "Fools. That's who. Fools."

"It's not right," one man said. "A man's got to have his dignity. You tricked him. Tricked us. What else are you hustling?"

"Shut up," a second man said. "She gave you back your money. We ought to buy her a beer."

Camilla scooped up her ante and tucked the winning money into the front pocket of her frayed jean shorts. "Nice playing with y'all."

The three men circled her. "What's your hurry?" When one of the men grabbed her arm, she jerked away. "Don't touch me." Her gaze darted from man to man. Swallowing hard, she took in a deep breath to mask her fear, then released her breath and squared her shoulders.

"Little lady, we know how to take care of a woman as good as any dude from the south."

"Excuse me." A tall, tanned man inserted himself into the group. Blond streaked his sandy brown hair, and a pale thin scar in front of his ear ran from his hairline to his jaw, adding to his ruggedly handsome looks. She guessed he was a businessman from the dark khaki slacks and crisply pressed, light blue shirt with a button-down collar. His eyes glowed deep blue. Camilla drowned in those eyes. Her mouth dried like someone had stuffed it with cotton. Stunned, she shook her head. "Gorgeous" ran through her brain as though it were the only word in the world she remembered.

"Honey, I've been waiting over by the bar. Thought you stood me up." He grasped her hand, hooked their arms together, and led her away from the group. Hypnotized, she followed his lead. He had her on an imaginary tether. They exited the billiards room, skirted the dance floor and headed toward a booth on the opposite side of the saloon. His touch produced pulses warming her entire body. She blinked, fighting off a faint. Never in her life had she fainted. Certainly not over a man. But this one made her wish for a veranda, sweet tea, soft music, candlelight, and a bed.

At least for one dance.

He pointed to a booth where a scantily clad, stunning brunette woman sat. She wore a man's sport coat draped around her shoulders. To keep her warm or to cover herself, Camilla couldn't be sure.

"Thank you, Jared," the woman said. "Those guys

could've gotten…difficult."

"You're welcome. Now, I've got to find my brother and get him to the condo." The man leaned down and shook the woman's hand. "See you soon." He nodded before leaving.

Camilla slunk into the seat opposite the woman. Dazed, she turned to watch Blue Eyes exit her life. Her fingers itched to rake through his hair, give him the just-from-bed look. Her rule since leaving home was only one dance, but dang if he wasn't the first man she'd break it for. Panic dredged a pit in her gut. How would she find him again?

The woman across the table interrupted her panic attack. "Hi. I'm Trixie. Are you okay?"

"Camilla Lind. Who's that?"

"Jared Richardson. I asked him to step in. One of the guys in that group…he likes to play rough." The woman's gaze swept over Camilla, and she tried not to squirm under the intense scrutiny. Trixie appeared at least ten years older with an air of complete confidence. When she offered her hand, Camilla reached out to shake it.

Trixie held on to Camilla's wrist and opened her palm. "You're like a redheaded Barbie in that peasant blouse, Daisy-Duke shorts, and cowboy boots…that guy thinking he's Ken. It's Friday night. Getting on to hookup time. This is a place for finding one-nighters, not life-timers." Trixie traced one of the lines in Camilla's palm. "Despite your appearance, you're the kind of woman who wants a man for keeps."

Camilla pursed her lips. The woman's uncanny ability to read her drove her discomfort mountain high.

Trixie laughed and released Camilla's hand. "My

dad owns this place. I've been watching the Friday night mating ritual since I was a young teenager." She pointed to stairs leading up to a landing and door. "We live up there. I've seen it all."

"How do you know…Jared?"

"He came in to finalize some details. I'll be the entertainment for the bachelor party. Belly dancer extraordinaire."

Camilla's stomach clenched. The man was getting married? The image of her private dance with him sprouted wings and flew away. Just as well. No sense in breaking the rule when she was so close to leaving Jackson and going home. Home to prove how much she'd grown up. How much she'd changed.

Her mind fell in line behind that kind of thinking and threw daggers at her curiosity and yearning.

He isn't married yet.

But her heart had a plan of its own. Before she left Jackson, she'd somehow manage to have a turn around the dance floor with Jared.

A tiny voice in her head shouted, "Remember your sister and Steven?"

****

The next night, Camilla slid booted feet into the stirrups of the saddle anchored on a barstool. She grabbed the horn for support, rose up, and waved a shot glass at the man behind the counter. "Fetch me another one, bartender!"

The large mirror over the bar offered a panoramic view of the scene behind her. An energy of eagerness rippled in the air. The atmosphere danced with promise, the kind that teased cowboys into believing they'd get lucky on Saturday night, maybe at pool, or on the dance floor, or better still after the bar closed if a beauty decided to take them home. Gazing in the mirror, the face she sought, the one who'd captured her interest never arrived. A small hollowness opened in her chest. At the very least, she wanted another chance to drown in his blue eyes for just one dance.

"I love the Wild West!" She clunked the small, empty glass on the bar and began to move it around until it sat squarely over a silver dollar inlaid on the bar top.

"Camilla," Mack, the bartender came to stand before her, "you told me to cut you off after two. I gave you three. No more tequila, even for the sexiest southerner in the place. The well is dry. Cup of coffee?"

Flipping her long hair over her shoulder, she plopped into the seat of the saddle. "Ouch. That's hard." She rubbed her butt. "I'm the only southerner in this place. Did you know that where I'm from Camilla Lind is known for drinking others, even grown men, under the table?"

"Maybe," Mack said, "but here, we don't know a Lind from the wind. You want the coffee or what?"

She shook her head. "Coffee would ruin the taste of the liquid gold you poured from that bottle behind you. Coffee's a terrible suggestion."

"Then say yes to one of those guys who keep bugging you to dance. It's a good way to sober up."

"Nope. My time in Jackson will soon be over. Not interested in finding a man."

"Maybe they want a dance, not a date."

"Ahh, I can see you truly haven't learned anything about me all summer. I have a way of attracting the perfectly wrong guy every time. I always choose prize-winning jerks."

"The irony"—the bartender poured coffee into the shot glass before her—"if that's true, you've got a streak going, and if I choose a guy for you, that wouldn't mess with your averages."

She gingerly picked up the shot glass—it wasn't as hot as she imagined—and downed the dark liquid in one big gulp. "Thanks, Mack." She clunked the glass, then slid it across the bar top. "I think I'll call it a night. Get off this wooden horse, and walk off into the moonlight."

"I'll find someone to walk you home." The concern in his voice was touching.

"I'll be just fine, cowboy." She offered a wry smile and a wink.

"See you same time tomorrow night." Mack tipped his cowboy hat.

"I'm that predictable. I'm going to surprise you soon and ride south into the sunset."

"Sun sets in the West, little lady."

"Except in New Orleans, there it rises over the West Bank. I'll be heading there in exactly six weeks."

"I think you're drunk. Walk a straight line, toe-to-toe. If you make it to the front door and you're still upright, you can go. Otherwise, I'm finding someone to walk you home."

Thoughts of home sobered her. Jackson, Wyoming, could never be home. Just a pleasant respite to the painful scene she left behind at Fleur de Lis. The pain of her disgrace rooted deep in her brain and her heart over the last year. Betraying her sister made her no better than a cattle rustler or scum floating on water in the bayou. Had Branna truly forgiven her?

"Go on. Walk." Mack shooed her from the bar.

For his benefit, she exaggerated the toe-to-toe walk. When she reached the front door, she turned and curtseyed, as any good belle would do at a southern ball, before slipping out of the big double doors.

Entering her tiny apartment, she wiped makeup from her face, stripped down to her underwear and crawled into bed. Before coming west, she never pulled the covers up before eleven p.m. on a Saturday night. Change had commandeered her life. Hopefully, the path of "the mostly straight and very narrow" would prove to her family she'd changed.

Hope springs eternal. She had that. The bayou beckoned.

Resisting the call—pointless.

Chapter 2

Camilla yawned and turned the key in the front-door lock to the Mountain View Diner. Sunrise at five a.m. in Jackson Hole had taken getting used to. The good thing about it, early light served as a natural alarm clock. The hour of her shift would shock her mother.

"Maybe a photo of my timecard will prove how much I've changed." She pushed open the door, then laser-sighted the coffee machine behind the counter.

"Coffee," she groaned with delight. Someone had started it brewing. Who or when didn't matter, they got a gold star in her book. Like a zombie grunting after prey, she headed for the back counter. The sooner caffeine pumped through her veins, the better. She grabbed a mug and poured in hot steaming java, delighted with the scent hitting her olfactory senses. A deep inhale of the aroma cranked up her addictive craving.

Slurp!

The sound echoed against the tile and shiny stainless steel surfaces of the diner. Camilla winced as her grandmother's voice drifted into her head, "So unladylike."

Only then did she notice Darcy. Bathed in clear morning light, the owner's daughter sat in the last booth lining the long bank of windows that faced the street. Though surprised to see her there, it was too early for

Camilla to ponder the reason. Not enough coffee yet.

She slurped again.

Darcy was up to something. Dressed in a crisp light blue waitress's uniform. Long blonde hair in a prim bun at the nape of her neck. Minimal makeup. A shocker in contrast to Darcy's usual five pounds of biker-chick cosmetics. Only one reason a woman changed her routine so drastically. A man.

Camilla walked back around the front counter and leaned against it, momentarily pondering what man Darcy had set her sights on this time.

"You always early?" Darcy rose from the booth, then positioned herself next to Camilla and gazed out the window.

"Momma wouldn't believe it." Camilla chuckled under her breath.

"Every time I see you, you always look like you've walked out of a photo shoot—so put together and perky, even after a long shift. How do you do it? Or is it in the DNA of all southern belles?"

Camilla shrugged. "I guess you catch me coming and going on good days." An ironed uniform and white apron helped project the image she wanted to convey. Clean and wholesome. The nice girl-next-door. To be called *good* would be a stretch unless sarcasm was involved.

"You're as prompt as that cowboy." Darcy nodded toward the street. Beyond the diner's windows, a man dressed in a black t-shirt and sweat pants jogged on the asphalt street.

Holding the mug with both hands, Camilla took a long sip of coffee and relaxed into the caffeine infusion. Beside her, Darcy drooled. Camilla's gaze drifted to the object of Darcy's stare.

She swallowed. Her heart fluttered into her throat. She recognized the eyes. The man from the Lucky Seven. Blue Eyes. Jared, Trixie had said. Camilla focused on the view. Vibrations rose in her chest as though someone had added vinegar to baking soda and fizzy sensations rose to her brain. If he'd crooked his finger at her, she'd be out the door and following him.

His stride was long and even, his legs moved effortlessly as his arms pumped rhythmically with his legs. She imagined him as a proud buck bounding across an open field in sync with natural surroundings. She sighed. A reaction she hated. No one would *ever* describe her as a simpering belle. Usually she didn't give blond guys a second glance. But this one…clear blue eyes, the color of a Wyoming sky, grabbed her. If he stared into hers and promised her magic beans or a ride on a magic carpet, she'd believe every word he said.

"Look!" Darcy cried. "He's been by here every morning for the last week at exactly the same time." She offered an eager wave in return to the jogger's quick one. In her enthusiasm, she bumped Camilla's arm and coffee sloshed over the side of the mug.

"Hey, watch it." Camilla took a step away and reached for a napkin. "How do you know he's a cowboy and not some accountant from Philly in for a two week vacation?" She wiped her hand and the spill. "Even they wear old Tony Lamas and slightly stained felt hats when they come for breakfast here." A stab of anguish slid into her gut. Darcy had set her sights on the one man she wanted.

"Just do." Darcy shrugged. "I can smell a phony

from forty paces."

"Guess it's like knowing the difference between a Cajun and a Creole," Camilla replied, trying for nonchalant. It wouldn't do to show interest in the man. Darcy had a mean streak, but what did it matter if she wanted him, too? In six weeks, she'd be leaving Darcy and Jackson behind for good.

She headed toward the kitchen to punch in for her shift. She set her jaw. If her family ever knew she sighed over a man, they'd never let her live it down. Jared. A solid man's-man name. Why hadn't she asked the belly dancer more about him?

"What? Creole?" Darcy called out.

"Never mind." Camilla shoved her timecard into place. The clock clunked loudly and printed six a.m. on the card. She waved at Tom, the morning cook, then scooted back through the swinging door to ready the diner for the regulars. The same five men arrived at six thirty a.m., every day like clockwork. They were old timers and diner celebrities, she'd learned soon after starting the job at the Mountain View.

As she readied her station, her mind settled on the man who'd rescued her on Friday night. He didn't fit in with the Stetson and jeans crowd at the bar. He'd presented himself as the perfect gentleman, but she accepted Darcy's word about Blue Eyes as gospel. If the woman said he was a real cowboy, then he had to be. She never lied. Could a cowboy pass for a cultured man?

Camilla shook her head. People always tried to put her in a slot where she didn't fit. She wasn't the perfect hostess like her sister. Nor the talented photographer like her cousin. Didn't fly planes like her brother and only male cousin. Her competitive streak was born from always trying to break from the southern mold she'd been poured into. So why would she try to put Jared into a slot when he clearly didn't fit? Cowboy and culture could work.

Could he be a rich rancher with another life and only in town for the summer? Darcy had informed her when she started at Mountain View that summertime brought the overly conscious health-set to Jackson Hole, Wyoming. They brought money to spend, and sometimes left attitude instead of gratitude in the form of gratuities.

Hmmpf. A couple of times back in St. Louis, customers had tipped her with their haughty sense of entitlement, but that rarely happened now. Experience was the best teacher. She'd worked in a fine dining restaurant in St. Louis, a steakhouse in Kansas City, and bartended in Denver before the Mountain View Diner in Wyoming.

"Last time he was in town—it was before you worked here—he came in every day at the same time. I wonder what brings him to town now." Darcy tugged off her sweater and hung it on the old-fashioned coat rack by the door.

"Yay-ya," Camilla drawled imitating her New Orleanian grandmother's accent. She'd perfected it, exaggerated it, and delighted most of the male customers with it, who in turn, left their phone numbers along with a large cash tip, which tickled her.

"So we're clear, I'm taking morning shift so *I* can wait on that cowboy when he arrives. Exactly at seven thirty. I'm betting on it."

Camilla nodded. No other hints needed. Darcy was

making her claim, marking territory. Rarely had the first daughter of the diner stepped into the dining room to work on Sunday mornings. Darcy, a great short-order cook, ran the kitchen like her life—full-throttle energy, take no prisoners, and everything was a competition during her twenty-six years. She'd lived in the slightly younger woman's world. Mapped it. Traveled those roads, running headfirst into disaster.

"You think you've figured out his type? As I understand it from Trixie, he's getting married. She's the belly dancing entertainment for the bachelor party."

"But he ain't married yet, right? Besides, she might have told you that to keep you off his scent. Fine looking man. Prime. I think he's fair game until he's got a ring on his finger."

"Fair game?" Camilla squeaked. Darcy always remained true to form, whereas, all she'd risk was a dance with the man at Lucky Seven. That showed marked change in her thinking. She used to share Darcy's no-holds-barred attitude…until her sister and Steven.

"Yep. I'll consider it a wedding present to the groom." Darcy smiled.

Her attitude bored under Camilla's skin like a chigger bite that needed scratching. Jared had rescued her, not Darcy, like Robin Hood. His mere touch scorched her skin and set her heart fluttering on overdrive, fast enough to send her to the moon.

With one hand on her cocked hip, Camilla patted the back of her hair and flashed a coy grin. Not that she would allow it to lead anywhere—but the woman beside her could use a little friendly competition. "Game on." A shiver of excitement raced up her spine.

Darcy frowned.

Camilla ignored her pout. Flipping on the lights, the diner lit up like City Park in New Orleans at Christmas time. In her mind, a voice yelled, "Camera! Action!"

Yes. Her life had become just that surreal. But the challenge of teasing Darcy and flirting with the cowboy added the dose of reality she needed. The old guys she'd met in Jackson, ranchers mostly, referred to a woman that caught their eye as a *filly*. She hadn't heard the term *stud* used in a long time, but if ever a man deserved the label, it was Jared. Lean, strong. Handsome in khakis and sweat pants. She might faint if she saw him in a pair of butt-hugging jean.

"Men. Such trouble makers…and such lovers." Camilla sighed and turned her attention to work. She placed five mugs bearing the Mountain View's logo on the counter in front of five stools, starting at the far wall. Grabbing utensils rolled in a red-checkered bandana from a galvanized bucket, she placed them beside each mug. Any moment now, Tom would holler for her to pick up fresh cinnamon rolls delivered by two little old lady bakers. The Fivers as everyone called them, ate the homemade baked goods before ordering a protein breakfast. They claimed the benefit of being old was eating dessert before their meal.

Almost finished with setup, Camilla walked through the second door to the kitchen heading for the walk-in fridge. She needed a carton of cream to fill the china cow creamers.

After pushing hard on the walk-in door to close it, Camilla stopped. She scanned the large open kitchen expecting to find Tom at the flattop grill prepping home fries and hash browns. No Tom. No Haley either. The dishwasher was late again.

Camilla's breath hitched in her chest when daylight slid across the kitchen's concrete floor. Someone had opened the back door. A complete no-no once the front door had been opened for business. She froze statue-still.

"Hush, now."

Camilla strained to determine the voices. Tom's whispers reached her ears.

"You go home. I'll call Mary and tell her to call another dishwasher into work."

Sniffles increased into a strangled sob.

Unable to ignore whatever was taking place out of sight, Camilla set the carton of cream on the worktable. She stepped closer to the corner. "Hello?" No one responded. Sounds of a squelched sob drifted to her.

Unable to restrain concern and curiosity, she rounded the corner. Framed in the doorway, sunlight like a halo around the pair, Tom patted Haley on the top of her head like a man terrified of a teenaged girl's tears.

"Oh, look, Haley. It's Camilla." Tom waved her over. "I'll take care of your Fivers if you'll take over here."

Tom stalked away without a backward glance.

"Haley," Camilla said softly. "Honey, whatever it is, it can't be that bad."

Haley's hands hid her face. Her shoulders shook as she whimpered and sniffled. "Go 'way. Don't look at me."

Uneasiness gripped Camilla's gut. "Let's sit you down." With an arm around the teen, she guided Haley to the chair outside the manager's office. "Sit."

Haley did as ordered.

"Now, let me see."

When the teen lifted her gaze to Camilla, involuntarily she gasped, "Oh, God!" Her stomach clenched tight like someone ringing a wet mop dry. Haley's cheek shined bright red. Her right eye was puffy, headed for swollen, and slightly discolored. A thin cut stretched from her hairline, across her cheek and stopped on the bridge of her nose. Had someone wearing a ring backhanded her?

Camilla ran. She grabbed a hand towel from the stack on the shelf. Raced to the ice machine. The lid crashed against the side with a *bang*. She scooped ice into the towel before sprinting back to Haley. "Put this on your face. Now!"

Haley obeyed. "Owww!"

Camilla lifted the teen's chin to examine the rest of the girl's exposed face for evidence of further injury. A dribble of blood had pooled at the corner of Haley's mouth.

"Girl, I've warned you about him. You can't tell me you *fell* into a door," Camilla insisted, anger igniting in her gut. "Nor can you tell me that you *fell* on the stairs at your mother's condo. I've had it with excuses. The evidence doesn't lie." With her fists on her waist, she stalked to the back door, then back to Haley, "You're going back to Cody, home to your daddy."

"Nuh uh."

"I don't know that language. You, young lady, are leaving town. Today." She turned to look over her shoulder and glanced around. Had she spoken those words? What spewed from her mouth sounded exactly like her mother. So it had come to that.

"But—"

"Don't you dare 'but' me, Haley O'Connor. And, keep that ice pack on your face. He could *kill* you next time. This has escalated each month. Besides, I'll bet I could have him arrested for statutory rape."

"Nuh uh. I'm old enough."

"You're not eighteen yet." Camilla strode to the large medicine box hanging on the wall near the office. She pulled gauze and individual wrapped cleaning swabs, then stood in front of the teen. "Move the ice pack. Let me clean up that cut. If you need stitches, I'm calling an ambulance."

Gently, she wiped Haley's face.

"Oooo."

What she though was a cut was more of a surface scrape. It should heal without leaving a scar. Haley, she'd learned in recent weeks, had many. The invisible kind, not apparent to the naked eye.

"Your momma's out of town again?"

Haley nodded.

"I'm sure by now Tom has called Mary. She'll get someone to take your shift. Don't worry about this dishwashing job. And, unless you want me to call the police and have them investigate *him*, you're going to march yourself over to my apartment, keep ice on your face—lie on the couch, then after my shift, I'll figure out how to get you home."

Haley hung her head low, then bobbled, yes.

"Good. Now, give me your cell phone. No chance are you calling that scum-bag. Here are my keys. Keep the ice on your face. I'm going to stand here and watch you enter my apartment. And you better stay put until I get there…or I swear, I'll grab the next cop, and we'll both hunt you down."

Camilla waited at the diner's back door until Haley walked the next block, then climbed the stairs to the apartment. The teen waved before entering, and Camilla waved back. Everything in her being said the scum knocking Haley around would—sooner or later—hurt the girl so bad she might not recover.

She never thought it possible, but some scumbags were worse than Steven Sterling. That was another something she'd add to her checklist of life's lessons learned.

"Camilla!" Darcy yelled. "If you're done playing nursemaid, we need you upfront. Now."

Shaken out of her musing, Camilla closed, then locked the back door. She washed her hands and grabbed the carton of cream. Before she pushed on the swinging door to the diner, she heard the chatter of customers. The Sunday early birds had arrived.

"Hey, y'all." She greeted the Fivers at the dining counter.

They waved or nodded and continued their morning debate.

She turned to find the ceramic cow creamers lined up, waiting to be filled. Darcy or Tom must have pulled them from the shelf above. Carefully, she poured cream into them.

Darcy scooted up and bumped shoulders with her, which caused her to spill cream on the countertop. "Camilla, he's here early, today. I've got the customers covered at table ten and eleven, but here"—Darcy shoved food tickets at her—"take care of the tables so I can take care of him. I'm waiting on Blond Honey."

"Blond Honey?"

"The cowboy," Darcy said insistently, then thrust the tickets into her hand.

"Oh. You mean, Blue Eyes? Sure. Good luck." But she didn't mean it for a minute.

A second later, the tinny bells over the front door tinkled when the door opened and in walked the cowboy she and Darcy waited to see. He looked rugged in faded jeans, black cowboy boots, and black cowboy hat. Camilla fanned herself and tried to avoid staring. His hotness ignited a flame inside her. His tanned face and just-from-the shower shaggy hair framed eyes so blue she couldn't look away. She recalled his grasp on her arm at the Lucky Seven and the sensual sensations that raced through her, making her want to tangle with him between some sheets. A private tango for two. But he was off limits.

Jared smiled in her direction and gave a short wave.

Camilla's cheeks burned like fire. If he could read minds, what would he think? She couldn't pass for the wholesome girl-next-door. Rather than face him with embarrassment emblazoned on her face, she entered the kitchen to hide. Through the small window in the door, she reluctantly gawked at his rugged beauty with awe.

His eyes reminded her of the blue waters of the Gulf of Mexico…and home. Maybe she was more than a tad homesick.

"Camilla," one of the Fivers called out. "More coffee, please."

"Coming, darlin', I aim to please." She pushed open the door, grabbed the coffee carafe and poured.

"Coffee all around."

"Say, young lady," another man called out. "Where'd you say you were from?"

"From down where they drink sweet tea." So far, she hadn't met a person yet who could stick a pin on a map and hit Bayou Petite, Mississippi.

After filling mugs down the row of Fivers, she snuck a peek at Blue. Darcy preened as she seated him at the corner table. If this were still untamed territory, the owner's daughter could be called at worst a jezebel, at best a tease. The woman had dumped all her other customers for the chance to cater solely to one man. That wasn't good business. It smacked of impoliteness, something her mother would never stand for.

Good manners were the only thing Momma had ever expected of her.

Camilla couldn't pull her attention away from Jared. She swallowed, but her mouth remained dry. Uninvited, he'd entered her dreams last night. The intrusion had left her unsettled. When she woke, her pulse pounded like a bass drum with a double beat. The man sparked excitement that flamed to exhilaration deep in her gut.

But he was getting married.

And she was going home.

"Nothing can come of this," she muttered dejectedly.

She started another pot of coffee brewing to stop gawking at him.

Never again would she do to another woman what she'd done to her sister. While she had no defense, she'd learned her actions with Steven had been rooted in years of jealousy and competitiveness. Her feelings for Jared were virginal by comparison.

"Yeah, as if anyone could ever utter virginal and my name in the same sentence." The past bore down on her like a vise. Grandmother Lind had cautioned her about her wild ways, yet in the face of her past despicable behaviors, she had been the only one to offer unconditional love. Grandmother Lind was old South.

Camilla considered her time away from home a self-imposed penance and a voyage of self-discovery. Yet some of her old habits still died hard. When comparing Jackson Hole to the South, where things were counted as centuries old rather than mere decades, it was the Wild West. She had tried to squelch her competitive side—it always gifted her with trouble. The Wild West thrived on competition—proof of the rodeos every night up in Cody.

She had to leave at the end of the summer season, wanted to go home, and didn't need any reins holding her back. However, Jared made her skin tingle and her insides hotter than a roaring fire in winter. If the situation were different, she might consider changing her plans just to see where the journey with him would take her.

"For now, flirting won't hurt." She nodded to convince herself. She'd played plenty of games in the past to draw the attention of a man. She wouldn't cross the line with Jared. One dance couldn't hurt…on the dance floor at Lucky Seven. Nothing more. But Darcy didn't need to know her plans.

She smiled, then whispered, "Darcy, let's just see if you are able to keep up in a Wild West game of tug-of-war over Blue."

Chapter 3

Jared entered the mostly empty Mountain View Diner with a small package tucked at his side. Aromas of coffee brewing and bacon frying triggered his hunger pangs. A quick scan of the place made it clear that his older brother hadn't arrived, which he expected, and it allowed him a few minutes of private time. His brother needn't know he sought a woman with the loveliest face when she smiled. He wanted her to cast that magnetic look of delight again in his direction.

After Trixie had pointed out a woman in need of rescuing at Lucky Seven, she insisted he play knight-in-shining-armor and liberate the woman from a group of pool-playing roughnecks. His conscience urged him to answer Trixie's plea, but then sadly, he'd been forced to a quick exit from the saloon, after which he kicked himself for not getting her name and number. Playing babysitter to his brother was hell, but someone had to ensure Ryan wouldn't overdo beer and tequila shots. Later Trixie called and said her intuition had a message for him. She gave him clues like they were playing a TV game show. After some irritating finagling, she opened up when his patience hit a wall, but not before making him promise to draw plans to redesign the kitchen in her home, upstairs from the bar, before he left Wyoming. She gave him the name of the smiling woman he'd disentangled from a potential brawl and shared where the woman worked. This morning, he came to the Mountain View on a specific mission—to ask Camilla for a date.

But it had taken twenty-four hours to come to that decision.

Uncertainty bothered him. He preferred calm decisive action in the face of every event. "Move it along" had been his motto for years. People who waffled over what to do in any given situation made him nervous. They didn't trust themselves, and he sure couldn't trust them, especially if a life was on the line. Like in a rodeo ring with a pissed-off bull, on a trail in the mountains where bears roamed, or in a bar where guns could show during a bar fight.

Yet he'd hesitated a full day before determining a course of action regarding Camilla. That irked him. His current plans didn't include entanglements with a woman. But something weird happened Friday night when he touched her arm. A sizzle shot up his spine. When she smiled up at him, his focus blurred, his mind blanked. He floated somewhere other-worldly, lost in her radiant smile. When her face lit, it set off oohs and ahhs in his head like fireworks exploding on the Fourth of July.

It made no sense.

He'd be a fool to try to explain the effect the southern woman had on him. Something that had never happened with any other woman.

That made even less sense.

However, a strong hunch about Camilla had egged him forward. Now with family business settled and his brother heading back to the ranch that afternoon, he intended to follow up on his inklings and focus on getting a *yes* from the woman who had snagged his attention and invaded his REM sleep for the last two nights.

While waiting to be seated, he studied her. She leaned over the counter and whispered something to an old-timer, then poured coffee into the man's mug. The older guy's belly laugh sounded as though he tried too hard. But who wouldn't when Camilla followed up with a wink and a grin.

"Hey, there." A blonde waitress greeted him with a menu in hand. "Table for one?"

He glanced in Camilla's direction. The empty stool at the counter was an option, but not conducive to finalizing his best man wedding responsibilities with Ryan. "Table, yes. For two." He stepped back when the woman's eyes lit up with an eagerness that could start a bonfire.

"This way." She grabbed a second menu.

She led him to a corner booth near the front door, an easy spot for Ryan to find him, whenever his brother managed to show up. Ryan had turned partying into the likes of a rodeo competition last night. Hard liquor always kicked his older brother's butt.

"Coffee, please. Black," he told the waitress as he slid into the seat.

She handed over the menu. "I'm Darcy, and I'll be taking care of you today. Coffee for now. Anything *else* you need, I'm here."

Those same words carried an entirely different meaning from other waitresses who had waited on him. He got her double entendre, but didn't care for it. If there was any doubt about her intended meaning, the saucy shift of her shoulder and her wink clarified her point.

He nodded. “Sure thing, *ma’am*.”

The woman drew back, her surprise very clear. He smiled broadly at her. Politeness had the added benefit of keeping some women at arm’s length.

After the waitress departed, he openly scrutinized Camilla. A subtle cut of her eyes and tilt of her head suggested she was aware of his scrutiny. She licked her lips, then smoothed the front of her crisp white apron with her hands.

Those lips and those hands were ones he wanted to know.

Her accent and sassy comebacks to customers intrigued him. She reminded him of southern hospitality his New Orleans grandmother had taught him. While Camilla appeared completely confident and at ease, slight movements gave her away. Her blush spoke the loudest. He’d learned to read folks when he started in the construction business. Eye contact, a handshake, and the way a person held their head told more about them than a signature on paper.

“Your coffee.” Darcy slid a mug in front of him and blocked his view of Camilla. “Are you ready to order?”

“I’m gonna wait a few more minutes. My brother should arrive shortly.”

“You mean there are two of you?”

He wasn’t quite sure what Darcy was asking. He and Ryan weren’t twins. In fact, they didn’t have the same mother. Just shared the same crotchety old man for a father.

“Two Richardson boys in my family,” he told her hoping that satisfied her curiosity.

Before she departed, she nodded in a manner suggesting she might have hit the jackpot—double or nothing.

While he waited for Ryan, he pulled out a folded half-sheet of paper from his jean's back pocket and reviewed his Jackson list: Final punch list for grocery store construction project—check. Spices for Felicia—check. Saddle ordered for Chuck—check. Tuxedos rented—check.

Rock'n R Ranch was hosting its first wedding in ten years. The last one had been when his father married for the fifth time. That had been a large gathering, a complete cowboy roundup. Ryan's wedding would be the exact opposite. Nicole Wilson, his soon-to-be sister-in-law, planned a big-city-type formal wedding, the kind written about in magazines. He fully expected her mother to have reporters and TV cameramen present, along with the wedding photographer and videographer.

He was trying to do his part. Hell, he'd gone online and researched best man duties. It wouldn't bode well for him, or Ryan, if they messed up Nicole's dream event. She and Felicia were the only two women who lived at the ranch fulltime. Winter often dragged on long. It could be an especially bitter and cold one if Nicole was unhappy. Happy wife equaled happy life. The men of Rock'n R depended on the women for cooking and cleaning. They brought a civilized feminine touch to an otherwise motley group of confirmed bachelor cowboys.

Jared looked up when the door to the café opened.

"Hey." Ryan slid into the booth wearing sunglasses and his hair still damp from a shower. No one ever took them for brothers. Ryan carried weight like a linebacker with wide shoulders and thick forearms. Jared could win at arm wrestling, but was more the skiing and hiking type. His urge to ride broncs or bulls was short lived. His eight-second rides always bruised his pride as much as his backside. Ryan, on the other hand, had his own rodeo fan club made up mostly of women with Nicole as their queen.

“Let me look at you.” He reached across the table and poked Ryan in the chest. “You sure you’re alive?”

“Barely. Coffee.” Ryan grunted, then raised his hand and called out weakly again, “Coffee?”

“Ryan, man, you can’t load a year’s worth of fun into one night. Why don’t you come out with me every once in a while? You ooze with responsibility. All work and no play…just say’n.”

“Coffee?” Ryan repeated, sounding like a man in a desert dying for water, then glanced over his shoulder and waved as though trying to catch someone’s attention. “Don’t talk, Jared, or don’t say anything I’m supposed to remember until I’ve had coffee.”

Jared smiled when Camilla sauntered in their direction. She approached the table with pots in hand. Her smile lit up the diner and for a moment made him forget everyone else in the room.

“I’m so sorry, y’all. Darcy will be right back to get your order. In the meantime, regular or decaf?”

“Leaded,” Ryan whispered hoarsely. He slid the mug close to the edge of the table and held tightly to the handle.

Camilla poured. Ryan retrieved the cup, lifted it to his lips and sipped.

“Ah, thank you. You’re a goddess,” Ryan sighed

between sips. "If I wasn't already engaged, I'd marry you right now." Ryan slouched in the booth and appeared lost in a world with only his coffee.

Jared pushed his mug toward Camilla, but stopped half way. "I've been waiting for a private moment to talk to you."

Camilla's brow furrowed in puzzlement.

"I was wondering if you'd have dinner with me tonight." He waited for her warm smile to shine on him. She'd say *yes* to the date, and he'd present the gift he'd brought especially for her. That was the plan.

"I'm sorry. I don't date regulars."

She was turning him down? "I'm Jared. I'm not a regular here. I only came in today to ask you out."

"You've been in before, according to Darcy. Whenever you come to town. That makes you a regular."

He could see her point, and her sidestep added a challenge, however, he wouldn't accept defeat. "I'm not from here—"

"Most aren't, I'm told."

"I'm here on business."

"Wedding business," Ryan interjected. "He's going home this week. If you don't say *yes* now, he'll be gone for another month. Until the bachelor party."

"Shut up, Ryan. Drink your coffee," Jared growled.

Camilla smiled sweetly. "Gee, I don't mean to put a hole in your cast net, but I don't go out with about-to-be-married men. I have a very strict, *exceptionally* strict, rule about that."

Before he could correct her, Darcy skidded to a stop beside Camilla.

"Tom needs you in the kitchen. Now."

"Yay-ya," Camilla drawled. She departed without the coffee pots before he could argue his point.

"Hey, there. You must be the brother. Welcome to Mountain View. Are you guys ready to order?" Darcy winked at Ryan.

"I need something to soak up all the booze still floating around in my system." Ryan raised his sunglasses and squinted at the view beyond the windows. He promptly dropped the shades back in place. "Yep. Those are mountains."

"Is there a special?" Jared asked. He kept his gaze on the spot where Camilla had disappeared into the kitchen.

"No. How about steak and eggs? Eggs Benedict? Waffles with fresh blueberries? You name it."

Ryan groaned loudly. The few other customers in the cafe turned to look at them and frowned.

"I'll have an egg-white omelet, turkey sausage, and fruit. He'll eat buttered toast for now," Jared quickly told Darcy.

The waitress scribbled on a small note pad. After sliding it into her pocket, she hoisted the two coffee carafes. "More?" she asked.

Jared nodded. She poured dark liquid into his mug. Across from him, his brother's shoulder hitched downward. Ryan had fallen asleep.

"Thanks," he told Darcy as she left the table.

If last night's antics were a predictive barometer of what he could expect from his big brother, then he needed to host the bachelor party the week before the wedding, and not the night before. Ryan's bride-to-be would be fit to be tied if she faced a hung-over groom at the altar. Later, she'd see to it that he was tied, too.

Hog tied.

He kicked Ryan's leg under the table. His brother jerked upright, scrubbed his face with his hand, knocking his sunglasses to the table with a clatter. Heads turned again in their direction.

"I think you're gonna have to take the express bus back today. You're not fit to drive. I've got stuff to send with you, including a surprise for Felicia."

"You know that woman would fall at your feet if you gave her a chance." Ryan opened the menu on the table in front of him.

"Not interested. She's a nice lady. She needs a nice cowboy who wants to stay on the ranch. I don't exactly fit in those boots. No sense in taking a path I already know is a dead end."

"Shit, Jared. What difference does that make? Gus has been married five, count 'em, five times. Your life didn't end when Cheyenne died. Dating is not a death sentence." Ryan raised an eyebrow and looked down his nose at him.

"Nice choice of words," Jared said dryly. But he had plans he hadn't shared with anyone yet. Plans that involved leaving Wyoming for the winter. And maybe longer. The calendar had no whip or ball and chain to keep him from changing his schedule.

"Shit. Sorry about that. Stupid on my part. I meant—"

"I'm sure Nicole would love to know you have no objection to divorce. Be careful about that. If she had the notion, that woman could take you down. Make you weep like a baby. I know how much you love her, and she you, though, I was surprised she agreed to the prenup after her specifics about everything else." He raised an eyebrow at Ryan. There would be no discussion of Cheyenne. That subject was closed.

However, Nicole's wedding details were tattooed on his brain. Ten bridesmaids in long dresses carrying roses. For the men, Windsor ties, full vests, black tuxedos with a single button. Nicole was very specific. The concession she'd made—Ryan could wear a new black cowboy hat, but none of the groomsmen could. All her mother's people from back east were making the trek to Cody, Wyoming, and she expected to present an impressive catered event to all.

"Gus insisted on it. Nicole wants to get married. Nicole signed on the dotted line. She understands that no one without blood ties ever gets their hands on Rock'n R."

"Thank God Gus didn't set his sights on her. Each stepmother we've had has been younger than the next. Gus doesn't function well alone. He's a rooster that needs a hen. At least he takes them one at a time. He's trolling for wife number six, but who'd have him?" Jared said.

Ryan shrugged.

"Food's here," Darcy sang out. She deposited toast in front of Ryan, then the omelet, sausage, and fruit in front of Jared.

"I'll take steak medium rare, eggs over easy, home fries, and a biscuit if you got any." Ryan lifted a fork and reached for Jared's omelet.

In a flash, Jared held up a butter knife blocking Ryan's advance. "You might be bigger, but you aren't faster. Back off, big brother. Wait for your own food." Jared pointed the knife in Ryan's direction and stabbed at the air between them.

Darcy stepped back. “Okay,” she said hesitantly. “Steak and eggs coming right up. Anything else, guys?”

“Yes. Send Camilla over, please,” Jared said.

“But—I’m your waitress.”

Jared raised an eyebrow.

“What do you need? I’ll take care of it.”

“Please, send Camilla over.”

Darcy folded her arms on her chest, huffed out a breath, and stormed away.

“Ryan, look at what’ve you’ve done. It’s one thing for folks to think you’re a donkey’s backside, it’s another thing to prove it.”

“Me? You’re the one who pissed off the waitress.” His brother grunted, then picked up his sunglasses lying on the table and slid them onto his face.

“You really need to come out with me once in a while. You’ve lost your civilized manners.”

“Your momma was the one who taught me—”

“Well,” Camilla said as she arrived at the table, “is the problem that your momma didn’t do a good job of it, or do you have a problem retaining information?” She planted her fists on her hips. “I don’t know what you did to Darcy, but she’s pissed at me, and she’s the owner’s daughter. Trying to get me fired? I won’t stand for roughhousing in the diner. Take it outside.”

Jared shook his head. “You’ve got the wrong impression of us. I’m sorry.” He kicked Ryan, who then piped up. “I’m sorry, too.”

“What do you want? I won’t take any crap from either of you. I’ll call the cops as quick as I can hit 911 on my cell.”

“We’re jerks. Forgive us. My brother here spends too much time on a horse and not enough time with humans."

Ryan nodded. "Sad, but true."

Ding! Ding!

The cook behind the kitchen window hit a bell.

"No more trouble, guys."

"Promise." Jared held up three fingers, flashed his best Boy Scout smile, and hoped she would forgive him. She raced away before he had a chance to ask his question again.

A few minutes later, Darcy plunked Ryan's food on the table and left.

"Don't know what you want with either waitress, but you're gonna have to beg the spicy southern one"—Ryan said between bites—"if you plan to talk to her."

Jared finished breakfast in silence. The diner began to fill with after-church customers. The five old men parked on the stools at the counter departed and others quickly filled the empty seats. Camilla and Darcy moved at a steady pace serving and watching over their customers. Darcy kept his and Ryan's coffee mugs filled. Camilla never returned to talk with him.

"I'm going back to the condo to sleep. Come get me in time to make the bus. We'll figure out how to get my truck back to the ranch later." Ryan rose from the booth. "Pay the tab, will ya?"

"I'll consider it part of my best man duties. Now get out of here."

The moment after the door closed behind Ryan, Camilla dropped off the bill. "I'm thinking you're *not* going to skip out on this."

"No. Absolutely not." Jared placed cash on top of the bill. "In fact"—he rose and reached for the package on the seat—"I have a peace offering for you. No strings attached, although I'd like you to reconsider having dinner with me."

Camilla started to protest, but Jared placed a finger to his lips. "Shh."

"What?"

"If you won't have dinner with me tonight, what about tomorrow? Take a look at the present. Here's my number. Call me. Or I'll be by for breakfast again in the morning, regular like. I'll sit at the counter, and we'll talk about where I can take you for a nice meal."

He took Camilla's hands, mere contact with her warming his blood. He closed her fingers around the package. Turning, he sauntered out the door carrying a mild stab of regret. What he would give to see her face when she opened his gift, treats his grandmother had sent from a sweet shop in New Orleans.

Sweet for a sweet.

How could she refuse him now?

Chapter 4

Camilla leaned in and wiped down the last booth in front of the bank of windows. The lunch rush had thinned to a single man nursing a cup of coffee at the counter. Finished with her side work, she had time to run home to shower and change before putting Haley on the express bus to Cody. If her luck held, she'd still make it in time for the fly-fishing class on the Snake River. It seemed a much tamer sport than learning to ride a horse. Rodeo riding, beyond barrel racing, made no sense at all. Recently, she saw a cowboy with a t-shirt that read, "Ride Bulls—Meet Nurses." That about summed it up.

"What's this?" Darcy called out, her tone more accusing than curious. She lifted a rectangular package, the size of a Saltines box, from behind the counter.

Camilla turned. She rushed forward and plucked the cardboard container from Darcy's grasp. "Pralines. You snooping in my cubby?"

"Where'd you get them? You didn't have them when you came in." Darcy's eyes narrowed and lips thinned, her annoyance shouted in the small space between them.

"A customer gave them to me." If she tiptoed around the subject, maybe she could sidestep it without full disclosure. No sense in pissing off the owner's daughter more. And as much as she wanted to get a dig in at Darcy, she needed her job more. No telling what Darcy would do if she learned Jared had asked her out for dinner. "They're from New Orleans. It's where my father's side of the family is from," she said, prying them from Darcy's hands.

How did Blue Eyes get them? The man definitely ruffled her insides. The old Camilla never embraced restraint, but she'd changed. The magnetic pull of the cowboy made her want to toss caution to the wind—like an addict wanted a fix—but after meeting his brother, apparently both of them were getting married. She wouldn't let history repeat itself. The deep sadness in her sister's voice whispered in her brain. The betrayal she perpetrated on Branna had been the most shameful act she'd ever committed. Even if she wanted to get in a dig at Darcy over Blue Eyes, doing it at the expense of a bride-to-be crossed way over the line.

Flashing her best hostess-with-the-most-ess grin, she asked, "Would you like one? I'm happy to share." She opened the lid of the box exposing the individually wrapped, round sweets, the color of caramel. Her mother was right. You always get more with sugar than vinegar.

Darcy's expression softened. "I've never had one. What exactly are they?"

"Southern candy." Camilla pulled one out. "As a kid, I ate them all the time. Greta, the woman who takes care of my great grandmother, makes a batch at least once a month for the family. Every now and then, she sends me some. They're good with *café au lait*."

Gingerly, Darcy reached across the counter and plucked one from the box. She opened the clear wrapper and nibbled one edge of the candy. Nodding, she said, “Very sweet.”

“Hope you like it.” Camilla turned and scanned the diner. “I’m done for the day. I’m going to punch out and go.” She rounded the end of the counter and headed for the kitchen door with the box tucked under one arm. With her foot, she held the door open, reached around to the time-card holder, and then pulled hers from a slot.

“Haley’s not waiting in your apartment.”

Clunk. The machine stamped her card. “What did you say?”

“I saw Haley cross the street more than an hour ago.”

“What? No. Grrr. I’m going to…” Camilla clamped her jaw tight as she closed the kitchen door.

“Don’t get involved. You need to stay out of other folks’ business. Nothing good ever comes of it. Just a little free advice.”

“I can’t stand by and do nothing!”

“You can’t rescue everyone, Camilla.”

“I—”

“Just like you tried to butt in with me and that cowboy. I don’t care if he’s engaged.”

“I didn’t—”

“The person you need to be saving is yourself.”

“What? You’re wrong. We can talk about this later. I’m going to find that girl and put her on a bus. In fact, I have her cellphone. I’ll call her dad on my walk home.”

“Whatever.” Darcy shrugged.

Outside the diner, Camilla stopped and pulled Haley’s phone from her pocket. Flipping through the list of names and numbers, she located “Dad.” It had to be the one she sought. She shaded the phone’s touch screen from the afternoon sun's glare, then pushed a button. When the phone began ringing on the other end, she continued her trek toward her apartment with sunshine warming her face while silently praying Darcy was mistaken, and that Haley waited inside with ice on her face, exactly as instructed.

"Hey. How's my little girl today?" A deep male voice vibrated from the phone.

"Mr. O'Connor, I'm Camilla Lind. A friend of Haley's."

"Something wrong?"

"I'm trying to do the right thing for Haley. I'm putting her on a bus and sending her to you."

"What the—"

"Her mom's traveling again. Haley's here alone, and I don't think it's the best thing for her."

"Who'd you say you are?"

"Camilla Lind."

"You sound older than my daughter. How exactly do you know her?" The man's suspiciousness came across perfectly.

"I'm a waitress at the Mountain View Diner where Haley works."

"So a waitress is going to tell me what I should do with my daughter? Where's my girl? Why do you have her phone?"

Camilla breathed in deep and let go of the breath slowly. On a back street, away from the tourist spots, she looked around. No one was near enough to hear her conversation. "I don't want to alarm you, but I think her boyfriend is bad news. Haley showed up at work today, and I think the redness on her face will turn to bruises."

"Boyfriend!" The voice from the other end of the

phone bellowed in her ear so loud she moved the phone away. “What do you mean, bruises on her face?”

At the bottom of the stairs leading to her apartment, Camilla paused and adjusted the package under her arm, then grabbed the railing as she climbed the stairs with the phone locked between her ear and shoulder. “Hang on a moment, I live across the street behind the diner. I gave Haley the key and sent her there. Let me get the door open, and you can talk to her.”

She said another silent prayer that Haley waited inside. What would she do if Haley had wandered off, or worse yet, run back to the jerk who hit her? A spasm cinched her gut tight.

Turning the knob swift and hard, she opened the door. No sound came from the television. The radio definitely wasn’t on. She crossed the threshold to her apartment and almost every inch of space became visible.

Relief flooded Camilla.

The teenager she sought sat on the floor, ice pack to one side of her face, munching a soft taco as though she had no concerns.

“No. Food. In. Fridge. Hungry,” Haley said between chews. She squinted with each downward clamp of her jaw, obviously in pain.

Camilla set the box of pralines on the table, then put the phone on speaker and offered it to Haley.

“For you.”

Haley brightened, swallowed, and dropped the ice pack to the rug. “Hello? Mitch?”

“The hell! This is your father. That lady says your face is bruised and your mother’s traveling. What’s going on Haley? We had a deal."

"Sorry, daddy." Haley's eyes welled with tears. She tossed the phone to Camilla and raced from the room. The door to the bathroom banged closed.

"Haley?"

Camilla sank into the old denim covered couch and kicked off her shoes. "Mr. O'Connor, she ran into the bathroom. I'm guessing you heard the slam."

"I'm Sean. Thanks for looking out for my little girl. I was against sending her to her mother for the entire summer. That woman…Does Haley need a doctor? Is she really okay? I'd come and get her, but your plan to put her on the bus sounds better. It will get her home quicker."

"There's a three p.m. express bus. No stops. I wanted to be sure you knew she was coming and you'd be there when she arrives."

"Who. Is. Mitch?" Sean's voice was deadly calm and quiet.

Camilla paused. How much should she reveal about Haley's relationship with the biker dude? She'd never been a parent, but through her short friendship with Haley, her mothering instincts had nudged their way in, bringing a better understanding of the angst and frustration she'd put her parents through. Since the incident with her sister, Branna, she'd tried hard to live the straight and narrow. No more pranks or competitions. Do the right thing. Not that it was always easy… In this instance, the issue at hand was Haley's safety, right? Rather than revealing whether or not Haley was sleeping with some guy no sane parent would approve of…God! Had she turned into her mother?

"I don't know him. Seen Haley with him a few times. Let's just say I know enough about Haley to know he's not the company I would want her to keep if she were my daughter. I don't want to judge, but looks alone—he gives me the creeps."

"How badly is she hurt?"

Anguish seized Camilla. Sean sounded desperate. Not like the disinterested father Haley had painted him to be.

"As I said before, her face is bruised. Nothing appears broken. Clearly, she's been slapped around. If I thought a doctor was needed, I'd have missed work and taken her right away."

"Thank you, Miss Lind. I owe you. I'll be here waiting. I'd appreciate it if you'd call me to confirm after the bus has left."

"It's Camilla. I'm happy to help. And, yes, I'll call once she's safely on the bus and it's pulled away."

She ended the call, then called out, "Haley, girl, I've got to shower. Come out here. Let me look at your face again."

The bathroom door creaked open. Haley appeared, eyes red from crying. "Why'd you call my dad? I thought you'd help me," Haley wailed. "You've made it worse. What kind of friend are you?"

Camilla rose from a comfortable slump and tugged on Haley's hand. "I'm trying to do what's best for you." She examined the teen's face closer. Icing the injuries had stopped some of the swelling, but discoloration made Haley look as battered as she was. "It will all heal soon." She pulled the girl to her and hugged her tight. She stroked Haley's hair. "You'll be safe with your dad. He's worried about you."

"Mitch didn't mean it. He promised not to do it again." Haley stomped her foot. "I…don't wanna…leave."

"How about this? I'll arrange to get two days off from work together. I'll come and visit you. I might even let you put me on a horse. You've been bugging me to learn to ride. Your face glows when you talk about your dad's ranch. You can show it off when I visit."

Haley let go of a groan and pulled away. She held up a finger. "One—my dad is over-protective. Two—my mother ignores me. Three—fun is here! I don't fit anywhere." Haley's anger masked hurt. Tightness grabbed Camilla. The pain of it sank into her stomach. If anyone understood the feeling of being an outsider in one's own family, she did. Maybe that's why she'd adopted the teenager from their first meeting.

"Aww, Haley…" Camilla sighed.

"You probably think I'm a child." Haley sniffed and shoved her hair back. "But I'm not. Next month, I can register to vote. Join the military. I am as much an adult now as I will be then!"

"I'm not disagreeing with you."

"What? Then why force me to go home to Cody?" The teen wiped her eyes and plopped on the couch.

"Because I can't stand by knowing how this kind of thing can escalate and watch you get hurt. Now, grab a book or watch TV while I shower quick. Then, let's get you on that bus. Oh, do you want a praline?" She opened the box and offered a candy, hoping to diffuse the angst hanging in the room like Spanish moss on an old magnolia tree.

With shoulders slumped as though she'd been an

abused prisoner, Haley plodded toward her, closing the distance between them.

"What did you call it?" Haley wrinkled her nose as she peeked inside and plucked one out. "Where'd they come from?"

"We pronounce it *prah-leen*. A customer gave them to me."

"The box says *pray-leen*. You aren't eating one?" Haley asked, then took a bite.

"No. Is it good?"

Haley nodded. "You once told me you love these. Somebody sent you some. Why aren't you eating one?"

"Nut allergy. It's mild most of the time, but pecans are the worst." She pulled an EpiPen from her purse. "I carry this just in case." Jared had no way of knowing his treat could be deadly. Just as pecans were off limits to her, he had to be, too. Besides, what kind of man brought a present to ask a woman on a date? Especially if he was engaged to be married! Was he a rogue rather than a Robin Hood? Perfect. She had to say *no* to a date with him. At least that would break her losing streak.

Haley continued to nibble on the candy. "Allergy. That would be really bad, since this is really good." Haley shoved the remaining candy into her mouth. "Um, I need to go to my mom's and get some of my stuff. You're busy. I can call Mitch—"

"Absolutely not! You stay parked right where you are. I'll be ten minutes. If we have time, we'll swing by your mom's, but otherwise, I'll make sure she sends you what you want when she returns."

After her shower, Camilla dressed in cargo pants, a tank top and grabbed a soft, chambray shirt from her closet. Her waders were stored in her car, ready for her fishing lesson, along with her fly fishing rod and tackle. She toweled dry her long hair, ran a comb through it again, and pulled it back into a ponytail. Nothing worse than fishing with hair falling in her face. She'd lost a fish during the first class because of messing with her dang hair.

Her cell phone vibrated on the bathroom counter. A new email came from her sister: *Call me. We have to make plans.*

A pang hit Camilla. Branna. Would things ever be truly okay between them? She missed her sister, her family, yet time away had done her good. But dropping back into her old world was risky. Maybe she needed a ceremonial funeral to bury old habits. Maybe a visit to a voodoo priestess in New Orleans?

A second message came through. This one from her cousin Biloxi. *Return my phone call! We have to talk.*

Camilla exhaled deeply. Was she strong enough now to resist the web of family dynamics? Tradition ruled life at Fleur de Lis. Even Branna hadn't escaped that. The Old Aunts might be old, but they were still strong. However, something was going on at home. Her sister and cousin sending emails at the same time. It couldn't be truly serious. Otherwise, her mother would've called with news. Worry wedged a nagging pain into her brain.

She applied tinted moisturizer with UV protection while canned laughter from a TV show drifted to her from the living room. Her first concern had to be Haley. Branna and Biloxi were more than competent to take care of things. Thank goodness Haley had the good sense to heed her instructions. Well, at least she listened part of the time. Had she minded before, Camilla mused, Mitch wouldn't be at the top of her hate list now.

Pulling on thick socks to keep her feet from numbing in the ice-cold river, she wondered if Jared fished or hunted. He had to do one or both. In this part of the country, those activities were necessary survival skills, not just sport. Tugging at the hem of her pants, she called out, "Haley, I'll be a minute more. I don't think we have time to stop on the way."

When she entered the living room, the TV played while Haley slept on the couch looking younger than seventeen. Peaceful. Serene. Being a push me-pull me doll between divorced parents had to hurt, that and knowing your mother insisted to everyone she was your older sister. Mothers came in all sizes and temperaments, and she'd gained an ocean of appreciation for her own in the last year. Macy Lind had hidden angel wings. Camilla missed her with an ache she never thought possible. She missed her father, too, but her brother, Carson, was his favorite, just as her older sister, Branna, remained their mother's. Life sucked for a middle child, Camilla lamented, then clicked the TV off.

"What?" Haley asked grumpily, then stretched long on the couch, rubbing her eyes. "I was watching that."

"Time to go, sleeping beauty. No time to stop at your mom's place." She picked up the box of pralines for Haley to carry home with her. A momentary smile played on her lips over Jared's thoughtfulness. No one had ever offered sweetness as an enticement for a date.

She herded the girl downstairs and into her Subaru. It got her through her first winter in cold country. The old Honda she'd left home with would have never made it through the ice and snow of a western winter. Too much southern rust.

"Don't be mad at me," Haley said tentatively, "I did something I had to do." She picked at her black nail polish. Her gaze remained glued on her fingers. "You've been telling me I need to be empowered."

Camilla glanced in the girl's direction as she backed onto the street. A sudden chill made her shiver involuntarily. What was the old wives' tale? A chill meant someone walked over your grave? She opened the car window to let in the afternoon heat and clean mountain air. Maybe the uneasy feeling would fly away on the wind. "What's not to like?"

"Mitch."

"Aww, Haley," Camilla groaned. "What about him?" A blanket of dread wrapped around her and like a corset pulled tight. Scenarios flashed in her mind of all the things that could go wrong for Haley with Mitch. The flashes served as warning signs. Something that never happened until she finally came to understand the consequences of her actions when she betrayed her sister. She never wanted to be that person again.

"He…might be…" Haley's voice cracked. "Waiting…at the bus station for me?"

Camilla pulled the car to the curb and put it in park, then popped the trunk release. Getting out, she left the car door open. In the trunk, she rummaged around and found her pocketknife. It was all she had. She slid it into the front thigh pocket, then climbed back behind the wheel. Given Mitch's size and girth, she'd never take him down, but she could try to scare him off until Haley was safely on the bus.

"You, missy, can wave good-bye and throw him a kiss. You may talk to him on your cell phone for as long as you have a connection. But let me make myself perfectly clear—" She paused to glance around looking for her grandmother. She now channeled Grandmother Lind? "—you will have no direct contact with that man. If he wants to see you, he can make the ride on his bike to Cody and meet your dad."

Haley slumped in her seat. She crossed her arms over her chest and frowned. A low growl emanated from her, though her jaw remained locked tight. "You don't understand. I just want to say good-bye."

A song on the radio drowned out the silence between them. Arriving at the bus station, Camilla noticed Mitch immediately.

A steely determination gripped her. She patted the knife in her pocket. Never before had she pulled a knife on a person, but to protect Haley from the biker she was willing to change.

Chapter 5

Sunglasses shielded Jared's eyes from the sun's direct light. He maneuvered the Chevy Silverado into one of the few parking spots on the side of the bus station. Shaded by tall, blue spruce trees perfectly landscaping the property, it was quieter there than the main parking lot. Even the bus station boasted the rustic western look of Jackson. In the truck's backseat, Ryan snored, a low timbre barely audible over Montgomery Gentry singing "Gone" on the radio. Rather than wake his brother, Jared climbed out of the truck with the engine running and closed the door with a light *click.* After he rounded the front of the Silverado and stepped onto the sidewalk, he stopped. The woman who'd been on his mind stood framed inside the doorway of the bus station's ticket office wearing a frown.

Was this his lucky day or what?

Camilla couldn't use customers or work as an excuse to not speak to him. Had she enjoyed any of his special gift? His grandmother's care package had arrived just in time. She'd be pleased to know someone in Wyoming knew what a praline was.

Camilla's hand rested on the handle of the metal-framed glass door. Her frown deepened. Eyes narrowed. She gave the door a hard push, bumping it open farther, then she exited the building crossing the threshold with a determined stride. The door slammed closed behind her. Glass rattled. "Riled" described the waves of angry energy rolling off her, like a bull waiting to bust out of a rodeo shoot. That look on her face, he'd seen it before on other women. Total concentration. Clear defined intention. He pitied the person on the receiving end of her fury. She was a woman on a mission.

He followed her stare to the blue car parked one space away from his pickup and surmised that the wiry biker dude leaning in through the open passenger window talking to the girl inside was fixed in Camilla's cross-hairs. Jared shifted his gaze back to Camilla. When she reached into the pocket of her cargo pants, she pulled out a small, red Swiss Army pocketknife, one like he might use to sharpen a pencil. Uneasiness grabbed the muscles between his shoulder blades into a tight spasm. He'd learned always to trust that warning sign of danger.

In a fast trot, he cleared twenty feet and jerked Camilla by the shoulders, swung her around, pushing her back to the log walls of the building and pinned her there.

"Let go—" Camilla shouted.

Her yelling stabbed his eardrum. When she started to open her mouth again, he silenced her with a kiss. The action surprised him as much as it must have shocked her, however, in that split second it seemed like the best way to subdue a raging woman. Lovely full lips melded against his. A zip of hot energy shot through him, blowing out his mental circuits. Unable to resist, he deepened the kiss. Camilla responded like a woman more than a little interested.

Lightheaded, he blinked as his brain kicked back

into gear. His hand stroked from her hip toward her hand and made contact with the hard edges of the pocketknife. She let go of it. He clutched it tight. However, she surprised him when she deepened the kiss more. The sensation of her lips against his blinked his mind to nothingness. Blood roared in his ears. The sensation washing over him could only be that of drowning. But only in the best way. He pulled her closer.

Then a sudden hard shove against his chest made him stumble backward.

"Don't ever do that again!" Camilla shouted at him.

Stunned, he struggled to see through a fog. Her eyes were wide and wild. Behind him, loud, slow clapping sounded. He turned slowly, but he kept one eye on Camilla, in case she tried to shove him again.

"Bravo! Little brother, I said you needed to get back in the saddle, but didn't expect this." Ryan's grin mocked. His brother stood on the running board of the truck with the back door wide open.

Jared frowned.

Camilla glared past him, then shouted, "You! Mitch! Get away!"

Jared flinched from her shriek. What was with her yelling?

Camilla turned, pushed past him, snatching the knife from his hand. The biker dude at the car window straightened, snorted, but had the good sense to back away several steps. Yet he remained close enough to reach the girl in the car with little effort. The girl crossed her arms over her chest and slunk down in the seat as though that somehow made her invisible.

When Camilla reached the spot where the sidewalk sloped to the road, she launched herself at the leather-clad guy. “You stay away from her, Mitch! I swear if you touch her again, I’ll—”

Jared shook his head. An image of a knife in Mitch’s thigh gave him the strength to wrestle her around the waist, her back to his chest. He lifted her off her feet. Her arms flailed. Her feet kicked. She was stronger than she looked.

“Enough!” Jared roared. He hugged her tightly to keep her from attacking the guy and caught a whiff of the soft sweet scent she wore. Another time he would explore the softness of the woman in his arms.

Mitch rolled his eyes, yet stepped farther away from the car, all the while staring hard at Camilla. His hands raised limply in surrender.

“Keep going,” Jared ordered. “Back up.”

“I could have you arrested for what you did!” Camilla lunged, but Jared held her tight.

“Don’t get excited. She called me.”

“Look, dude, leave the ladies alone.” Ryan jumped down from the truck. He stood halfway between the rear of the car and Mitch with his arms crossed on his chest.

“She said she was eighteen. You can’t try to pin anything on me,” Mitch snarled in a low tone. He shoved his hands into his jacket pockets and lifted his chin in defiance. “It’s a free country. I’ve got a pass to get on that bus to Cody.” Mitch produced a slip of paper and waved it in the air taunting Camilla.

As though on cue, the loudspeaker blared, “Three o’clock bus to Cody, Wyoming. Loading begins now.”

Landscaping blocked Jared’s view of the loading

zone, but not the *swoosh* of opening doors of the bus. Anyone mingling in the front of the station was unaware of the battle taking place only yards away.

"Fifteen minutes until departure!" someone yelled. "Bus always leaves on time. Got a schedule to keep."

"If I let you go, you promise to remain calm?" Jared asked Camilla.

"Yes."

He released his grip on her waist, and she jerked away.

He motioned Camilla closer with his finger. "Want to tell me what's going on?"

"That"—Camilla stabbed the air in Mitch's direction—"abused Haley. She's in the car. I'm sending her home to her father. On. This. Bus."

"I see." Jared nodded. "Ryan was going home, too, but I think, for safety's sake, you need to get on that bus with Haley. Ryan and I will detain said offender."

"I have an idea. Do what you cowboys are so fond of doing," Camilla drawled sweetly.

Puzzled, Jared tried to follow her line of thinking. "What?"

"Roping, of course. Lasso that sucker, and tie him up. Call the sheriff. If I get near him, no telling what I might do," Camilla huffed.

"I have the complete picture," he assured her. Guys like Mitch created a stench in the clean mountain air.

"No. I'm betting you don't. You haven't seen Haley's face."

"Stay right here." Jared pointed to the asphalt beneath Camilla's feet. He crossed the short distance to the car and peeked inside. "You're Haley?"

She wasn't a girl, but a teenager. She nodded. Her

eyes remained cast downward. She didn't speak. The last time he'd set eyes on her, she was a scrawny kid on a horse and could've been mistaken for a boy. Not anymore. She was a greater beauty than her mother, the ex-rodeo queen. He remembered seeing Haley at the diner, collecting dishes and wiping tables. Only then, she didn't have swelling over her eye or colorful bruises on her cheek and jaw.

"You're O'Connor's kid, aren't you?"

Haley nodded.

The thought of the blows producing the darkening discoloration to the girl's face sickened him. He narrowed his eyes and locked his jaw. "Look more this way." Jared reached for his phone and clicked over to the camera, snapping a few pictures of the girl. Mitch needed to be hogtied and dragged through the woods. Or better yet, given a sample of his own medicine. He and Ryan would be happy to oblige, but if they did and any hint of Mitch's lesson ever leaked out, their cousin, a sheriff's deputy, would show no mercy for their actions. He always cautioned them about playing vigilante. In the end, doing the upstanding-citizen thing would have to do. The authorities could handle the scumbag biker.

"I'm going to tell you the ending of this story," Jared said as he turned from the car and faced Mitch. Beads of perspiration dotted the guy's forehead. Jared took his time. He enjoyed Mitch's discomfort, but it was probably due more to the heat of the afternoon and the guy's leather jacket. His kind never showed fear.

To Jared's left, fifteen feet away, Camilla remained true to her word. She stood glued to the spot where he'd left her. "Camilla is going to get what she needs out of her car. Mitch is going to give Ryan the bus ticket. Camilla will get on the bus with Haley and escort the young lady to Cody."

Mitch drew back like he might rebut the plan. He scowled, then opened his mouth to speak, but Jared cut him off. "I just took some photos of Haley. We happen to have a cousin with the Teton County Sheriff's Department. I could call for a deputy now, if that would make you happy, or you could work the plan I've laid out. Where are you from?"

Mitch turned his head and stared off into the distance.

"Look asshole, you can make this hard on yourself, or save yourself a trip to jail. Where are you from? Easy question. One word answer. If you don't tell me, I'll still find out."

"Casper." Mitch muttered and glared.

"Then make like the ghost and vanish."

Mitch snorted. "You think you're a funny dude. Not like I haven't heard that before, stupid."

"Go back to Casper." Jared motioned Camilla to her car while Ryan continued to stand guard.

"Get what you need. I'll drop your car off at the diner," Jared told her.

"No. I live in the apartment building behind it. Leave it there. Let's go, Haley." Camilla pulled her purse, jacket, and the box of pralines he'd given her from her car. The fact that she'd brought them along pleased him. Maybe he was making headway with the feisty southerner after all.

Haley hung her head as she exited the car. Her gaze remained on the ground. She never snuck a look in Mitch's direction. It was as though her long hair hanging in her face created a cocoon for her, a world of her own.

"Awe, baby," Mitch whined. "You know I didn't want to hurt you."

Jared tensed when Haley stopped and turned in Mitch's direction with a pained expression. Jared feared the teen was on the verge of bursting into tears.

"I know," she said softly. "But nonetheless, you did this to me. I'm trying to figure out why."

"Haley, honey…" Mitch shifted his weight, leaning in the teen's direction.

Camilla slipped her hand into Haley's and tugged the teenager through the trees and toward the bus and the sound of passengers loading along with the driver tossing baggage into compartments.

"Ryan, take the ticket from Mitch." He didn't dare let Camilla near Mitch.

"Hand it over, dude."

Wordlessly, Mitch complied. Then, Jared took it from Ryan. He walked to where Camilla stood at the end of the line.

"Safe travels," he said, taking her hand and tucking the paper into her palm. That single touch, an innocent gesture started his heart pounding. Her eyes widened. She nodded.

"How about a private and personal thank-you?" He admired her conviction, her loyalty to the kid, but the heat she caused in his blood distracted his mind and hardened a particular part of his body. He shifted his stance not wanting to give her the wrong impression.

"Mitch should be thanking you about now," Camilla said pointedly. "I'm confident if he tried to put another hand on Haley, I would've hurt him good.

Besides, you got your reward."

Jared cocked his head. He had?

"The kiss."

The line of passengers moved quickly. As a tall man held out a hand to assist Haley onto the bus, Jared reached for Camilla to stop her. "Once again, how about you thanking me proper tomorrow after you get back? Dinner at seven?"

"I don't go out with married *or* engaged men." There it was again. Conviction to principles. She wrinkled her nose in disdain. The expression confused him.

"Wait. You think… No. Not me. I'm not married or engaged."

"Yeah," she huffed. "Whatever. Heard that story before."

The driver coughed. "We gotta go, ma'am."

When Camilla took a step away, then paused, the bus driver boarded the bus.

"It's just dinner. I swear, I'm not married or engaged." Jared waited for her response. After all he'd just done, a meal with her had to be his reward.

"I don't know. Maybe. Maybe not. We'll have to see what tomorrow brings." She boarded the bus without a backward glance. His heart sank.

As his father always said, "Tomorrow never comes. By then, it's today. Tomorrow is always out of reach."

Jared sighed and shook his head. Would Camilla be like tomorrow?

Chapter 6

Camilla squeezed by a man standing in the aisle and plopped into the plush, high-backed aisle seat next to Haley. An exhausted deep sigh escaped in a rush. "I can't believe what I just did."

The aftermath of adrenaline from confronting Mitch and Jared's kiss made her weak-kneed. Her hands trembled as she tucked her purse and the box of pralines in the back pocket of the seat in front of her, and she wished one of the pralines concealed a sprinkling of Xanax for anxiety instead of life-threatening nuts. Her heart stuttered as though trying to find a regular beat. The thing she wanted most and the thing she needed least was Jared's lips against hers. The cowboy could kiss.

Across the aisle, the man who'd helped Haley on the bus, raised an eyebrow and gave her a quizzical look. He appeared harmless in his golf shirt and khaki slacks, but she wasn't about to explain to the dark-haired stranger what had happened to Haley. She forced a thin grin, shrugged, and shook her head before turning to the teen beside her. Never in her wildest dreams did she imagine herself as a teenaged girl's self-appointed protector.

"Hope you know what you're doing," Haley said flippantly. "It's a long ride to Cody. And just so you know, I'm not talking with you about Mitch." She crossed her arms over her chest and slumped down in the seat.

"Now I know why children are to be seen and not heard," Camilla muttered under her breath.

"What?"

"We'll make the *best* of it." Camilla drawled sweetly.

Whoosh. The bus doors closed.

"Hope you enjoy the ride," the driver said as the bus rumbled, then swayed like a hulking beast away from the station. Camilla strained to see Jared. He'd already climbed into his truck. Sunlight illuminated his silhouette. He reached for a cowboy hat and plunked it on his head. His truck started backing up and that's when she lost sight of him. Mitch, thankfully, was nowhere to be seen.

"I can't believe you pulled a pocketknife. I don't know if I think you're brave or stupid." Haley snorted.

Camilla sighed again. Her shoulders relaxed a tad. Jared had saved her as much as he'd saved Mitch. What had she been thinking? Pulling a tiny pocketknife on someone? Someone with a three-days' straggly beard, hard square jaw, and piercing eyes that appeared as though they'd seen too much in a short life. Plus, he was twice her size. Madness had consumed her when she caught Mitch talking to Haley. Every cell in her body contracted and morphed her into a she-bear wanting to protect her cub.

Thankfully, Jared stepped in and saved her from having to back up her threat. He was strong as a bull, though lean and muscular. His build made her want to swoon like her southern female ancestors had, even if it was only to have a man come to the rescue. This man oozed calm confidence, an attractive asset that drew her like a magnet. He was comfortable in his own skin. No need for cocky or arrogant.

And he'd given her pralines. Very sweet, him and the candy.

But why? And how did he know she even knew what they were?

She'd fantasized about him, both awake and asleep since their first meeting. The past moments made her curiosity meter rise more for him than for any man in the past. That kiss… An adrenaline rush of deliciousness. It shook her to her toes. It had been a long time since she'd sincerely admired a man or experienced such a strong reaction to one. Maybe he could be trusted. Maybe he wasn't getting married.

But if he was?

A dinner could be just dinner. Nothing more. No. Good manners dictated she reject the invitation outright—she wouldn't allow anything more between them. Couldn't, more than wouldn't. He was a planet to someone else's sun. Coals in a fire too hot to touch. Or sunken treasure off the coast of Grand Isle, completely out of reach. Engaged.

Yet, on the off chance no woman claimed the title of his fiancée, getting tangled up in something emotional would only make leaving worse. Soon she had to wave good-bye and head for home.

"Grrr," she groaned. Why had life suddenly become so complicated? The kiss shouldn't have happened. The electrically charged connection with Jared blew out half of her senses.

For now, Jared fit into the western boots of a hot-blooded, all-American man, and after that kiss, her need for more of the same sent shivers of delight down her spine. If he wasn't engaged, had he ever been in love before?

"Love?" Camilla sputtered. "Where did that come from?"

"What?" Haley grumbled. "I'm trying to sleep over here."

"Nothing." Camilla squirmed in her seat. Exactly how did someone fall in love? Men had always been a game, a pastime, a good time. And none of them had ever used the word "love" with her, either. Though she was no stranger to dating drama, most of which her parents remained blissfully ignorant of thanks to Branna. Her older sister knew minutia of details and protected her secrets. She might have learned what it meant to have true self-respect—something beyond pushing boundaries just far enough to break the rules, yet avoid punishment—had Branna shown tough love instead of always enabling. But she couldn't blame her older sister. Everything in life came down to choice…and she had to take responsibility for her own actions. The fallout between her and Branna rested solely on her own shoulders.

"Those that can't do, teach," she muttered. She might not have her own life in order, but she was qualified to coach Haley about "don'ts." She could impart a lesson on self-respect without alienating the poor girl. The four-hour drive gave her plenty of time to cover various topics. At least as much as she knew about them.

She gazed out the window while she gathered her thoughts before channeling to Haley wisdom from generations of southern women whose voices echoed in her head. The bus window framed a landscape of open green plains running to mountains so high their peaks weren't visible unless she leaned over the teen, pressed her nose to the window and craned her neck to take in the view. Brush strokes of airy white clouds painted against the bluest sky she'd ever seen. A deep pang of homesickness hit her. She missed everything about the south. The humidity against her skin, the sway of palm trees in the breeze, the scent of honeysuckle growing in the garden, soft white sand between her toes, and the noise of her chaotic family whenever they gathered. The next big event hosted at Fleur de Lis would be the Labor Day cookout. All of the town would turn out—minus one. She longed for a sip of strawberry soda.

Beside her, Haley snuggled into a ball. Her eyes were closed, but the girl wasn't sleeping. Camilla brushed a stray hair away from the teen's face. She'd allow Haley to play possum while she figured out how to explain about men. A lecture wouldn't work. Nothing worse for an obstinate teen than to be patronized.

Camilla patted Haley's hand. "Where's the ice pack? Did you leave it in the car?"

The teen nodded. Her eyes still closed.

"Girl, what am I going to do with you? Thankfully, the bruising will go away soon. You're a magnolia about to blossom. You're going to have lots of opportunities with guys. You can be selective. I want to talk about self-respect. If I could buy it at the general store, I'd buy you a case. See, the thing is, you've got to demand respect from others, but first you've got to have self-respect."

Haley opened one eye. "Is that something your

mother taught you?" she whispered. "Does she have that same funny accent, too?"

Camilla frowned. "Boo, you mockin' me?"

"Boo?"

"Something we call children, where I'm from."

"I'm not a child. Your accent isn't that marbles-in-the-mouth sweetness. It's something between southern and Boston. Yes, I've been to New Orleans, and Boston, too. My mother *does* take me with her when she travels—sometimes."

"Hold that thought." Camilla held up her finger. "I've got to call the diner and let them know that I won't make the early shift tomorrow. Then we talk."

Camilla pulled her cellphone from her purse and flipped through to find the contact number. The man across the aisle stood up. He bumped her arm. She looked up at him and frowned.

"Sorry. Excuse me," the man said, then reached above his seat, rummaging in a bag.

She nodded, then refocused on her task. Finding the number she needed, she tapped the cell phone's screen. Ringing started on the other end.

"Hello?"

"Darcy, it's Camilla. I need to talk with Mary."

"She's not in. Can I give her a message?"

"I'm on the bus to Cody. With Haley."

"So?"

"I won't make my early shift in the morning. Do you have someone to cover for me?"

"Camilla, I told you not to get involved with that girl. No, I don't have anyone to swap shifts with you. I'm going to have to work it if you don't show. I'm going to make this real plain. If you're not here when you're supposed to open, then you're fired."

Stunned, Camilla looked at the phone, then put it back to her ear. "Don't you think that's a bit harsh? I should be able to make it back for the dinner shift. Surely someone can switch with me."

"That's not how we do things here. Schedules are made a week in advance. You know that. Penny is sick, something she can't help. If you'd minded your own business, we wouldn't be having this conversation."

"Darcy, please," Camilla pleaded. She was on the verge of begging. Losing her job now could ruin all her nicely knitted plans for returning home.

"Either you're here or you're not. You have a job or you don't. It's all up to you."

"There's not another bus back tonight. What do want me to do?"

"Again, Camilla, your problem," Darcy said in a sing-songy voice. "I warned you."

"Yeah. You did," Camilla said flatly. "Thanks for nothing."

"Anything else?" Darcy asked sweetly.

"Yes. Just so you know, your cowboy asked me out. He kissed me at the bus station. It melted my bones and curled my toes. Thought you'd like that news flash." She hung up the phone with Darcy sputtering on the other end. Clutching the phone in her palm, she pounded it on her leg. She liked her job at the diner, had hoped it would be her last place of employment before heading back south. The jab at Darcy was catty, but she couldn't stop herself.

"Problems?" Haley asked.

"Nothing I can't handle." What were her options? Stay or go home. She shuddered. She couldn't face her family just yet. She had a plan. Needed to work it. Stay the course. But the unwanted change in circumstances threw a twist into her well-structured blueprint that had included cool summer days surrounded by the mountains bumping the sky of the Cowboy State.

The last eighteen months in the school of hard knocks taught her working for someone else always put her at their mercy. She absolutely wanted her own business. To be her own boss. Life experience provided the key ingredient that pushed her to strive for her dream rather than a college classroom or a corporate boardroom. Her journey from home had opened her eyes to a path in life, one offering a sense of purpose. Giving up wasn't an option. Besides, her cousin, Biloxi, counted on her.

Determination shored up her bruised confidence. Could there be another summer job with her name on it?

A tap on her left shoulder caught Camilla's attention. "Yes?"

"Here." The man across the aisle shoved a small, plain brown paper bag in her direction. "I think you might need this. For your sister."

She accepted what he offered. "She's not—" Her fingers grasped the top edge of the bag, and she reached with her other hand to support the weight of it. Opening the bag, she peeked inside. A clean cotton cloth and a small plastic bag of ice. She turned to the man and smiled wide. "This is perfect."

"I overheard the predicament. So, this ought to help during the ride."

"Thank you."

"Here's my card. Butch Moore. I'm a sales rep

headed up to Cody."

"We appreciate this, Mr. Moore." Camilla nudged Haley. "Don't *we*?"

Haley leaned forward and gave a curt wave to the man. "Thanks."

After wrapping the ice bag with the cloth, Camilla motioned for Haley to sit back. Once the girl situated herself in the seat, Camilla placed the pack on the girl's bruised face.

"Ouch," Haley winced.

"The ice will help the pain."

Someone, somewhere behind them on the bus, opened a bottle of soda. Camilla's mouth turned dryer at the sound of escaping carbonation. She regretted not having even a bottle of water and swallowed. Then, a tearing sound came from behind, followed by the crunching of chips. She wanted something to munch on, but pecan pralines wouldn't do.

"I need an ice cube from your bag," she said to Haley. "Something to wet my whistle, as you folks up here say."

Haley unwrapped the cloth and opened the bag. Camilla pulled out a small cube. "Thanks."

"I've got a water bottle in my jacket, if you're really thirsty."

She eyed the teen hard and allowed the melting water to sooth her dry throat. "Thanks, I'll make it."

"Suit yourself." Haley shrugged.

Uncertainty swam through Camilla's brain like a fish swimming against the currents. How to begin the discussion she wanted to have? Folding her hands in her lap, she looked straight ahead rather than to make direct eye contact with the girl beside her. "Haley, I'm not anyone's mother. In fact, the only time I ever babysat was for my cousins, who proceeded to burn down a boatshed trying to roast hotdogs. So, I don't have much experience with…mothering."

"I've got a mother. She sucks."

"Maybe so, but she's the only one you've got. And you acting out, doing things you know are wrong, isn't going to make her a better mother."

"How do you know?" Haley challenged. "She could change."

"I'm going to be straight with you. I'm going to talk to you like you're an adult, like you're a friend. I know it's soon, but you'll be eighteen when?"

"Next month."

"Not far away." Camilla paused. If she were to take a poll from her friends and family, they would probably say her transformation from spoiled party girl to a responsible business owner—not very likely. Change required a willingness to look deep into the darkness of one's self.

"People can change, if they want to, if they work at it. However, in your almost eighteen years of experience, has your mother changed in the ways you wanted?"

When Haley didn't respond, Camilla reached for her purse and pulled a small mirror out. "Take a good look at your face." She pushed the mirror toward the girl. "Do you want be *the girl* folks whisper about?"

The teen slunk further down in the seat.

"Becoming an adult comes with responsibility. It's better to choose the kind of person you want to be in life and live right on *that* path, otherwise, you'll always be rowing against the current…I can't think of a cowboy analogy to help all of this make more sense."

"Maybe like trying to prevent water from running downstream?" Haley brightened. "It takes a lot to build a dam."

"Yes, like that. Now, I'm not going to tell your father about the…intimate nature of your relationship with Mitch, but I also won't lie if he confronts me."

"Thanks." It was the most sincere thing Haley had said all day. "You'll like him," Haley continued. "Dad's a good man. Everyone says so. You can ask Jared. They know each other."

"Why bring Jared into the conversation?"

"I saw that kiss."

"He's…I'm betting he's engaged."

"Is that what you think?"

"Back to your father," Camilla insisted. "It doesn't really matter if I like him or not. I will act respectful toward him because that's the kind of person *I* am."

Haley squirmed in the seat, leaned her head and rested it on Camilla's shoulder, then replaced the ice pack over her bruised eye. "What happened to you to make you so smart?" the girl whispered.

"Water over the dam," Camilla mumbled.

Haley sat upright. "I have an idea. Dad can find you a job in Cody. And the two of you could date. He's never remarried. Maybe it's about time he climbed back into that saddle."

Camilla rolled her eyes. "Don't get any ideas, Boo." After all, the only guy she had an interest in dating may have promised to marry another woman. If so, he was no better than Steven Sterling. She would despise him for that. But for the moment, she could daydream of him. His kiss. The feel of his arms around her. However, in truth, any feelings she might harbor for Jared had to be “water over the dam.”

And she fully intended to tell him that.

Chapter 7

In the distance, thunder rumbled. Jared circled around the bus station and turned right at the light. “I’ve got a hunch.” He gripped the steering wheel harder. The gnawing in his gut churned more.

“You’re like a blood hound,” Ryan groaned. “Can’t stop once you’ve got the scent. Take me back to the condo. I want sleep. You robbed me of my bus ride.”

“You whine worse than an old woman. This will only take a minute. Besides, look at those thunderheads. It’s not like I want my truck hailed on.”

“Damn your hunches. Can’t remember when you’ve ever been wrong. If you only had them when they counted. Like at the casino in Vegas. There I could use you.”

Jared punched his brother’s arm. “Sleep can wait. I think Mitch is hanging out near here.”

He made a block-by-block search. Small cottages with neatly manicured lawns displaying colorful flowers and tall evergreen trees dotted each street. No other cars passed them. The only person they saw was a cyclist.

A few minutes later, he spied his target. In a strip mall’s empty parking lot, Mitch rummaged around in the trunk of an older model black car, a motorcycle parked next to it.

“Ryan, take down the tag numbers. Car and bike.

Let's give the info to Dax."

His brother pulled out his cell phone and snapped a few photos. "Got it. Do you want to open a can of whoop-ass on this dude now, or what? There's no one else around. I'm too tired to help, but I can referee. At the very least, make sure it's a fair fight. No guns. *And* no knives."

"Very generous of you. I hope talking will solve this problem."

Jared stopped the truck, blocking the black car in the parking lot, and rolled down the window. "Mitch," he called, leaning out. Another two feet and he could touch the guy. He didn't want trouble, but wouldn't shy away from it if the guy wouldn't listen to reason. "I didn't properly introduce myself back there. I'm Jared."

Mitch ignored him.

"I'm telling you, whoop-ass is the only language that guy will understand," Ryan said, dryly. Jared shot his brother a glare, threatening him not to instigate more trouble.

Mitch cast a bored glance at Jared, then looked away as he wadded up a leather jacket and stuffed it into the saddlebag on the motorcycle. Returning to the car's trunk, he pulled out black rain gear.

"I'm speaking to you," Jared said, trying to remain patient.

Mitch turned in Jared's direction again with eyes narrowed. "Yeah. So?" The biker pulled on the rainsuit over his clothes.

"I want you to leave Haley and Camilla alone."

"Free country."

"Let it go. Don't go looking for trouble. I've got your tag numbers. Going to give them to my cousin, the deputy sheriff I told you about. His name is Dax Richardson."

"Whatever. Leave me alone."

"Which won't be a problem, if you leave the ladies alone. Remember the name—Dax Richardson—so when you come face-to-face with him you can be polite. Or…you can save yourself some trouble. Don't follow that bus. Your choice."

The biker zipped up his rain gear, then slammed the car trunk closed. "Storm's coming," Mitch said, looking toward the darkening sky.

Jared tightened his grip on the steering wheel and relaxed it. Did the guy think irony would somehow save him? A storm of trouble would rain down on Mitch if he continued to pursue Haley. Or hurt Camilla.

"The only storm I'm concern about is the one you're causing to folks I care about," Jared said flexing a fist. A physical fight never solved anything, but it was often the language of the land. It could be the only thing Mitch respected…or feared.

The younger man climbed onto the motorcycle and positioned a black helmet, face-shield flipped up, on his head. He turned a key on the bike. It roared to a start. He revved the engine several times and a wide grin stretched over his face as he deftly maneuvered the machine away from the car and Jared's truck.

"Can't stop a storm," Mitch shouted, then flipped the helmet shield down and took off burning rubber in the parking lot. The bike fishtailed. Mitch zoomed across the asphalt, then turned onto the deserted street while waving his middle finger. He never looked back.

"Asshole!" Ryan shouted.

Uneasiness settled in Jared's belly. He pushed his

cowboy hat back farther on his head. "I smell trouble, same as I smell the rain headed our way. Hope that fool doesn't find himself over the side of a mountain. Wonder if he's got any next-of-kin in Casper."

Blue and red lights flashed from a white SUV pulling into the parking lot. Bold gold letters spelled out *Sheriff* on the side of the vehicle.

"I sent the pictures to Dax's phone and our location. He's on duty. I gave him the asshole's first name. You forgot to politely ask for his last," Ryan pointed out.

The SUV stopped in front of the truck. Jared climbed out of the pickup and Ryan followed.

"You're a little late, Officer." Jared chuckled as he shook Dax's hand.

"You"—Dax poked his finger at Jared's chest—"always seem to find trouble. Now, you're involving Ryan?" He turned to Ryan. "That won't sit well with the bride-to-be or your old man. After all, you're the favorite son."

"Give Jared some credit," Ryan joked. "He saved the man from a knife fight."

"What? Jared, I thought you were dumb when you took to riding broncs instead of bulls. Breaking up a knife fight? Stupid." Dax frowned. "Anyone get hurt? Would the other man in the fight be the owner of the bike?" Dax pointed to the black marks streaking the parking lot.

"One and the same," Ryan replied. "Only the person starting the fight was a woman."

"A woman? How *does* trouble find you?" Dax shook his head. "I haven't run the tags through the system yet. Is there something I need to know?" Dax adjusted the holster on his waist.

"I think the guy is following the express bus to Cody. I believe he's got a thing for O'Connor's kid, Haley. Remember her? I hadn't seen her in a long while. She's pretty grown up now. Tall like her dad. Prettier than her mom. Not sure if she's eighteen yet, but I'm guessing not," Jared explained.

Dax shook his head. "What's with your sudden interest in this girl? Do I need to be concerned about you?"

"What? Damn! No. It's not like that. She's a kid."

"Ahem," Ryan interrupted. "It's the woman *with* the girl he's interested in."

"O'Connor's ex?" Shock registered on Dax's face. "That'll piss off your old man in a flash. Are you brave or stupid?"

"Noooo," Jared said slowly. "The ex-Missus O'Connor isn't on the bus. Camilla is taking Haley to Cody. Darla was strictly a one-time thing."

"Camilla?"

"Yeah," Ryan said. "She's a waitress at the Mountain View. You may have seen her. The one with the southern accent. I think that woman's used a cattle prod to trip his heart. It's beating again."

"You know my motto," Jared said dryly.

"Measure twice, cut once," Ryan responded. "You're a builder at heart. But you've been measuring for five years. It's about time for you to do some cutting. Rebuild your life."

"They say 'Married men live longer,' Jared," Dax said. "Or at least my wife reminds me every time she reads some dang woman's magazine. Besides, one bad marriage shouldn't turn you against the whole institution."

The litany was nothing new. A repetitive song played over and over, especially since his older brother's engagement, and since their father began shopping for wife number six, they peppered him at every opportunity with advice bullets as though he were a paper target at a firing range and understood nothing about women. If their prods were knife nicks, he'd die from a million little cuts. Hell, he had more nicks than a practice board used by a sideshow knife thrower.

"Look, when I said, 'For better or worse,' to Cheyenne, I meant it. Once was enough. I'm many things, but always a man of my word." Jared leaned against the SUV. The past was the past, and he refused to rehash old history in the parking lot with a storm closing in. "Dax, if you run the tags and find out something—like Mitch has outstanding warrants or prior arrests—let me know. He's headed to Cody, I know it. I'll phone O'Connor and let him know his daughter is coming with company."

"Right," Ryan chuckled. "Even if you're offering good news, that's one man who won't want to hear from you."

"Do you think he's carrying a grudge about that old incident?" Dax asked.

"Dax, you call him. I *don't* want to rehash this with him or the two of you," Jared said, heading toward his truck. Irritation sprouted a bud in his gut. If they kept at him, they'd feel the power of its bloom.

"O'Connor caught you with his ex," Ryan said. "The scene was pretty damning. Couldn't be mistaken for anything else than it was."

"White, glow-in-the-dark butts." Dax laughed.

"That may be true," Jared said, clenching his jaw and fighting back mounting irritation. "However *ex* is the key word in that sentence, Ryan."

Jared climbed into the pickup and yanked the door closed hard. His brother's jabs pestered him more than he liked to admit. Yes, they'd caught him in the back barn at the rodeo three years ago enjoying the company of a woman who'd hounded him for months—since her separation from O'Connor became official. That night, after the bronco bounced him in the rodeo ring, a soft woman soothed his pains. If he couldn't score in one ring, he could score in another. She came on strong. He had no energy to resist after the humiliating rodeo performance.

That night met a *need* in the moment.

Camilla, he was certain fell into the *want for a lifetime* category, but he had to step up his moves to be certain. Measure twice, cut once. He had a hunch about her. She could be the one. If so, could he convince her of that?

"It gave new meaning to shining a light into the darkness." Ryan laughed.

"Even I have some standards. I wouldn't make it with a married woman. Ryan, let's go."

"But I love telling the rest of the story"—Ryan slapped Dax on the back—"O'Connor wasn't married to the woman anymore. He didn't know the divorce had been finalized the day before because he never showed in court for the final hearing."

"Let's go." Jared revved the engine. A muscle in his jaw ticked. In a minute, he'd have to punch Ryan out.

Dax wandered over to the driver's side of Jared's

truck as Ryan climbed into the passenger's seat. "Just a word of caution," Dax said. "We all know O'Connor is fiercely protective of what's his. If your Camilla is escorting Haley home, he might think she needs his protection…including protection from you. Be wise. Be careful."

"She's never even met the man—"

"Be wise. Be careful."

"Yes, Officer. Advice duly noted. Catch you at the wedding Labor Day weekend.

Jared followed the same path as Mitch across the parking lot and turned onto the street. "Ryan, Dax is right. We need to go home now." Drops of rain sprinkled the windshield. Thunder rumbled.

"I'm gonna give you the same advice you gave Mitch," Ryan said.

Jared cocked his head. "Yeah?"

"Don't follow that bus."

"What are you talking about?" Jared frowned. Sometimes he could predict Ryan's thoughts before words ever came out. Sometimes.

"The storm is almost upon you. Having witnessed the unfolding *melodrama,* I get your attraction to…Camilla is her name, right?"

"Yes. Are you going to tell me what you're talking about or do I have to arm wrestle it out of you?"

"Southern. Louisiana, I'm betting," Ryan said. "All your momma's folks down there, right?" He nodded and Jared nodded, too. "There's something about a southern gal that draws you like a bee to a flower." Ryan grinned wide. "She could be one of those carnivorous ones."

"I think I've seen her worst moves—a

pocketknife." Jared turned on the radio to dissuade his brother from continuing. Jake Owen belted out "The One That Got Away."

Jared shook his head. He and Camilla hadn't yet had a summer romance, but it would happen. However, unlike the girl in the song, Camilla wouldn't get away.

Ryan tipped his cowboy hat low, the brim shaded most of his face, and he slunk down in the passenger's seat. "It's been a while since Cheyenne died, but maybe I've been pushing you too hard, all my hints about marriage."

"Hints? Those were hints? More like declarations just shy of *orders* the old man issues."

"I've got a hunch of my own. Camilla is the name of a hurricane. She's blowing a storm into your life."

Jared grinned. "I'm going to invite her to be my plus-one for your wedding."

"Heh. The woman won't even go out on a date with you."

"That settles it. We'll go pick up your gear. We're headed for Cody *and* Camilla tonight."

Chapter 8

Rain splattered the windows. Ahead, the lights of Cody glistened in the gray overcast evening like jewels holding a promise of good fortune. Inside the bus, Camilla tapped her finger in a slow beat against her chin. Her brain whirled round and round like a hula-hoop. Uncertainty attacked her confidence like snaking vines taking it hostage.

“Are we there yet?” Haley stirred beside her. She patted the teen’s head resting on her shoulder.

“Soon.”

Soon she’d be flat broke. Soon she’d have to leave.

She lived like a frugal nun, saving every cent possible. At the time, it had seemed like a good idea to deposit her earnings into the café’s account set up by her cousin, Biloxi. Now she had no cash reserve. Since her name wasn’t on the account, for a very good reason—money washed through her hands like water—withdrawals were impossible. The bank balance showed evidence of her invested commitment. A proud accomplishment. Nothing could persuade her to use the money for anything other than its intended purpose—the Fleur de Lis Café. But without a job, she’d be out on the street, unable to make rent, which meant she had to head home soon.

Options? There had to be some. She rejected each thought leading to a long, lonely car ride home to Fleur de Lis in the dog days of August. She could sell her car and catch a flight out of Jackson. Her family would celebrate if she returned. Going back a changed woman would earn her big points. They would throw her a party, the prodigal daughter returned. She could finally make peace with her sister and finalize the business plan for a café on the grounds of the estate with Greta and her cousin. Adding her recent bar and restaurant experience to Greta's cooking expertise and reputation, then stir in her cousin Biloxi's business savvy, the bank would surely lend them the rest of the money to launch the business successfully. Leaving Wyoming would not be defeat. Leaving could be the smartest of all options.

But it would deny her the pleasure of one dinner with Jared. Leaving a man she barely knew shouldn't be a problem. Except for that kiss. Except that his blue eyes had trapped her soul. In his arms, her every nerve reached a fevered pitch of hypersensitivity. Just thinking about him sent her pulse into a quickening throb that scared her as much as it fascinated. Not normal reactions. And there was that little matter of his engagement. Was he or was he not getting married? Her stomach lurched.

He's the last man on earth to let into your heart.

Ha! It's too late for that.

Good kisser. Charming. Manly. Strong. A date with Jared, even only one, could take her down the path of more shame and self-loathing. Her stomach knotted. Maybe fate had a sardonic sense of humor. It could be a test. Maybe Jared had landed in her life as a yardstick for her to measure how much she'd changed. Giving in to building desire and urges of seduction with a man about to be married would prove she hadn't changed much at all. If she shamed herself now, no one but she would know. But she *would* know.

Then home would be out of reach. She couldn't face her family. It would ruin all chances of truly healing the relationship with Branna. Camilla shuddered. She'd be a woman without a country…death might be preferable to never returning home.

Waves of homesickness carried her under. She'd been away too long. Fate was cruel to split her heart in two. Karmic punishment was hard to swallow.

Jared or home and family?

She sighed deeply, tapping her chin with her finger increased to a staccato beat.

"You're going to bruise your chin. Dad's going to think both of us were assaulted."

Camilla leveled a hard stare at Haley. "I thought you were asleep. You play possum well. So, you finally admit the truth. Mitch hit you."

"Yeah, but you don't understand. You've never let me tell you the story of what happened. He didn't *mean* to hit me. Not really. He meant to scare me. And it was my fault."

Camilla fought to keep her voice level, which required wrangling anger surfacing faster than a NASA launching rocket. However, to keep the teen talking and maintain open communications, she couldn't get preachy or too motherly. "Tell me how *his* lack of intention makes it *your* fault."

"I'm ashamed to say. Can't we drop it?" Haley's chin dropped to her chest. Her shoulder hunched.

"I won't press you right now. However, we need to talk about this, get it all out in the open. You'll feel better. It's not good carrying shame around. Trust me, I know all about it."

"What have you ever done that was so awful?" Haley challenged.

"Cody," the bus driver called out. "We'll arrive at the station in a few minutes."

"Since I promised to treat you like an adult, I'll explain when we talk about it later. You have to face the problem and deal with it, before you can really move on," Camilla said. "Let me look at you"—she lifted Haley's chin—"ice works wonders. Not too bad. Run a brush through your hair and smear on some lip-gloss. Smile wide when you see your dad."

"I'm afraid, Camilla," Haley whispered. She brushed her hair in quick strokes. "My dad's got a temper."

"Has *he* ever hurt you?" Camilla squeezed her hands tightly together waiting for the teen to answer. Had Haley been abused by her father? Is that why she continued to defend Mitch's actions?

"He's blustery"—she shoved the brush in her purse and pulled a tube of peach balm—"bossy, too, but he's never laid a hand on me. Though, he did try to shoot Jared once."

"What?"

Haley puckered her lips, spreading gloss over them.

The doors of the bus opened. "Please exit safely. We're behind schedule because of the rain, so please exit quickly. There's a busload of passengers waiting to head up to Sheridan." The driver stepped off the bus.

After Camilla gathered her purse and box of sweets, she started to rise, but Butch Moore stepped into the aisle on her left and towered over her.

“If you’ll give me your number, I’d like to call you. Take you out for dinner. Here or back in Jackson. I didn’t mean to listen in, but I overheard you talkin’ to your friend, there. I really admire you. You’re a good woman. A good one is hard to find.”

Haley stood up and squared her shoulders. “Thanks for the ice, Mr. Moore. Camilla’s going to be busy while she’s here.”

“Well, then…when you’re back in Jackson.” Butch smiled, apparently undeterred by a teenager’s sass.

Still sitting and sandwiched between the two, Camilla’s neck ached from gazing up at them. “Mr. Moore—”

“Butch.”

“I have your card. Thank you for the invitation. If I have time before I go, I’ll give you a call.”

“Go where?” Haley demanded. “You got fired from your job. You have to stay here. With me and my dad.”

“So you did hear all of the conversation. I’ve been planning to go home. Mississippi. Louisiana. Where my people are from.”

Butch held out his hand and helped her to rise from her seat. He gave her hand a light squeeze. “You’ve got the accent, all right.” He made room for her and Haley to pass.

“Thank you,” Camilla said. “Again, if there’s time…” Butch’s manners were perfect, but no sizzling reaction came when their palms met. However, she’d received two sincere offers for a nice dinner in one day. That hadn’t happened before. Momma would be impressed. Men could actually think of her as a lady. Wait until her sister heard that.

Haley stepped off the bus in front of Camilla.

"Daddy!" Haley squealed.

Camilla stepped down. While a big black umbrella blocked her view, she heard the exchange between her young friend and her father.

"Haley. I'm glad you're home. Let me look at you."

The umbrella lifted, then closed. Haley ran to Camilla. The teen tugged on her hand. "Come on. Come meet my dad."

Camilla took two steps forward and stopped at the sight of Sean. Square jaw. Intense dark eyes, tinged with tiredness or maybe worry for his child. Haley had his same shiny, thick brown hair. A shadow of a beard made his tanned face look ruggedly handsome and full of character. The kind of face her cousin would love to photograph.

"Welcome to Cody." Sean reached for her hand. "Camilla, I can't thank you enough for bringing Haley home."

A touch on her shoulder made her pull her gaze away from Sean. She turned slightly.

"Call me, ya hear," Butch said. He tipped his imaginary hat at Sean before walking away.

"Dad, I'm hungry. Let's go." Haley headed toward the parking lot at a fast trot. "Camilla, you can ride up front with Dad. You're the grownup. I'll ride in the back."

"Haley, slow down," Camilla called, though she understood Haley's avoidance tactics. If the girl had no time alone with her dad, it diminished the chance of an interrogation or any lecture he may have planned.

"Oh my gosh! I forgot to call you," Camilla cried.

"So sorry. After what happened at the bus station…I got on the bus to see Haley home—"

"All is well." He gestured for Camilla to follow in Haley's wake. "Let's go have a quiet steak dinner. There's an old establishment in town."

Once in the car, Haley chattered endlessly, barely taking a breath. She talked of her dishwashing job at the diner, how much she missed her horse at the ranch, and then glowingly explained about the blowout party her father hosted for her sixteenth birthday. Camilla rubbed her temples. She'd never heard the girl go on and on and on.

"And I'm so hungry I could eat a whole cow," Haley announced.

"This restaurant is an institution." Sean pointed ahead. "Been around since the turn of the last century." He pulled into a parking spot under a colorful animated neon sign of a cowboy riding a bronco. The horse appeared to buck, and the cowboy appeared to wave his hat. Nothing said "Wild West" louder than that sign.

"But…Babette's? It's named after a woman?" Camilla cast a glance around at the western motif when they entered the restaurant. Log walls. Scuffed wooden floors with sawdust scattered around mixed with peanut shells. She'd entered a different universe, one where the clock remained stuck more than a hundred years in the past.

"Mr. O'Connor, how many for dinner tonight?" a hostess in a plaid shirt, jeans and white cowboy hat asked.

Sean raised three of his fingers.

"Please follow me. Do you want a booth or table?"

"Booth," Haley said, then followed the woman

through the dining room. Camilla trailed behind with Sean bringing up the rear. Peanut shells littering the wooden floor crunched underfoot.

The chatter of other diners didn't drown out the band warming up in the next room singing Toby Keith and Willie Nelson's version of "Whiskey for my men. Beer for my horses." A waitress carried a sizzling steak, the size of which Camilla had never seen, to a nearby table, and she resisted the urge to follow the sound of the sizzle and scent of the char-grilled beef to snap a photo of the platter in front of the man. The baked potato's size matched the steak's proportions. It was as big as any size-nine sneaker she'd ever owned. The platter would forever define steak and potatoes in her mind.

"Camilla, I think it's cool what Babette did—the woman who started this place," Haley said with a backward glance over her shoulder. "She was a known prosti—"

"Lady of the night," Sean interrupted in a low voice from behind.

"Dad"—Haley stopped and turned, then rolled her eyes—"she slept with men for money. It's no big deal these days."

"Is that a fact? Well, let me tell you something, young lady—"

Camilla turned and frowned at Sean, who discontinued his sentence.

The hostess placed three menus on the table at a booth. "Your server will be right over. I hope you enjoy your dinner. And…it sounds like your conversation will be *stimulating*." The woman smiled and left them.

Haley climbed into the booth. Camilla slid in next,

her fatigued body waving a white flag of surrender. After the day she'd had, she craved a good, strong cup of coffee and chicory with condensed milk, a carryover from her childhood. Greta always led her to believe the drink was a special secret between the two of them until the day she caught Greta serving the creamy beverage to her younger brother. Though the memory lifted her spirits a bit, her coffee brand wasn't on any menu outside of Louisiana. And Haley's incessant chatter was about to step on her last good nerve.

Sean slid into the booth across the table and sat in the middle of the bench seat. His eyes widened when he looked his daughter over. His jaw clamped shut. A muscle ticked. He leaned across the table and caught Haley by the chin, turning her face from side to side.

Tears welled in Haley's eyes. Camilla cringed.

Yet around them sounds of diners and the band drifted across the restaurant. "*We'll raise up our glasses…evil forces…whiskey…*"

Unable to stand the building tension, Camilla smacked her hand on the table. "I think I need a glass of whiskey." When Sean continued to stare at Haley, she reached across the table and rested her hand on his arm. Gave it a little squeeze. "So in your opinion, what's the best brand?" She hoped Sean would take the hint and let the issue drop until they were in a private place more conducive to a father/daughter discussion.

"Excuse me, please, Camilla. I need to leave the table for a minute." Haley jerked away from her father. Camilla quickly scooted out of the way. Before the teen stalked away from the table, she turned back and said, "Dad, why don't you tell Camilla why you tried to shoot Jared."

Camilla snapped her full attention to Sean. “What?” Haley’s startling declaration stole Camilla’s breath away. She shook off the shock. The girl was lashing out from pain. No better way to deflect attention than to throw it on someone else, only Haley’s words set off a firebomb of questions in her mind. Sean tried to shoot Jared? She shook her head. How in the world could she protect the teen from the wrath of Sean?

“She’s the only child I have,” Sean said, as though that explained everything.

“I would prefer to discuss this with you in a less public place.” Camilla dropped back into her seat, hoping the rest of dinner would be a peaceful affair. Her stomach rumbled. Her mouth watered from the aromas trailing behind servers delivering food.

Sean’s cell phone rang. He pulled it from his the clip on his belt. “This ought to be real interesting. O’Connor here.”

Sean’s eyes narrowed, then he raised one eyebrow. A forced smile appeared on his lips, the kind a cat might flash before pouncing on a mouse. “Here’s what I will do, Richardson. After I have dinner with a lovely lady and my only child, we’re going home. If you want to pay a visit to the lady, you can come by tomorrow. Not tonight…No,” he said forcefully, “not tonight. She’ll be my guest. Not that it’s any of your business.”

Camilla wet her lips. Her stomach fluttered. Jared was talking to Sean? He had followed her to Cody?

“Ah, Sean?” Camilla raised her finger to get his attention, but he clicked the phone off and set it on the table.

“Do you and Richardson have a thing?” Sean asked pointedly.

Camilla furrowed her brow. "No, not exactly. I didn't even know his last name."

"My advice to you lady, stay away from him. He's a skunk and a bear lover. Not a rancher or hard worker like Ryan."

"But—" She started to contradict him. Darcy had said he was a cowboy. Cowboys and ranchers are different. But a skunk and bear lover? What the heck? Her relationship with Jared, or lack thereof, was none of his blasted business.

Haley returned to the table with the waitress following close behind her.

"Basil Haden neat for the lady and me. Lemonade for the kid. Two filets—for the ladies. One medium. And how do you take your steak?" Sean asked.

"Medium rare," Camilla answered. The man had some nerve ordering for her without even asking. The rib-eye steak was more to her liking. Jared might be a bear lover—and why that was a bad thing, she intended to find out—but she wasn't about to challenge the bear of a man sitting across the table from her. He scared her more than a little.

"Dad, I can order for myself."

Sean ignored Haley, finished ordering, then turned to Camilla. "I think it best that you stay at our place tonight. I just assumed it was understood. But I can see from my daughter's glares I may have overstepped my bounds. So I'm asking if you'll be our guest."

"I think, father dearest, you need to know she's got the hots for Jared," Haley said. "Did you tell her yet about the time you tried to shoot him?"

Camilla's eyes narrowed. She scrutinized the teenager next to her. Haley, back rigid and head cocked, stared hard at her father. Anger radiated. The two were tethered by a conduit of electricity. Clearly, Jared was a hot button with the O'Connor family. But why?

A man in a plaid shirt with pearl buttons, jeans, and a black Stetson arrived with a small tray. "Drinks." He correctly placed each drink on the table.

"Good to see you, Sean," the man said. "And with such lovely company, too." The man winked at Camilla.

"Don't get any ideas. She's a friend of Haley's visiting from out of town," Sean replied gruffly, then began talking ranching with the man.

Camilla lifted her glass. Sean did the same, but he continued his conversation as though she and Haley were not seated across from him. He *clinked* his glass to hers. Camilla gulped her first taste of the amber liquid. She needed all the fortification Basil Haden might offer. The whiskey was smoother than she imagined, but not smooth enough to erase the anxiety plunking a tune in her gut.

While Sean and the man continued their discussion, Camilla leaned over to Haley and whispered, "Are you purposefully trying to piss off your dad?"

"Yep." Haley nodded. "If I rile him up about Jared, then he'll be too busy being mad about that to get all *parental* with me…at least for tonight."

"So you're using me."

"Not intentionally."

"Only about as unintentional as Mitch hitting you."

"That's not fair," Haley protested.

Camilla started to reply, but stopped when Sean's conversation pricked her curiosity.

"—yeah, Richardson wants to argue water rights again. Them's fighting words."

"Speaking of fighting words," a very familiar voice sounded behind her. Camilla's breath hitched in her throat. Tingles traveled through her body like someone had plugged *her* into an electrical current.

Sean's eyes narrowed. All conversation at the table died. He glared at a spot just over her shoulder with anger so intense she flinched.

"I need a few minutes to speak with Camilla." Jared said it matter-of-factly, as though it was an everyday, ordinary request.

Under Sean's glare, Camilla gulped air. Her palms moistened. She grabbed her glass and knocked back the rest of the whiskey, almost choking as it went down hot. She sucked in a breath to smother the rising sense of doom in her gut.

Men! She refused to allow two men to asphyxiate her into a stupor. Jared was the one man she definitely wanted to see, but just not at that exact moment. She had settled on a course of action and intended to call him later to share her plan. In a few days, once she settled things with Haley, she'd allow herself one dinner *only* with Jared, then leave for home, removing herself from all temptations.

Sean slid from the booth and rose, his fists at his sides. Camilla imagined the bear of a man tearing into Jared. She shuddered. Sean O'Connor had to be as tough a man as she'd ever seen. As tough as any *hombre* she'd watched in old black and white cowboy movies.

"Wait." Camilla scooted out of the booth. She stood in the aisle like a fence between two bulls.

Tension radiated around her like a tornado. It fried her remaining nerve. Stuck in a mechanical press about to pulverize her would probably be more fun.

"Sean, I'm very sorry for the interruption"—she turned and faced Jared—"now isn't a good time. How about I call you tomorrow?" She raised her eyebrows and frowned hoping to send him a very clear message. This was her choice. Not his or Sean's.

"Take the lady's offer, Richardson. This is a private dinner," Sean growled.

Camilla laid her hands on Jared's chest, took a step and pushed him back, then took another step, forcing him back farther.

"Please, Jared. This can wait until tomorrow. I've got all I can deal with right now."

Jared quirked his mouth to one side, then snorted. "Okay. Tomorrow. Just write your cell phone number on my hand, *then* I'll go."

When Camilla turned to find her purse, a pen appeared from over her shoulder. "Little lady, I think this is what you need." A waitress handed over a permanent ink Sharpie. "You don't want that man washing your number away. At least not easily."

In a rush, Camilla scribbled her phone number on Jared's palm. She looked up, but before she could speak, Jared leaned in as if to kiss her. She jerked back in surprise and stumbled into the waitress. Sean grabbed her around the waist and helped her regain her balance.

"I'm sorry," Camilla told the other woman.

From the booth, Haley rested her chin in her hands and giggled.

"Until tomorrow, Camilla." Jared tipped his hat at

her and walked away without a look back.

Camilla sighed. She hated clichés, but Jared had to be the best-looking hunk of man she'd wanted in a very long time. Maybe ever.

And tomorrow, she'd tell him good-bye.

Chapter 9

The next morning, Jared woke alert as though someone had pumped him with adrenaline that shot straight to his brain. A rooster crowed in the far distance, but the natural alarm clock didn't usually bring him to full military attention. Sleeping in a bunkhouse, he'd learned to ignore errant sounds. Now faint noises disturbed his peace and grabbed him from sleep, ruining a dream of a sweet, brown-eyed woman with the most kissable lips and an accent that dripped like honey. With a minute more in dreamtime, he would've had her beneath him in bed. Instead, wide-awake, he turned on his side, moving out of an uncomfortable position.

"Damn bird," Jared muttered. "That rooster better be thankful it lives to see another day." If the dream had continued and crowing woke him in the middle of the best part…the henhouse would be looking for a new head male, pronto.

He stretched out long on the bunk with his hands behind his head and gazed at the underside of the mattress above him. The bunkhouse often reminded him of summer camp. He'd been a teenager at a coed camp for the first time down south, near his grandparents' home, the last time a dream gifted him with a nocturnal hard-on. That was when he truly learned all about primal instincts. Raging hormones, a fierce tornado of desire, mixed with more girls in bikinis than he'd ever known existed left him over stimulated for two solid weeks, so much so he could've run coast to coast like *Forest Gump* only stopping to pee and drink.

Somehow, Camilla had reduced him to that boy at camp. Wanting her topped his list of desires. He wouldn't take *no* for an answer and would use all his charm and persuasion. But was that taking unfair advantage? Nope. Not when love was at stake. He had measured twice, and now it was cutting time.

That kiss from Camilla sealed everything. He picked up the cell phone beside his pillow and scanned email messages. No reply from Camilla to his good-night note.

"Why didn't you answer?" he murmured. Disappointment pricked his heart. Except for one real kiss—he'd tasted her lips in his dreams—she had shut him down last night when he went in for a second one. Other women never treated him like that. He'd never faced that problem before. His problem was the exact opposite. Women didn't like to take no for an answer.

This woman was twisting his insides like saltwater taffy on a pulling machine. Everything Camilla said and did, very politely at that, during his waking hours shouted *Stop!* like a flashing red neon sign.

Except he couldn't.

Her combination of sweetness, like the way she chatted up the old timers at the diner, her mother-bear instincts with Haley, and the smoothness of her southern accent charmed him, and that's how he planned to describe her to his grandfather. The old man was in for a big surprise.

Swinging his legs around and planting his feet on the ground, Jared sat up. The cool cement floor didn't cool his ardor. He raked his fingers through his hair. Any thought of Camilla and his gut churned with a deep gnawing ache, something Tums or Rolaids couldn't cure.

He'd played it too safe. A slow flirtation had been the plan. When Trixie told him where Camilla worked, he was happy about the coincidence. He always ran past the diner on his jogging route whenever he stayed at the Jackson Hole condo. Yesterday, to his surprise, he caught her staring when he went running past. He praised fate for stepping in. The morning's choice of eatery had everything to do with her and nothing to do with the food.

Her smile, especially her dimples, snagged his full attention. She was attractive in a wholesome way. She played coy at the diner, yet her subtle actions clued him, and when she spoke, her voice wove a magical web. She was a Pied Piper, and he had no choice but to follow her tune.

After their random Friday meeting, he'd allowed the undercurrent of attraction to swirl for a full day, just to be sure hormones weren't turning him into a randy old goat. He wasn't like his father. He had to be sure there was more than physical attraction, though clearly his body intended to overrule any possible objection. Lucky for him, before he'd left to go jogging, he caught sight of the contents of the package from his Louisiana grandmother. The pralines set his course of action—he could offer them as a gift, his first definite move to charm the woman who captured his thoughts. Dinner would've been next. What followed should've been a slow seduction in bed at the finest hotel in Jackson. Not her on a bus to Cody. Nor her as a guest at O'Connor's.

Coulda. Woulda. Shoulda. It got him in trouble every time.

"Damn it," he groaned. His frustration over her simmered while soft snoring from five men asleep in the bunkhouse intruded on his daydream. He flopped back on his bunk, but the snoring prevented sleep and sank his hopes of plugging back into a Camilla phantasm.

Rolling to his side, he punched a fist into his pillow. Instead of exercising his manly prowess with the Southern belle haunting his every thought, he lay listening to a concert of snorts and snuffles produced by gruff, grown men. It was the first time since Cheyenne had died that he wished he were back in his own home and in his own bed…with Camilla's company, of course. But that wouldn't work now. He'd made the bunkhouse his primary residence whenever living in Wyoming and given Felicia an annual lease on his house rather than let the thing sit vacant.

Click. The timer on the automatic coffeemaker turned it on. In seconds, the aroma from a dark brew drifted through the bunkhouse to Jared's nose. Giving up on any hope of more sleep, he surveyed the room. Six bunk beds he'd built with his own hands. At the rear of the room, spanning the entire width of the wall, another of his works—a clothes closet. A local artist had painted a mural on it and unless someone knew the closet was there, the entire wall appeared to be a painted western scene of mountains, trees, and animals.

His father had taken a risk on him and given him his first, professional commercial project. Until then, he'd only built houses. The old man had his faults, but where he lacked in fatherly skills he made up for it in others, like agreeing to every detail of the construction plan. The long rectangular building had been constructed out of milled timber harvested from the ranch and designed to appear authentically western on the outside. Inside provided full modern amenities, including a shower room like one found at big city gyms, restroom stalls, and a locker room for dressing. The kitchen opened up to an eating and living area that Nicole made sure was cleaned regularly, which was the only reason it didn't look like a frat house with beer cans everywhere.

A pillow flew at Jared from across the room and before it hit he caught it.

"You up already?" Ryan called out, his voice raspy from sleep.

"Yeah." Jared rose and walked to the closet. "Let's go check on the old man. He needs office help to keep the ranch moving, especially with you leaving soon."

"Last night, Nicole told me he fired his recently hired assistant," Ryan said sliding into his jeans.

"When will he get it in his head that *office assistant* isn't a euphemism for wife number six?" Jared yanked a t-shirt over his head, then pulled on his running shorts. He finished with his socks and sneakers.

"Well, what do you do when the same plan works five times in a row? I guess in his defense, you don't fix what ain't broke. All of his wives started as employees."

"Would you two shut up?" groaned one of the ranch hands in the bunks.

"Time to get up. Summer lasts only so long." Jared

raised his voice to his brother. "Talk about grumpy. I'm going running. Meet you up at the big house when I'm done."

"Since you're here, I want you to take Nicole to my house to do a walk-through. You're the builder. I want my bride to be satisfied. That damn house better be ready for occupancy when we get back from our honeymoon."

Jared bent and stretched, starting his warm up. "Plenty enough time. After all, you're taking two weeks. Are you sure you can stand the stress of being away that long?"

"Two weeks," Ryan grumbled. "I couldn't convince her a week now and a week in the islands in the dead of winter. The ranch will survive, but will I? I'll be back for the cattle drive. Best part of ranching." Ryan grinned. "So how'd it go last night? Invited Camilla to the wedding yet?"

"Plan to do that today," Jared said, jogging in place to continue warming up. "Sean wasn't cool with me talking to her in his company. If I don't hear from her, I'll go over there on my way out of town. I'll take Nicole up to the house before I leave, then I've got to get back to Cody to check in on the grocery store. Occupancy certificate should be ready tomorrow after the final inspection today."

"I'll make a wager on whether or not the little belle will say *yes* and be your date. It'll liven things up a bit. Just so you know, my money's on you."

"Better be, big brother," Jared said, dryly.

"Say, any more news on the bear?" Ryan asked, pulling on his boots.

"Spotted one a few times, but never close enough

to know if it's *the* one. Not able to get a bead on its location. I'm positive Sean hasn't found it and killed it. He would've called just to gloat. Got to go."

"Just watch out for bears," Ryan hollered.

Jared nodded. He'd pay close attention. Bears were foraging for their upcoming hibernation, which made it a bad time to tangle with them. He grabbed a water bottle from the kitchen, then jogged into the morning light. Fresh air filled his lungs and buoyed his spirits the same way helium gives life to a balloon. He purposefully shut Camilla and work out of his mind and focused on the old horse trail that meandered for miles along the fence lines of the ranch. His father and brother ran about six hundred head of cattle there. With the herd grazing on federal land all summer, the fields waved with hay waiting for cutting that would commence any day now.

The old man thought running for exercise was just fool crazy when riding a horse and working the ranch pulled a hard sweat from a man and strained muscles until they ached. He never came out and said, but if asked, would admit he believed running was for sissies.

Before Jared, the path sloped subtly downward. He kept a steady pace. After the first mile, he neared the ditch. In the distance, a dust trail from a truck caught his attention. The guy behind the wheel, a ditch driver checking the water source, slowed and waved. Jared waved back. Neighborly guy. It was about the only thing the south had in common with Wyoming. The semi-arid western land, a place where water rights could spark a civil war, differed greatly from the water-laden air of Louisiana where growing up he'd spent half of each summer, caught in the war between his father and grandparents. The South and the West never reached a compromise. As a kid, the pain of it all had seeped into him the way pickling spices changed cucumbers to crunchy pickles. The battle changed when he'd reached eighteen, and he vowed to live his own life…one that didn't include ranching.

His maternal grandparents still lived in New Orleans in the Garden District. Proper. Polite. And political. They provided him with exposure to the finer things in life and dangled the carrots of riches in front of him each time he visited. It was as though he'd been raised in two different countries and two different cultures. But, to everyone's dismay, he refused to choose one over the other. He became his own man. A contractor, then developer. Would his mother be proud?

He barely remembered her. She died when he was five. There was a marker for her grave in the Richardson cemetery up on the mountain, but her body rested in a family tomb in New Orleans. He had a few good memories of her and could describe her from photographs, but her face remained fuzzy in his memory the way a watercolor blurs hues one into another. Her perfume, however, a sweet and floral scent, always grabbed his attention whenever he recognized the fragrance on another woman. Ryan took her passing even harder after having lost his own mother when he was a baby.

"Ugh!" Jared grunted when his foot came down hard on a raised stone slamming into his arch. He slowed his pace, then stopped to shake out the momentary soreness and finish the bottle of water. Back to normal, he continued at a regular steady pace though quelling the urge to run wide open across the field and all the way to Sean's house just to see Camilla.

Maybe the stuff he'd read about commitment avoidance had a note of truth. Since neither he nor Ryan ever had a stable, female role model in their childhood, they didn't understand what commitment meant to a woman. Cheyenne had told him that, in fact, she'd shouted it at him in front of a packed rodeo stadium. He wanted to prove her wrong for the sake of his pride. Little did he know back then the woman had baited him. He'd married her to prove her wrong, confusing bruised pride with love.

"Pride goes before a fall." His fell when Cheyenne cheated on him the first time…and then later, cheating had cost her her life. When he buried her, condolences from friends and family made his skin itch with the same uncomfortableness as an outbreak of poison ivy. His relationship with Cheyenne had been her sham, and he was too much of dumb ass to know until after he'd said, "I do."

Girlfriends. Wives. Mothers. Women confused him. For some reason, his father, big strapping man that he was, only seemed to feel fulfilled when he had a wife. A girlfriend didn't cut it. Five wives in one lifetime. A dizzying thought.

At least he'd had one less stepmother than Ryan. After his mother died, he and Ryan suffered through two additional stepmothers before leaving for college, and one more after that. Their stepmothers were pretty, dainty women from some eastern city and thought the west had magic it didn't. All of them divorced their father. The revolving door of women in the old man's life made him and Ryan leery of marriage, though he *had* made it to the altar with Cheyenne.

Jared slowed his pace at the halfway mark in his run. No bears or even bear track sightings. The sun's slow ascent hadn't burned off all the low-lying fog. He jogged around three large boulders near the edge of a tree line, then stopped when movement caught his eye. About fifty yards away, he spotted Hunter. Satisfaction rolled over him the way water rolls over rocks in a stream, fast and steady. A glistening black coat rippled with movement whenever the bear lumbered across a field or down a trail. He'd nicknamed the animal the Wyoming Game and Fish Department had been trying to trap for relocation. He wanted it done before Sean took matters into his own hands.

In March, after hibernation, the black bear wandered too close to Sean's horse barn and spooked the stock of horses. A hired hand ran the bear off. No damage to horse or property resulted; however, Sean had it in his mind the animal was a nuisance in need of exterminating. When news reached Jared about the confrontation, he paid a visit to Sean and ended up arguing with the man against killing the bear. He insisted relocation could work, but Sean disagreed and had stated outright the government had no business digging into his. He'd kill any bear to protect his home, family, and livestock. Since then, Jared had been on bear watch.

The bear paused. Stretched its neck. Sniffed the air. The omnivore snuffled for the scent of food, or maybe danger. Did he recognize Jared as friend or foe? Unarmed, Jared remained wary but unafraid. Black bears weren't the hulking beasts that maimed and killed like grizzlies. Then, as though satisfied no danger lurked, the bear moved farther away while Jared made a mental note about where to return to track the animal. Humans had encroached on bear territory, not the other way around. Bears became a threat usually due to carelessness of humans. Wild animals were never intended to be pets.

Moving at a slow jog, then picking up speed, Jared ran toward the big ranch house and the expected confrontation that waited. He intended to discuss his offer to scout for a new office assistant. One that had no possibility of being stepmother number six.

Then he'd have to explain why he wouldn't be returning for the winter.

Chapter 10

Camilla yawned and padded barefoot across a thick woolen rug, enjoying plush softness underfoot. When her feet met the cool wooden floor of the large guest room, she scrunched her toes and continued toward the window. Slivers of daylight haloed around the edges of the room-darkening drapes. Mornings in Wyoming dawned early, and she usually rose with the sun. A habit she'd fought against at first but come to love. Except this morning when the opulence of a king-size bed and a down comforter surrounded her like warm, soft cashmere in winter. Life at Fleur de Lis ran on a different schedule, and she'd miss the early morning quiet once she returned home.

Earlier a rooster had crowed way off in the distance; she ignored the pesky bird's call to order. Her brain incorporated the sound into a scrumptious dream involving Jared during his morning jog, just as when she first saw him running. His inner strength radiated calmness. He reminded her of a lighthouse on the beach in Biloxi, Mississippi, that steadfastly flashed a white light at night, cautioning ship captains and boaters about dangers ahead. The beacon remained strong in hurricane-strength winds. The lighthouse was the unique landmark uniting the town. But she couldn't imagine Jared in that setting.

Tugging on the drapery cord, Camilla wished for a

day better than yesterday. One that included a few moments with Jared. A private good-bye to a man who gave her the gift of making her feel feminine and ladylike. Yet her resolve to look but never touch tightened like a cinching rope around her heart. There could be no more kisses. She had to remain strong. In her mind, a crack of a whip flicked near her ear as a warning—do not kiss the man again, let alone think of hokey-pokey or hanky-panky with him, ever!

She dropped into the upholstered chair near the window. Whenever her thoughts drifted to Jared, tingling delight washed over her, head to toe, like silk buffing her body, which caused the imaginary devil on her shoulder to dance an Irish jig and coo, "Sensually delicious!" while the angel on the other shoulder *tsked* in dark disapproval.

"Good morning, world." She squinted at the brightness flooding the butter-colored room, then dove back beneath the covers, slithering into warmth. The large Hello Kitty t-shirt she'd borrowed last night from Haley bunched around her waist. She wiggled between the sheets to straighten it while wondering if Jared were out there running now, his strong legs carrying him along wild country trails. Maybe even with a dog running beside him for company. Yet the image didn't hold quite the same appeal as watching him in person. A smile played at her lips. He might definitely be in the department of "look but don't touch." However, thankfully for her, admiring never hurt anyone. Giddiness swelled in her chest. If nothing else, she would enjoy the delights of the pull of attraction to the man.

Taking in the scenery beyond the bedroom

window, her body relaxed at the sight of splendor. Images in books and movies paled by comparison to the real thing. The mountains rose higher. Greenery appeared in so many shades that any artist would be energized by the palette. No one had ever accurately described the clear blue hue of the sky. Just like Jared's eyes. When she returned home and repainted her bedroom, she intended to match it to that particular shade, though she doubted the paint guy at the hardware store would be familiar with the color "Jared blue."

She listened for noises in the house, signs of anyone stirring. A peaceful silence pervaded. As much as she wanted coffee, traipsing downstairs underdressed in Haley's t-shirt and running the risk of bumping into Sean made the need for java less appealing. In a while, she'd wake Haley, and then rummage through her closet to borrow a few things to wear until returning to Jackson. With no job, she had no reason to rush back. Spending a few days on the O'Connor ranch might benefit both of them. However, Haley was taller, so jeans would need a temporary hem, but skirts and shorts would probably fit okay. Even though the diner owed her a final paycheck, her funds wouldn't stretch for spending on anything but the trip home, which she might manage if she charged expenses on the emergency-use-only credit card her mother had sent a year ago.

She cringed. There was nothing worse than a family handout given in pity. She'd left home to change, to prove her maturity and independence to all of them…and herself. Taking money, even in the form of credit, blemished her plan like a big black ink spot splattered against pristine white paper. If the worst came, she could sell her car and buy a plane ticket home.

Bzzz. Her phone received an email. She grabbed her phone and read the message from her sister.

Been trying to call you. Call me. NOW @FdL

Humph! Camilla snorted. Aggravation locked her jaw. Her older sister may have grown a stronger spine when she ended her engagement to Steven. After all, it took guts to cancel the wedding everyone in Bayou Petite dubbed “the wedding of the century.” However, Branna’s bossiness hadn’t diminished a bit. In fact, it may have grown worse since her engagement to James.

Fighting the urge to delete the message without responding, Camilla bit back a snarky retort and instead answered honestly.

Barely have service. Will call later. I’m in Cody, Wyoming.

She tossed the phone on the bed. One thing that hadn’t changed. She still hated taking orders from her sister.

Knock! Knock!

Two loud raps sounded on the closed bedroom door. Camilla rolled over in bed wondering if Haley, Sean, or the housekeeper he’d mentioned stood on the opposite side of the door.

“Yes?” She glanced at the clock on the wall. It was almost nine, and she wondered if Darcy had enjoyed opening the diner alone that morning. Had the woman missed her morning treat of watching Jared running? Served Darcy right for firing her. Camilla’s giddy-meter rose more than a tad at the idea of Jared returning home to Cody for a date with her.

“Breakfast,” Haley called out. The cheerfulness in

the teen's voice touched Camilla. Even if leaving Jackson to escort the girl home had cost her a job, she'd done the right thing. Haley's chipper tone improved her mood and helped put the day back on track.

"I'll be down in a few minutes," Camilla said. "I'm so hungry I could eat a whole cow." She mimicked Haley's words from dinner last night.

"No. I've got it here on a tray."

"Breakfast in bed for me?" Camilla rose and pulled the t-shirt's hem, it almost reached her knees, before opening the door and peering around it to see if Haley was alone.

"Get back in bed. The tray has legs."

Camilla breathed in aromas of coffee and fried bacon, though a silver dome on the tray covered any hints of food. The scents lit her hunger pangs and, on cue, her stomach rumbled. She licked her lips and swallowed hard, anticipating the first mouthwatering bite. "I've never had breakfast in bed," Camilla told the teenager.

"Git, then."

As ordered, she climbed back into bed and stuffed another pillow behind her back. Pulling the covers over her legs, she folded back the top end, tucking it at her waist.

"Never?" Haley asked.

"Never what?"

"You've never had breakfast in bed. Not even at a nice hotel?" Haley maneuvered the wooden tray toward her and the bed, setting it down.

"No, not even in a hotel. I didn't know you could cook."

"I'm decent in the kitchen. Don't you travel and

stay in hotels where they have room service? I've never had a tray like this"—she pointed—"usually the food is rolled in on a moveable cart with a tablecloth and linens. I like it when they do this." Haley lifted the silver dome with a flourish.

"Wow! And no, growing up, I never traveled much. The typical grade school trip to Washington D.C.. A trip to the Smokey Mountains with the family once. I guess I'm more of a bayou girl than I realized. Home's got everything I want."

"Oh. Well, eat up. French toast, hot syrup, fried bacon and coffee. There's cream and sugar on the side." The girl plucked a white linen napkin from the back pocket of her jeans, snapped it open, then snuggled it into the space between Camilla and the tray. "No crumbs in bed this way."

Camilla looked over the food. "I'm so hungry I could eat a bear." Then she looked over the teen. The bruising on Haley's face had diminished a bit, but not enough to be unnoticeable. How had Sean dealt with the confirmation of his daughter's bruises? What would he do to heal the invisible wounds? She wondered how their discussion ended last night. Haley's eyes weren't puffy from crying. That was a good sign.

"Eat up. I already had mine," Haley said, plopping at the foot of the bed.

Camilla poured cream, then scooped sugar into her coffee. Last night, she'd excused herself from what she considered a private conversation. Sean started in almost as soon as they arrived at the ranch. Having been on the receiving side of many lectures, she opted to give them privacy. The last thing she wanted was for him to see her as an ally and take a two-against-one stand against the girl. Nor had she wanted to give Sean the opportunity to put her on the spot. She wouldn't lie for Haley, but also didn't want to be cornered into revealing information he could use as leverage against her.

"This is great French toast." Camilla savored the melding flavors of bread, egg, and syrup. "We have something called *pain perdu*. Greta—I've told you about her. She's the one who sends me care packages—she runs the kitchen, takes care of my great grand aunts, and is the *best* cook. But, don't tell Greta, this is right up there with hers." She took another nibble of the sweetened bread and two bites on the crisp bacon.

"Know how I learned to cook?" Haley's grin turned mischievous.

Camilla shook her head. "No. Tell me." She seriously doubted Haley's mother had anything to do with the teens culinary skills.

"Jared's wife taught me. She was my nanny when I was young."

Camilla dropped her fork. "Wait. Jared's wife?"

"I tried to tell you before. Jared isn't getting married."

"Of course not, not if he's already married." Her pulse quickened. She'd kissed a married man. In a parking lot. Where anyone could have seen them. Oh God! What had she done?

Thinking back to the conversation at the diner, Ryan talked of a bachelor party. It seemed a lifetime ago.

"Jared *was* married," Haley said in a sing-songy voice. "He's not married now."

"Divorced. Wow. Hadn't considered that," she said

between small bites of food. She didn't want Haley to think she'd lost her appetite, but somehow it had dribbled to nothing, like a creek drying up in the desert.

"No, he didn't get divorced. But just so you know, it's Ryan who's getting married, not Jared."

"Now I'm really confused." Camilla sipped coffee. Maybe a caffeine jolt would clear her head and drive away the muddling brain clouds. The facts about Jared didn't fit together. Instead, they were more like odd irregularly-shaped buttons tossed in a box. She could see them all, but they had no real connection.

"Cheyenne was my nanny…until she married Jared. They weren't married very long"—Haley's expression turned solemn and she leaned in close—"before Cheyenne died."

Camilla's pulse skittered, then bounced around like a pinball. Lights flashed in her mind. The woman had died? "How?" she asked quietly.

"Shot dead."

"Excuse me?" Shock hit Camilla squarely in the chest. She couldn't hold back incredulousness in her voice.

"I'm not supposed to know the details," Haley whispered conspiratorially. "But my mother isn't the discreet kind, you know. Mother said, a neighbor woman had shouted for her husband because she thought the bear on the porch of their house was a grizzly. She looked for a rifle, but couldn't find it and ran out the back door to the barn—to where they kept another rifle. The bear started after her, that was her story. She grabbed the gun. When the bear started to pushed open the door to the barn, the woman fired a warning shot to scare the bear, then heard a scream.

Startled, the woman turned in surprise and fired a second shot, hitting Cheyenne…who died instantly.

"When the woman went to check on Cheyenne, she discovered her husband amongst the bales of hay babbling over Jared's dead wife."

"What?" Camilla blinked. "You're kidding, right? This is a joke. Not funny, Boo."

Haley shook her head. "With his pants down."

Camilla flinched at the mental image. "What happened to the woman?"

"The police didn't press charges." Haley shrugged. "The grizzly bear apparently made a quick escape. Some of the men around here, my father included, tried to hunt it down."

Camilla covered her face with her hands. "Oh, poor Jared." She understood humiliation, had obtained a degree in it rather than an MBA at grad school. Shame of the past reared its head and bit at her tender heart so hard she was surprised drops of blood didn't appear on the white napkin Haley had placed in her lap.

"Camilla?" Haley said tentatively. "I thought you'd be happy Jared isn't married. Did I say something wrong?"

Camilla shook her head and folded her hands in her lap. "No, darlin', you didn't say anything wrong. It seems all the fault lies with me."

She wiped away the tears on her cheeks. Jared had suffered betrayal. Cheyenne's infidelity may have been worse because she was married, but in truth, there was little difference between her betrayal of her own sister and that of the betrayal of Jared's dead wife. He would hate her once he knew of her past.

Haley's news would've been good under other

circumstances. How could she ever be totally honest about herself with the man whose kisses made her insides melt like warm sensuous chocolate? Could he even look at her if he knew of her past transgressions?

"His wife betrayed him," she whispered. He would never want her now. The best way to avoid Jared learning of her shame—to leave without seeing him again. Her sins of the past had come home to roost once again. There was no sense in tempting fate. Jared couldn't help but despise her if he ever discovered she'd stooped so low as to betray her own sister, same as Cheyenne had betrayed him.

"Haley, lend me some clothes? Honey, I've got to go soon. I need to look up the bus schedule to return to Cody."

"Not before you see the ranch."

"I'm sorry. There's no time."

"Fine. Go. But I'm not lending you clothes. I'm not taking you to the bus station. You're just like my mom. Leaving me when I need you." Haley bolted for the door.

"No. Stop," Camilla called when the teen grabbed for the doorknob. She couldn't stand to disappoint her. "I'll stay and see the ranch. However, tomorrow, I've got to go. Deal?"

Haley beamed. "Thank you! Now finish your food, and I'll go scout out my closet. My bedroom is at the other end of the hall."

Camilla's shoulders sagged. What would she do if she ran into Jared?

Chapter 11

Jared jogged up the front steps to his childhood home, a massive log cabin built by his Grandfather Richardson in the 1920's. On the expansive porch running the front of the house, Nicole waited for him with a mug of steaming coffee. His brother was a lucky man. Nicole hadn't done too bad herself in capturing the full attention of the county's most confirmed bachelor. Their engagement announcement had produced a collective groan from all the single women around. Nicole and Ryan were touted to be the perfect picture of wedded bliss.

Envy burned in Jared's gut as though stuck with a hot branding iron when he'd learned the news of their engagement. He was happy for them, but wanted a woman in his life, one that was faithful to the core. Not a cheater or backstabber. He could never love a woman like that.

"As soon as you're done hashing out ranching problems with my soon-to-be father-in-law and groom, meet me at my new house. Let's get the walk-through done. I've got my punch list. There are a few glaring problems. So chop-chop. Time's running out," Nicole said, handing over the mug. "I expect my groom to carry me over the threshold of a fully completed house when we return from our honeymoon."

"Don't start on me, woman." Jared chuckled.

"Everything is right on schedule…for your new life." He kissed her cheek. "But not today. I have plans. Tomorrow, we do a walk through, I promise." He left her standing in the morning light looking as clean and fresh as any mountain Champlain rose blooming in August. Entering the cabin, he headed straight for the office, his favorite room in the house.

It smelled of leather and lemon oil from a recent cleaning. After a full minute of observing his father and brother immersed in spreadsheets, he made his presences known. "Morning."

Gus rolled away from the oversized, solid oak desk and eased back in the wooden captain's chair. Ryan stood beside the desk holding an accounts ledger book. The old man didn't stop Ryan from bringing technology to the business but still insisted on having a paper copy.

"About time," Gus snarled. "You're late. We've got ranch business to go over, if you're going to take Ryan's place while he's away. I will never understand jogging. Riding a horse. Throwing hay. Working a ranch—all the exercise a man needs. If I didn't know you, I'd think you were light in the shoes if I saw you trotting across fields all the time."

"As they say old man"—Jared slid into a brown leather club chair without spilling the hot liquid from his cup—"looks are deceiving."

"Don't try to turn this around on me," his father groused. "I'm not the pantywaist prancing about the countryside."

Ryan coughed. "Enough."

Jared glanced fondly at his brother and father. Gus was an older version of Ryan. Broad shoulders. Square jaw. Thick hair that had turned completely white like snow on the mountain tops. Women always commented on how Gus closely resembled the actor James Brolin. Those words fueled his father's ego, as big and wide as the Wyoming sky.

"I'm ready to begin. What's on the agenda? Price of cattle?" Jared asked.

"We're making a detour now that you're here," Ryan said dryly. "The old gentleman from the South called this morning. He provided interesting news. When were you going to tell us?" He snapped the ledger book closed. A loud *whack* echoed in the room when Ryan slammed the book against the desktop.

Taking a big gulp of coffee, Jared stalled the conversation. Two sets of angry eyes glared. Their old man being riled was nothing new, but Ryan being pissed made him sit up straighter and place the coffee mug on the side table.

"Exactly," Jared asked, "what did he say?"

"He talked about a job." Ryan raised an eyebrow. "And his pleasure at civilizing one of us. When were you going to tell us?"

Jared raked his fingers through his hair. If ever there was a good time for Camilla to return his message and interrupt the inquisition, now was it. He reached for his phone, but found no message despite having sent several emails to her.

He drew a breath and let it go long and slow. "I've been warning you about it all summer, but you ignored me. Selective hearing? Selective memory? I saved the confirming information for this morning's meeting. Granddaddy rushed the gun." He shrugged. "I knew full well that once I told you my plans were finalized, we'd have this discussion…I can't win for losing with the two of you. I tried to set a specific meeting with the both of you, but you brushed me off with 'Mucking up the routine. Daylight's burning. Ranch won't run itself.' So I waited for this morning."

"If I hadn't loved your mother so much, I'd fight you on this," Gus said. His mouth formed a thin line. He narrowed his eyes. Jared ignored the intimidation tactics. They hadn't worked in years.

"My house *will* be done." Ryan pinned him with a stare. "Before you leave again. No trips to Cody. No trips anywhere. Until my bride has her house just like she wants it."

"You're issuing orders to me?" Jared asked.

"You heard your brother," Gus said.

Jared stood. "Have I ever"—he pointed his finger at his father's chest—"failed to meet my obligations?"

Gus appeared to scroll through his memory searching for an example of a contradiction.

"That's not the point," Ryan interrupted. "You'll inherit a portion of this ranch. You can't oversee your investment if you're not here."

"Gentleman," Jared drawled, "my past performance is my best recommendation." He managed to partially impersonate his southern grandfather's accent. "I'm good for my word. I always do what I say. Ryan, you were born to run this place. I have other talents. Neither of you have any worries. Nicole will give Ryan sons who will grow up and run the ranch. Now, get off my back." He had never allowed them to dictate his life. He wouldn't start now.

"Better not have any worries," Ryan muttered. "Let's get back to ranch business." Ryan opened the ledger book again and pointed to the computer screen on the desk.

"So there's no elephant hanging out in the room, I'm telling you now, I won't leave until after you return from your honeymoon. In the meantime, I'm going to undertake the task of finding Gus an assistant ASAP. Maybe this time, we should look for a man to do the job."

"Not on your life!" Gus snapped, rising to his feet.

Jared and Ryan chuckled. Ryan winked. Jared relaxed. His brother's bluster was mostly a show for their father. Ryan might not agree with his decision to move down south, but in the end, his brother would support his choice.

"Let's get to work," Jared said.

The discussion of ranch issues lasted longer than Jared anticipated, but when it concluded he said, "You never bothered to ask what I'll be doing down south."

"Working for your grandfather," Ryan replied.

"I'm going to hire on as an apprentice with a craftsman who does historic preservation. Granddaddy is narrowing his architectural firm's focus."

"Sounds like a step down from developer." His father grunted.

"In the near future, yes, but it's a long-range career plan."

Ryan slipped into the chair next to Jared. After a few moments, he said, "You told me there would come a time when you'd only come home for roundups. I just didn't think this year was the start of that change. Your leaving impacts all of us."

A knock sounded at the door, and Nicole stepped into the room. "You're leaving?" Nicole asked, her head tipped to the side and she frowned. "Not before you finish my house, mister."

Jared sighed. "Retract the whip. I'm leaving *after* you return from your honeymoon." He chuckled. "Actually, I'm leaving now to pay a call over at the O'Connor place. Then, I'll start checking out candidates for your new assistant, old man." He had a mission to complete and a woman's heart to win.

****

Camilla shimmied into Haley's Dolce & Gabbana jeans. Her legs had never been sheathed in such expensive denim.

"Here," Haley said, appearing from her walk-in closet the size of Camilla's entire bedroom at home. The teen offered a white cotton peasant top with puffy sleeves.

"How much did that cost?" Camilla asked. She'd never heard of the designer, but that didn't mean much. Her older sister was the fashion queen with a Chanel fetish while her first choice for shopping was all-American Macy's.

"Just put the top on," Haley urged. She headed back into the cavernous closet.

Camilla fingered the lacy top, hesitating to don a thousand dollars' worth of clothes just for an hour of horseback riding. The teenager had a closet most grown women would kill for.

Peering at her reflection in the long mirror mounted on the wall behind the bedroom door, Camilla concluded there was something to be said for clothes with the right fit, *like a glove* might be trite, but still true. Never had she ever considered herself sexy in jeans because of the roundedness of her butt. Some celebrities might rock the look, but she always wanted to minimize her hind end. Running her hand down one side seam, she wondered if Jared would enjoy seeing her in something other than a waitress' uniform or fishing outfit, something that made her legs appear long and lean.

"Pick a pair of boots. I think these will fit you." Haley appeared with a slightly worn brown pair and a shiny pair of red ones.

"The brown ones are Mad Dog goat hide. Both are Lucchese. The red pair, very special, belly caiman crocodile with a python inset."

"Those red ones, boots or a pet?"

"Just pick," Haley insisted, holding the boots side by side.

"Nice." Camilla admired the brown ones. Unlike the jeans and top, she couldn't afford to replace the boots if anything happened to them.

"I've got about twenty pairs. Old Gringos, Luccheses, Tony Lamas mostly." Haley puffed with pride and set the boots on the floor.

Uncomfortable about borrowing anything other than Levi's, a Hanes t-shirt, and old riding boots, Camilla hesitated. "Got anything…less expensive? I've never owned twenty of anything. At least not clothes or shoes."

"Is your family poor?"

Camilla paused and glanced in Haley's direction. How could she explain to the teen about her large extended family and that a farming plantation required a lot of work and repairs due to the climate?

"I don't mean to pry, but you *do* work as a waitress."

"My family doesn't have money like yours, but

we're rich in tradition," she explained, sitting on the edge of the bed.

Haley handed her the brown boots. "Put them on."

"I'll *try* them on." She pulled the boots over the socks Haley had given her earlier. "We have an antebellum plantation home. The family once owned—I don't know exactly—hundreds of acres, but over time, much of it was sold off. I'd have to ask my sister how much is left to know the correct amount."

"A thousand acres. Four hundred head of cattle. Fifty horses. A passel of barn cats. Two dogs," Haley rattled off.

Surprised by the precise accounting, Camilla stared at the girl. "If you have all of that here, why would you work as a dishwasher at a diner in Jackson?"

Haley reddened and turned her gaze away. "You're one to talk," she muttered. "Why were you working there? You're a long way from a family you talk so much about."

Camilla kneeled beside the chair where Haley sat. "Because until the last year, I wasn't a very likable person. The only thing ever expected of me was to be nice and polite…but raising hell was easier. I needed to get away in order to grow up."

"I don't believe you."

"That's okay," Camilla chuckled. "In your soul you know I'm right about the things we talked about during the long bus."

"Self-esteem. Reliability. Accountability."

"Yay-ya," Camilla said. "Amen! You got it, sister."

A faint smile played at the corners of Haley's mouth. "All I've ever heard since I turned thirteen was how someday all of this would be mine. Then, when I turned sixteen, Dad started saying how it would be important for the man I marry to fit in with us. I don't fit in my own family. How could anyone else? He hasn't found a wife since he and my mom split. I'm too young to be thinking about marriage. I want to have fun."

"I agree. You're way too young to be thinking about walking down the aisle. *Fun is good*, just as long as the consequences don't haunt you all your life."

Haley's nod was reluctant, but clearly she was paying attention. "Can we go now?"

"Do you have any straight pins or a couple of safety pins? I can mark the hemline," Camilla said, lifting her foot to eye the boot heel and the amount of hemming needed. "How about a needle and thread? It'll only take me a few minutes to make these fit." It was time to leave the somber discussion behind. She'd promised Haley they'd go riding before she left. She might even catch the last bus of the evening back to Jackson.

"Just roll them up. Let's go. You're stalling." Haley jumped up and tugged on her arm, then ran on ahead.

"The number of times I've been on a horse, I can count on one hand and not need all my fingers," Camilla called after her. She might not ride well, but she would sure look good doing it. Too bad Jared wouldn't be around to notice. With one last check in the mirror, her butt looked exquisite, nicely wrapped in Dolce & Gabbana.

Ring. Ring. Camilla climbed across the bed to grab the cell phone and checked the screen.

Jared.

She tossed the phone on the bed like a hot coal from a campfire. The phone rang again. Again. She ached to talk to him but didn't trust herself. The man could be too persuasive. Unable to resist temptation, she grabbed the phone and answered before the last ring.

"No," she said.

"Hello? Camilla?" Hearing Jared's voice made her breath catch. Her sturdy defenses lowered a bit.

"Yes, it's me. No, is the answer to everything else."

"I haven't asked a question yet."

"That's okay. No need to ask. The answer is still no."

"Drinks?"

"No."

"Dinner?"

"No."

"A tour of my family's home? I'll even show you my childhood bedroom." His voice teased.

"Oh, *hell* no." Had she just said that aloud?

Jared chuckled. "You promised me a dinner date. If no date, how about a picnic and a ride?"

Alone with Jared in the wilds of Wyoming. Thick grass, shade beneath a tree. A quilt. Nice bottle of wine. Sandwiches or something to eat. A gentle breeze…her imagination carried her there. And then to the kissing that would follow. The man made her giddy. She sighed, and hated herself for it.

"Camilla?"

She shook her head. "No," she said more to herself than to him. "Some promises are meant to be broken. No date." She stopped short of telling him her plans to catch the bus back to Jackson. Her greatest fear was he'd offer to drive her…and then one thing might lead to another. Her restraint would pop like a balloon too full of air. She needed to add *appropriate restraint* to the list of things she wanted to instill in Haley.

"You can't come all the way to Cody without seeing some of the sights."

"I'm going riding with Haley."

"Well…think of me while you're galloping across the fields. We'll catch up later. I'm not taking no for an answer, even if I have to hunt you down like a grizzly bear."

Something about his cavalier tone tickled her brain like a yellow flag waving a warning, but she couldn't put her finger on why.

"Just don't shoot to kill," she teased.

"I only hunt with binoculars. I leave the tranquilizers to the state Game and Fish Department," Jared informed.

"I'm not sure if I should be happy or scared learning that part of the puzzle."

From the hall, Haley called, "Camilla, let's go. The horses are saddled and waiting. Roll up the hems." Haley burst through the door. "We can go riding sooner."

Camilla held up a finger to Haley, hoping the girl would remain quiet.

"Jared, I've got to go. Maybe if I'm ever back this way, I'll take you up on your offer. Bye, now," she said with her best southern drawl, then ended the call before Jared could argue. Or worse, talk her into doing something that would only cause her pain in the long run. She had to do the adult thing.

Her spirits plummeted, sliding to the bottom of a deep cavern.

Jared always set her heart pounding.

Somehow, she had to close the door on her heart.

Chapter 12

Jared wandered into the kitchen. Felicia stood in front of the stove, stirring something a large pot.

"What's that?" Jared asked. "Doesn't have much aroma." Steam rose from the pot and curled before disappearing. The blonde woman before him looked more like a long-legged colt dressed in denim than a ranch cook.

"I'm dyeing t-shirts for the kids coming for the Cowboy Camp Roundup."

"In the kitchen?"

"Do you need something, Jared?" Felicia asked impatiently. "You're dressed like you're going out on Saturday night. Best boots. Nice jeans. And a button down shirt. All you need is a new Charlie One Horse hat. Mothers will be throwing their daughters at you." She rolled her eyes, pasted a plastic smile on her face, then pointed a finger heaven-bound. "Wait, they already do that."

She stepped closer and ran that same finger along the scar on the side of his face. That gesture always irritated him. He pulled away. She only tried that move whenever she caught him alone.

"I came looking for lunch." He refused to take her bait. Felicia was tenacious, he'd give her that, but he wanted to avoid the sore spot between them. She had given him every clue and created opportunities for the two of them to change their relationship from employee and employer to something more intimate. However, over the years his father found himself married several times to women who had come to the ranch to work, and Jared promised himself he'd never mix business with pleasure. Never.

"There's food in the fridge. You missed lunch." Her voice was filled with accusation.

"I was in the attic going through old photos." He opened the door to the fridge. "What's good for a picnic?" In a bin, he found sliced ham and cheese. "Any chance there's a loaf of French bread in the freezer?"

"How many are you feeding?" Felicia bumped him, elbowing him aside.

"Three."

"Three?" Felicia scowled. "Three's a crowd."

Jared shrugged. "I'm hoping to meet two ladies. Haley O'Connor and a friend, their houseguest."

"Haley?" Felicia raised an eyebrow. "Really, Jared."

"Not that it's any of your business, but it's her friend I'm meeting. I want to show off our western hospitality. It's every bit as good as the South's. You'll make something I can take?"

"Yeah, I'll make you a picnic. Do you want bottles of water or are you going to fill up your favorite canteen? I thought Haley was in Jackson with her mother."

"Throw in three bottles of water. Haley can't be in Jackson with her mother, because it appears her mother's away on a trip, and now Haley is here. I'll be back in a few minutes. And Felicia…"

"What?"

"Thank you. I appreciate you doing this for me."

"I'm not doing it for you. I'm doing it for Haley…and the houseguest," Felicia grumbled.

Jared picked up the hall phone and pushed a button. "Sam, would you have one of the boys bring Zenith up to the house? I want the rifle scabbard, too."

****

Camilla adjusted her sore butt in the saddle—strapped to a horse rather than anchored to a barstool made a huge difference in how the leather cradled her backside. Her hips ached from the constant torque of the horse's gait. Her thighs, sweaty and sore, were grateful to be covered in Dolce & Gabbana. The scenery soothed her soul, but her mind ran on overload. Jared punctuated every other thought, and each time her hope sank more over the loss of what could have been.

"Hello?" Haley called. "Where are you?"

Camilla looked up, her face shaded from the sun by a brown cowboy hat. "The scenery is beautiful. Makes me want to be a photographer, like my cousin," Camilla said, trying to be a more attentive guest. And it was true, her cousin would love the texture of the craggy mountains, the greenness of the grass, the blue of the sky, and pure white of the few puffy clouds.

"You must think I'm completely dense. You were thinking about Jared."

"No. I was thinking about my sore butt."

"Liar. A soak in the hot tub at the ranch will help when we get back. I could ask Jared to join us."

Camilla narrowed her eyes. "You're absolutely *not* dense. Sneaky, maybe. I was thinking I might try to make the seven o'clock bus back to Jackson."

"No. You have to stay. I'll sell a saddle or

something to pay you since you lost your job over me. We could go to Yellowstone tomorrow." Haley bumped her horse's side, and the large animal cantered ahead. "Come on, keep up!"

Down the short hill and ahead in the distance in an open field, a small cloud of dust ran parallel to a ditch. The cloud moved rapidly in their direction. The sound of an engine sliced through the quiet as it drew nearer. Camilla slowed the horse. A ripple of unease ran through her. The horse beneath her backed his ears, then shying, began to back up while she tried to convince him to stand still.

"Haley?" Camilla cried. "Help!"

Already ahead by at least twenty yards, the girl slowed her horse and turned around. "Don't pull hard on the reins. A gentle touch. Be calm. Stay there. I'll go see who's coming." Haley took off like an arrow zinging from a crossbow. She and the horse were one.

"Good boy," Camilla cooed. She tried not to move in the saddle, not wanting to send a wrong signal to the horse, least the beast between her legs decide to take off like a shot from a canon. "I've got an apple for you as soon as I get down." His ears twitched, but he calmed some.

Camilla's gaze followed Haley crossed the planted green hay, the span of an entire football field. Dust swallowed the teen. Suddenly, the engine noise ceased. Camilla's anxiety inched up each moment the girl didn't reappear from the cloud of dust.

"It's okay," Camilla said gently, then patted the horse's neck and finally the horse stood still.

When the brown cloud cleared in the distance, Camilla gasped. "Haley! No!"

Before her, the biker at the root of all her trouble held Haley in a tight embrace, and if it had been another man, another time, another place, the scene would've been romantic as they kissed. Two long lost lovers separated by time and distance, longing for each other. But it had been twenty-four hours and these two had no business being lovers.

"Haley," Camilla groaned. "Oh Boo, what am I going to do with you?" Darcy was right. She couldn't save Haley. Couldn't save anyone, not even herself. Anxiety flooded her gut. Her stomach clinched and churned. What could she to do?

She flipped through her memories. What had her mother done to make her listen to reason? Talking had rarely worked. Maybe something with a dramatic one-two punch would startle Haley into reality. Could a "scared straight" help the girl understand what she faced? Did Cody, Wyoming, have a woman's shelter and a counselor who would explain life when living with an abuser?

The scene before Camilla continued. Mitch stroked Haley's face and kissed each bruised spot. He hugged her and playfully dipped her back, then kissed her once more. He took her hand, twirled her around, pulled her close and kissed her again. It was an awkward play of Beauty and the Beast. Haley moved with grace and elegance compared to Mitch, dressed in black leathers and clunky boots.

Had he not been the man who put his hands on Haley and harmed her, Camilla might have believed the guy was smitten as Romeo for Juliet. How could she get through to Haley? Alternatively, if Haley wouldn't listen, could she convince Mitch to seek counseling?

How would Sean respond if he discovered Mitch in Cody? Her brain teetered, about to explode with panic.

The horse beneath her took several steps. “Whoa,” Camilla squeaked, her tone as authoritative as a scared mouse. When she refocused her gaze on Haley, the girl had mounted her horse. Mitch mounted his motorcycle. Each headed back in the direction in which they had come…and away from each other. Haley’s horse galloped across the field as if escaping a fire.

The cinching in Camilla’s stomach eased a bit, making it easier to draw in a deep breath, but until Mitch was out of Haley’s life forever, she’d worry.

Flushed and glowing, Haley rode up, pulled on the horse’s reins, and stopped. “Whew. Kisses like honey. Let’s go or we’ll be late.”

“That’s all you have to say to me?” Camilla demanded. “Girl, we need to talk about what just happened. You played me. I stayed for you, and you’re using me as a cover to a rendezvous with…” She couldn’t utter his name.

“We’ll talk later. We’ve got to go.” Haley took off.

“Go where?” Camilla grumbled.

She refused to match Haley’s pace as the girl headed into the woods. Soon enough the teenager would figure out no one cantered behind her and return to finish what had been promised as a leisurely ride. But after a few minutes, the teen didn’t reappear.

“Let’s go, Galaxy. I must get a move on it. My departure is imminent.”

Camilla started in the direction where Haley disappeared. The horse picked its way along the trail, expertly missing protruding rocks. In the brush beside the worn path, fallen trees, now gray logs stripped of branches and leaves, lay scattered about. Decay took forever in the dry Wyoming climate, unlike in the south where humidity and bugs consumed wood quickly. Her thoughts drifted to home, a deep ache blooming in her chest. A wave of tiredness washed over her along with a new awareness about home. She wanted to go. Needed to see Fleur de Lis. But it meant leaving Jared and Haley behind. In a perfect world, she'd bundle them up and take them with her.

Except Haley had a family, as dysfunctional as it might be.

Jared would hate her once he learned of her betrayal to her own sister.

The only thing left to do was return home and create a new role within her own family. Like Biloxi had done. Except her cousin hadn't left a good friend and a heartthrob behind.

Camilla continued over a small rise and followed the trail to the right. She continued scanning the scenery for the teen.

"Over here!" Haley shouted.

Camilla caught a brief glimpse of the girl through the trees. She rested on some rocks near a stream. Her horse lingered behind her…along with a second horse.

Mitch? No. Couldn't be.

The path, barely a trail, opened into a small grassy pad. A blanket had been spread on the ground and paper plates, a picnic basket, and bottles of water waited.

"What's going on? Haley, I'm pissed at you." She started to speak again, but snapped her mouth shut when Jared stepped out from behind a tree.

"The lady won't come to dinner"—Jared crossed

his arms over his chest—"so dinner came to the lady." He casually leaned, resting one shoulder against a tree. A smug smile spread across his face. His gesture touched a spot deep in her core. She tingled with happiness, but her body relaxed only an inch. The level of tension she'd been holding hadn't been apparent until it began to diminish. She didn't dare tell him the only person to ever call her "lady" worked at an auto garage in St. Louis, and when he said, "lady," he'd delivered it with extreme exasperation over the poor care she took of her car.

Jared looked so good. Relaxed. Completely in his element. Perfectly worn brown cowboy boots peeked out beneath Levi's settled snug on his hips. The belt buckle wasn't dinner-plate sized, yet fancy, maybe even engraved silver. The light blue cotton shirt made his eyes appear a deeper sapphire blue. Hypnotizing. She could get lost in them forever. But his mouth captivated her attention the most. Smug, yet sexy at the same time. Where was the Grand Canyon when she needed it? The distance from one side to the other offered the barrier she required. If she kissed him again, she'd be lost forever.

"Ahem," Haley coughed and tugged on Galaxy's reins. Camilla released them while keeping her gaze fixed on Jared. He came to her side and assisted her down from the horse. His strength held her suspended, and slowly he lowered her. Her heart banged in her chest like a triangle clanged when a cook called ranch hands for dinner. She licked her lips. Her gaze remained glued on his. She feared that when her feet reached the ground, her knees would buckle.

"Ah…I'm going." Haley climbed onto her horse.

"I'd say, 'get a room,' but there isn't one for miles. I've got an errand to run and a date."

Haley's words snapped Camilla to attention. She pulled away from Jared and made a grab for the reins of Haley's horse. "Wait! You can't go out with Mitch. *No*. After all we talked about. Besides, I need you to get me back to your house. Remember, *I've* got to go."

"You're in good hands. Jared will see you back to the ranch in time for the hot tub before dinner. My father is expecting you. Don't worry about me. I listened to everything you said. Mitch promised he'd never hit me again, even agreed to meet my father." Haley jerked away and took off down the path, disappearing in a cloud of dust.

"Jared, you have to go after her," Camilla implored, wondering what words she could've used to cajole Haley into waiting.

"She'll be okay. She has a plan. You'll see her before you leave. I promise. Now, take a break from the drama and"—he tugged on her hand—"come over here with me."

"But, she's going to see Mitch."

"Actually, Mitch is going to see her."

"But he just did. They were just kissing a few minutes ago…in that field." She pointed in the direction from which she had come.

"Trust. Camilla. Have faith. It will all work out. She called me for a male perspective. She has a plan. The girl had a temporary lapse in judgment in Jackson; however, I think her common sense has returned since she came home. Thanks to you, I might add. Now, let's eat."

"Hard to have faith when I've seen Mitch's

handiwork. How is it you know what's going on with Haley and I don't? As my Granddaddy Lind would say, 'You bet on people like you bet on race horses—on past performance.' I don't trust Mitch. In fact, I don't trust Haley to take care of herself."

"You ever need a second chance?" Jared asked.

His question hit her squarely in her gut. She lowered her head, staring at the ground. "Everyone needs second chances," she said softly.

"I hadn't seen, let alone talked to Haley since she hit puberty. When I called her today, she rattled on about how fabulous you are. She understands the tension…between me and her parents, but she still took me into her confidence. So how about giving her a chance?"

The man could calm a hurricane. She couldn't *make* Haley do anything, but she could take Jared's advice.

"Okay," she agreed reluctantly.

Camilla scanned the secluded spot. With the plaid blanket laid out, the woven picnic basket set in one corner, and paper plates, the scene would be perfect for a photo in many magazines. But the day brewed trouble like Greta brewed tea—by the gallon. First Haley, now Jared. Alone with him invited problems she'd promised herself to avoid.

"Sit," Jared encouraged. "Let's see what my cook made for us."

Her every nerve went to war. Half battled on the "Oh, yes let's!" team. The other half on the "No. No. No." team.

"I…" She grimaced. "I don't know."

"What? I promise no food poisoning here. Felicia

is a great cook." He kneeled on the blanket and tugged again on her hand.

"Felicia?" she asked.

"She's the cook at the ranch. Roast beef sandwiches, fruit, and chips. Bottle of water? It's not gumbo or jambalaya, but still good."

She eyed him suspiciously. How did he know about Cajun food?

"I've traveled south quite a bit. Look, if you don't want to eat, at least have something to drink." Jared offered a bottle of water.

"I'll sit, on one condition."

"Name it."

She stalled. How did she tell him she couldn't risk kissing him again?

"We're only friends. Nothing more. Haley assured me you're not engaged…Ryan is the one getting married."

Jared drew back. "You didn't believe me?"

"At the diner, Ryan said you had wedding business. Trixie said she was going to be the entertainment for a bachelor party. So I thought…"

"I can see where that might have been confusing."

He had the good sense not to laugh. She credited him with that, though believing she'd kissed an engaged man—and loved it, had sent her anxiety soaring. But that was all he had to say? "Yes. Confusing," she huffed.

"So now you know there's nothing improper about my attraction to you." His lips curved into a sexy smile. He crooked his finger, then patted a spot on the blanket beside him.

Camilla stood rigid. The man oozed with

seduction. He didn't understand the war taking place inside her. If she surrendered now, it would be the same as tumbling ten thousand feet off Rendezvous Mountain and landing crumbled at the bottom. She had to leave. Had to go home. She didn't belong in Wyoming. Plus, she'd watched the agony her sister endured from a broken heart. Branna was stronger. Wiser. Had mended and bounced back.

But she wasn't Branna.

Emotions swirled like an eddy. Thoughts spun like a tornado in her mind. Love scared her more than she ever imagined. A broken heart just might kill her.

"And you enjoyed the kiss." Jared's eyes danced. He rose and stood behind her. Lifting her hair, he rained kisses on the side of her neck, and sucked ever so slightly. Her knees started to buckle. She wanted more.

And more.

"And…I enjoyed the kiss," she murmured. "Need to sit down." She lowered herself to the blanket to keep from falling, then snatched up a bottle of water, opened it and drank. Anything to keep Jared from kissing her again.

When he sat on the blanket facing her and reached for her hand, she reached for a bag of chips. "I said, we're only friends."

"And we are," he chuckled. "However, we both know there's more than friendship building between us. From the first moment we met."

"You don't know me," she protested.

"Then tell something about yourself."

Flustered, she didn't know where to begin. The man addled her mind. "Let's see. I have a big family. My father's side is from Louisiana. My mother's side is from Mississippi. Our family home is called Fleur de Lis."

"That doesn't tell me much about you. I want to know what movies you love. What books you read. What food you can't live without. What makes you dizzy with desire?"

"Even if I tell you that, you still won't really know me."

His expression turned to one of contemplation. "I do know you. You're a hard worker—at the diner. You're friendly and welcoming—at the diner. You're caring and compassionate—with Haley. You're protective and loyal—protecting Haley from Mitch at the bus station. You're brave—thinking a pocketknife would be useful in that situation. And you're nearly terrified of that horse, but for Haley, you went riding."

"That doesn't mean you know me. You know *about* me. Big difference."

"I'd never touched a woman and at first contact felt a connection. You looked at me with surprise, and I knew you felt it, too. I coaxed Trixie into telling me your name and where you worked."

"You did?"

"I'm a cautious man when it comes to women."

Haley's revelation about Jared's wife popped into her mind.

"Haley told me about how your wife…died. I'm sorry."

"It taught me to be clear about my choices. Made me wiser." There was something contemplative about his tone. "I've learned to trust my instincts." He took the water and the bag of chips from her hands, setting them off to the side, then leaned in close. When they were cheek to cheek, his breath caressed her ear. “We belong together,” he whispered.

All her reserve melted. She regretted many of her past decisions. But if she didn’t follow her heart now, didn’t give in to the longing and desire this time, would she regret it as much or more than any haunting memories of her past?

Chapter 13

Jared brushed his cheek against Camilla's. "I want to be closer to you," he whispered, then felt her breath catch. Turning slightly, he captured her lips with his. She resisted. Undeterred, he kissed her again, deepening the kiss. Her warm, soft lips finally gave in. His arm snaked around her waist and though the move was awkward at first, he lay back and pulled her with him, rolling her onto his chest.

He sucked in a breath. There was no way she could miss the hardness in his jeans pressing against her when she settled comfortably on top of him. He gave her a moment to adjust to the intimacy of their bodies. Taking it slow, he ran his hands over her ass, up her back and held her close. She needed to make the next move. No need to spook her and have her gallop away. Gentleness would wipe the wary look from her eyes.

"Where's your mind, Camilla?" he asked quietly.

She lowered her gaze. "At war with my heart."

"Which side is winning?" He kissed her nose.

When she squirmed, his groin tightened, yet his heart, his head, and his body perfectly aligned in their want and desire for her. The woman lying on him might need some slow coaxing; however, she was worth the wait and the time. Everything about her brought out a protectiveness he'd never experienced. He'd been in lust many times. Thought he might have been in love once…after Cheyenne, but when he applied his rule—measure twice, cut once—the connection didn't hold up. With Camilla, energy between them vibrated so strong that in her presence she was the sun, and he a mere planet in her orbit.

"I want…" she started.

He raised his eyebrows and grinned. "And I want to give you what you want."

"But you don't even know what it is."

"Me."

She crushed her lips against his and undulated her pelvis against his jeans containing his hardened manhood. He groaned deep in his throat and it reverberated in his chest.

Lifting up, she straddled him, then removed the top she wore, folding it neatly as though it were something more precious than she was to him. His hands instinctively went to her waist. Slowly they rose up the sides of her torso, stopping on her rib cage just beneath her breasts. Glorious breasts. Firm and pert. She brushed his hands away. He rested them back on the blanket and wondered what she would do next with the gravitational pull between them growing stronger.

Camilla licked her lips, leaned over and kissed him, her hair falling down to cocoon them. Then she began a slow unbutton of his shirt. He tried to catch her gaze. Tried to read her mind. Tried to get a sense of her struggle. She wanted him, but at the same time, she radiated a sadness he didn't understand.

"Camilla," he said, gently. "I want to make love to you."

Her eyes snapped and locked on his. Unhurried, she finished the unbuttoning and pulled on his shirt, releasing the tail from his jeans. Nimble fingered, she popped open the button on his jeans. Drove the zipper down. Pushing off from his chest, she stood, wiggled out of her jeans, then folded them neatly, too. She stood proudly, silhouetted by the sunlight from beyond the trees. Every fiber of his being wanted to capture her body beneath him and lovingly worship it. Clearly her heart had won the war and taken the sadness captive.

"I want you, too." Her voice was earnest and sincere.

He pulled off his boots. Slid out of his jeans and briefs and tossed them. A thrill of delight zoomed through him as Camilla's expression turned to one of appreciation when she raked her gaze over his nakedness. On his knees, he closed the short distance between them. His fingers grasped the silky material of her panties, slid them down, and she stepped out of them. Placing them on top of the folded blouse and jeans, he turned his attention back to her. As he rose to standing, his hands brushed over the smoothness of her legs, hips, and sides. Capturing her lips, he kissed her slow and deliberately. But she broke the kiss.

Her chest heaved as though she needed air. He needed her. He spun her around, plucked the hooks on her bra and the lacy garment dropped to the ground.

She backed to him. He wrapped his arms around her and captured her breasts, massaging the soft firmness of them.

"Oh," she moaned softly, covering his hands with her own, encouraging him.

"Is the war over?" he whispered, and pushed his pelvis against her ass.

"Yes!"

Camilla stepped away and reclined on the blanket. She rolled his jeans and made a pillow for her head. "Come here, cowboy." Her voice was low and seductive.

Covering her body with his, he peppered her face with kisses. He suckled her breasts. Her nipples hardened. She cupped his ass and squeezed. Moving into a more comfortable position, he settled his manhood between her legs.

She smiled with no hint of shyness, then she arched her back. His hardness found entry to the sweetness of her womanhood at the apex of her thighs. He moved slowly at first, a short withdrawal and a longer thrust. She rocked with him. Up and back. He moved deeper into her, reining in the urge to move quickly, instead he took it slow and rhythmically, fighting for his control. When her muscles contracted tightly around his hardness, the glorious sensation sent him to the brink of explosion.

Their first time together had to be perfect. He wouldn't finish without her. To keep his body in check, he focused on her face. She appeared entranced. Eyes closed, slightly fluttering. Lips barely parted. Jaw relaxed. When she licked her lips, her tongue moving in and out over the tip of her lip, he matched his thrusts to her pace. Then, thrust faster and harder. She surprised him when she moaned, "Ride, cowboy, ride."

Rocking against him faster and faster, she lifted her pelvis up higher. He quickened his thrusts. His energy shot sky high. She moaned louder when her core contracted around his manhood. His release began to give way. He arched his back. Together their orbits collided and stars shot through heaven.

"Jared. Jared. Yes," she cried, though her voice was barely audible over his own groan of euphoric surrender, a sensation so intense he drowned in happiness.

With his heart still thundering, slowly he drifted back to earth. Opening his eyes, he took in the heart-pounding sight of Camilla with her head lolled back, exposing the soft skin of her neck. She panted hard, her breath still as uneven as his. Unable to resist, he kissed, then licked the spot. "You're as sweet as a praline."

"You're one damn seductive man," she whispered between pants. "Around the world and back, you took me. I'd say something like you're hung like a horse, but honestly, I don't know what that means."

"Camilla, I'm falling in love you."

She lifted her head and pushed the rolled jeans back into place as a pillow. "You shouldn't have said that. That complicates everything."

Her expression closed. Shut him out. She lay very still beneath him. He hoped he'd captured her heart, but it appeared her mind wanted to war again.

"Why? Most people fight to find the perfect love."

"Please let me get dressed." She tried to move him, but he refused to budge.

"Perfect?" she snapped. "There's nothing perfect about me."

"Woman, I'm explaining that I love you. I want you in my life." He eased off her. She sprang up and grabbed for her clothes.

"I've got to go, Jared. I told you, you don't *know* me."

She was incorrect in her understanding. He knew about her. He knew her heart. She loved him. He'd been with enough women to understand Camilla was the only one he'd ever loved. Completely. Whatever made her freeze up and freeze him out would take some time to thaw. Yet in the end, he'd win the war over her battle with doubt.

She stood over him fully clothed as he finished dressing and pulled on his boots. Silently, he hoisted her up into the saddle, then untied Galaxy's reins, but rather then turning them over to her, he kept them and climbed on Zephyr. "We'll take it slow," he told her.

"I don't want to bounce out of this saddle, so slow is good."

He'd been talking about the future of their relationship. She was the one who misunderstood. All he needed was some time to convince her of the value of their love. She would be his plus-one at Ryan's wedding. Next, he'd take her south to meet his family, and then he'd meet hers. The plan would work. He could see their relationship in his mind like a blueprint for a building. One built sturdy and strong.

"I'll take you to O'Connor's," Jared said. "Mitch is coming to meet Sean. Haley wants you there for the meeting."

"I don't think I can handle that right now. I want to catch the bus back to Jackson."

"You want to, but you won't. You won't abandon Haley."

She glared at him.

Small talk didn't seem appropriate given all they'd just shared. It hurt that she'd iced him out. Nothing in her past could be so bad. Nothing could change the way his heart wanted only her.

"You have a gun on your saddle." Camilla

interrupted his thoughts.

"Yep. A rifle for protection. Just in case of a bear." He placated her desire to change the subject.

Camilla's gaze darted from side to side as though she scanned the terrain for a sighting. A flicker of fear passed on her face.

"Don't worry. You're safe," he said, dryly.

"Maybe," she said mostly under her breath. He doubted the words were intended to reach his ears.

"But my heart is breaking same as if you'd shot me," she mumbled.

The painful words hit his heart.

A clear, dead-on shot.

Chapter 14

Camilla brightened. Never was she so happy to see a red barn.

Riding in silence next to Jared frayed her nerves so badly that she fully expected to look into a mirror and see fringes of nerves hanging from her body.

"Have a good ride?" Haley asked. Her smile and her tone insinuated more.

"Enough to know I don't need to get on a horse again." Camilla leveled a stare, and Haley's smile dropped.

"Don't mind her." Jared tossed Galaxy's reins to the teen. "She just got stung by a mad bee."

"You did?" Haley's voice hitched with worry.

"Get that step thingy so I can climb down from here."

"It's called dismounting when you get off a horse. I checked the hot tub. It's ready. I promised you a soak to get rid of the soreness." Haley dragged the wooden, two-step platform from the side of the barn and set it on the ground beside the horse. "I brought a bathing suit for you to change into. It's in the pool house."

"Thank you, Haley. That's very thoughtful." She softened her voice. "Will you join me in the hot tub?"

Haley's eyes widened. "Sure. Jared? I can find something of Dad's for you."

"No, Boo, the man is leaving," Camilla said

quietly. “We’ll have a bit of girl time before I catch the bus.”

“Bus?” Jared asked.

“When I said I had to go, I meant leave Cody and return to Jackson.”

“But why?” Haley wailed. “I need you here. Mitch is coming to meet my father tonight. You promised to help me. It’s not like you have a job to go back to.”

“What happened?” Jared’s eyes filled with concern.

Inwardly she groaned. She wanted Jared to ride off into the sunset so she could hold that memory forever. Better he leave her life now than when he found out just how imperfect she was. Once he knew of her betrayal, he wouldn’t be able to stand looking at her.

“She got fired because she couldn’t show up for work this morning, which she couldn’t do because she brought me home. Darcy is a witch.”

“Now, Haley,” Camilla started, then paused when a stable hand appeared. What she had to say to the teen needed to remain private. She waited for the man to lead Galaxy away.

“Thank you for defending my honor, but it was a choice I made. Darcy has a business to run, and she can’t do it if employees are running out. I admit, I was mad when she fired me, but everything happens for a reason.” If she truly meant those words, then heaven needed to open up and drop a direct message about why her soul was dying. She’d never see Jared again. Was it karmic payback because she kissed the man when she thought he was engaged? She never allowed anything to go further until the truth of his situation had been revealed. That had to count for something. Or hadn’t she changed enough? Did she deserve happiness? Love? "As we talked about on the bus ride here, decisions and behaviors have consequences, sometimes not the ones we want."

"I sure learned that lesson today." Jared's mouth turned up into an irascible grin. "There's no reason for you to return to Jackson. I've a temporary job for you. You'll be the perfect assistant."

A temp job? If she didn't leave today, leaving Jared in a few weeks would be even harder. She shook her head. "I don't think so."

Jared turned his horse around. "You ladies go enjoy your hot tub. Camilla, I'll call you later and explain about the position."

As Jared's horse cantered away from the barn, Camilla stared, memorizing his every movement. She would file it away with all the ones she had collected since first meeting him. They'd have to hold for a very long time. Love, she was certain, just rode out of her life.

"Let's go," Camilla said. "Point me in the direction of the pool house, and then do me a favor. Run up to the bedroom and bring me my phone? I never called my sister back. She's probably complaining to our mother that I'm unreliable."

"Follow that hedge"—Haley pointed—"at the end you'll see the pool house. Door is open." The teen ran off toward the house.

The roof of the pool house rose above the tall hedge of evergreens. Soreness in her thighs complained with each step she took. A good soak might revive her and provide time to formulate a new plan. She couldn't risk being alone with Jared again. When he said, "I'm falling in love with you," the power of his confession grabbed at the core of her being. Flickers of joy started to spread. She nearly repeated the same words back to him, but the shouting of condemnation from her conscience drowned out joy, snuffed out hope. Jared was a good man. Solid. True to his word. And how would he look at her if he knew her secret shame?

Opening the side door of the pool house, she entered. A couch sat in the middle of the room flanked by chairs on either side. A coffee table rounded out the furniture. Behind the couch, were slatted doors. A dressing room? A bathroom, she guessed. Locating a colorful, one-piece bathing suit on the couch, she began to undress in the shadow of the room. She adjusted the straps, then scooped up the towel. As she walked barefoot toward the front double doors, the side door opened and startled her.

"I wanted to catch you before you joined Haley," Sean said.

Camilla turned slowly. "Hey there."

"Haley told me you lost your job because of her."

She shrugged. "I did what I felt I needed to do."

"I should've come down and picked her up. We've imposed on you. I want to pay you for your inconvenience."

Surprised, she didn't know how to respond. "I could use a ride to the bus station. I'm pretty set on catching the seven o'clock bus."

"Well, I guess I'm going to have to impose on you a little bit longer. *We're* going to meet Mitch this evening. Then, I wanted to take you to dinner…and maybe catch the last half of the rodeo. Show you some of what Cody has to offer."

“Camilla? Where are you?” Haley called out.

Conflicted, Camilla turned back toward the door. She felt Sean’s touch on her arm.

“Buses run tomorrow.” His voice carried a hopefulness she hated to squash.

“Thank you for your offer,” she said softly, “but I don’t have any clothes. No makeup. I’m going to spend an hour in the hot tub, then a quick shower. I’ll grab a burger on the way to the bus station.”

Then she hollered for Haley, “I’ll be right there.”

“If you think you can handle her tears…”

“Camilla, come on!” Haley yelled.

Sean raised his eyebrows. “Taking a horse to catch the bus?”

“What?”

“Sorry. I’m pulling out all the stops. You want to get to the bus station, you’ll have to ride.” He flicked his thumb in the direction of the barn. “If you change your mind, Mitch will be here about six. Can’t believe you’d want to miss that fun.”

“I’ll call a cab,” Camilla stuttered. The man would truly leave her stranded?

“Costs a fortune to have one come from town to pick you up.”

Panic flared. She couldn’t explain to him her need to escape Jared…or at least put the distance between them that Jackson offered.

Haley appeared in the door of the pool house. “What’s up?” she said impatiently. “Let’s go.”

“I think you’ve got that phrase tattooed on your brain,” Camilla said, dryly.

“Did he convince you to stay? I suggested the horse part.” The angelic grin on Haley’s face made her pause. She couldn't disappoint her.

"Okay, I'll stay. One more night. But we all agree, I'm on the bus tomorrow."

Sean smiled and nodded. "Deal." He walked around them and out of the pool house.

"Here's your phone," Haley said. "Now can we go?"

Camilla looked at the email messages. Three from her sister demanding a conversation, to which she replied, *I'll call you tomorrow. Promise.*

"Now we go."

The warm water and massaging jets would sooth her aching body, but what could she do about her aching heart?

****

Camilla wrapped a towel around her body and walked into the bedroom where Haley reclined on the bed.

"I pulled some clothes for you." The teen yawned. "A dress. Shoes. Makeup is on the dresser. Blow dryer is in the top drawer."

"The hot tub cured my pains." Camilla sighed deeply. She peeked at the label on the cotton navy and white dress. "Brooks Brothers. Very sensible."

"Shoes are snakeskin. Cole Haan." Haley tucked the pillow beneath her head.

"Aren't you getting ready?" Camilla asked, glancing at the clock. She racked her fingers through her damp hair.

"What for?"

"Mitch?"

"I doubt he's going to show." Haley rolled on her side. She seemed completely indifferent.

Concerned, Camilla sat on the edge of the bed near Haley's feet. "Why?" Her heart beat quickened. Haley, she was learning, had a sly streak, like a sidewalk magician.

"I've been listening to all you've said. You spent more time with me in the last two days than either of my parents in months."

"Haley"—Camilla shook the teen's leg—"what's going on? Tell me."

Reaching for the blanket at the foot of the bed, Haley dragged it over her body. "The reason Mitch hit me, and it was accidental, was because he was working out with the punching bag, bare-fisted. I kept nagging him to pay attention to me. When he ignored me, I jumped in front of the bag. That's how he hit me. I hate being ignored."

"You…had him hit you on purpose?" Oh Lordy, the girl needed love and guidance, otherwise she'd ride round and round on a carousel of abuse. "What about the other times."

"Those were legit. But today, I broke…some news…to him." Haley's eyelids dropped as she fought sleep.

"Haley O'Connor, wake up. What news?"

"I'm pregnant."

"What?" Camilla jumped up. She grabbed the towel to keep if from falling off. "What?"

"Shhh. It's not true. I watched you with Jared. I saw how he looked at you. I know he likes you. A lot."

"Explain, young lady."

"Mitch kissed me and apologized today. He'd never said, sorry, before. Then I told him I was pregnant, and I expected him to do the right thing, which included meeting my dad and us sharing the news together." Haley blinked. "I want a man to look at me like Jared looks at you. I want a man to do for me what Jared is doing for you."

"What exactly?"

"The old-fashioned word is *courting*. That picnic thing. Kinda cool. I saw fear in Mitch's eyes. I acted all giddy about him being a daddy."

"I saw that performance. I think you have a career in the theater. You're a damn good actress."

"You don't usually swear." Haley sat up wearing an expression of concern. "You mad at me?"

Camilla laughed. "Oh. My. God. I said the same thing to my mother the first time she swore at me. I must have exasperated her as much as you do me." Maybe there was hope for her after all. The schooling she'd learned at her mother's knee had burned deep into her subconscious.

Haley's mouth curved into a sheepish grin. "I like that I'm like you."

"So you never expected him to show all along."

"Not really." Haley shrugged.

"And it was easier to scare him off than trying to run him off?"

"I'm as much to blame as he is for what happened."

"No. He's responsible for hitting you."

"I meant about the sex."

Camilla wanted to cover her ears. The last thing she wanted was details and images in her head of Mitch and Haley together in bed. "Yes, you did make that decision."

"Enough said." Haley lay back down. "I'm really

tired. I'm going to nap. Dad will be waiting to take you to dinner. Take my jean jacket in case you decide to go to the rodeo. Don't want you getting chilly. The mutton racing is fun."

Haley drifted off to sleep as Camilla finished dressing in the outfit Haley had picked out. It gave her a look of respectability. After fluffing her hair, she slipped into the shoes, a low wedge, comfortable heel and grabbed the jacket before descending the stairs.

At the bottom, Sean waited.

Camilla smiled. A sudden wave of awkwardness bloomed. She didn't know this man, but he carried sadness in his eyes. He loved his daughter. She loved Haley, too. Leaving her would be as hard as leaving Jared. And she would miss the wide-open spaces of Wyoming.

Sean escorted her to his car. During the drive to town, he shared information about his ranch and expressed his guilt over how the breakup of his marriage impacted Haley. "She took it hard."

"Just don't give up on her. A little encouragement. Some attention. A dose of direction, and she'll do just fine," Camilla told him. "Everyone deserves second chances."

"She's going to be eighteen soon. Then off to college. Don't know how much influence I can have over her then."

"Call her. Every day if you have to. Show her you care."

"I think I'm hearing the voice of experience," Sean said quietly.

"Something like that."

"I tried to take it like a man," Sean gritted out,

"when she told me all about Mitch. It hurt like hell. I wanted to call the police. But Haley said she'd leave. And there's no real proof of…what she and Mitch did."

"I wondered how that went, but didn't want pry. I wanted Haley to share on her own."

"I admit I wanted to punch the damn guy. It's best he didn't show up. Shooting him would be too easy. But she's almost eighteen. I'll take your advice. I'll keep the lines of communication open. I blame her mother for some of this. She finally called looking for Haley today."

Wanting to sidestep the topic of Haley's absent mother, Camilla redirected the conversation to ranching in Wyoming.

During dinner, Sean shared the history of Cody, named for Colonel William F. "Buffalo Bill" Cody. "The town, officially established in 1895, is a living history to the man. The Buffalo Bill Center of the West is made up of five world-class museums."

When dessert arrived, she picked at the chocolate cake. "I'm sorry to miss Yellowstone National Park."

Sean reached across the table and laid his hand on hers. "Come back and visit next summer. Haley and I will show you the sights."

"Thank you. I just might do that."

"I have to ask…" Sean paused and squeezed her hand. "Is there something serious between you and Jared? A good woman is hard to find." Sean's gaze lifted to hers. "We might try dating…"

"Oh, Sean," she said, lowering her voice. "I…it's not a good idea. I have to go home." A little part of her rejoiced. First Butch Moore, now Sean O'Connor called her a "good woman." Twice in two days had to mean something.

"Just keep me in mind. You never know what the future holds. Now, are you up for the rodeo?" Sean asked, removing his hand and finishing his cognac.

Her cell phone rang. "Just a second. Sorry. It might be my sister." She rose from the table and stepped toward the ladies' room. The number calling was the Mountain View Diner.

"Hello?"

"Camilla? Darcy here."

"Yes?" What reason could prompt that woman to call?

"When I'm wrong, I say I'm wrong. I was hasty in firing you. Are you back in town? I need you to work. Crystal walked out today. Seems she found a husband."

"No. I'm still in Cody."

A pause turned into several seconds of silence. "Darcy?"

"Look, can you come back? I apologize. We could use you."

Darcy held the answer to an unspoken prayer. Now she could finish out the summer, and then go home with a few more dollars toward her goal. "I'll be back tomorrow evening. I can work the day after tomorrow."

"Take the morning shift. I've got to get some sleep. See you then. Well, I won't see you, but you know what I mean. Tom will be in the kitchen."

"I'll be there."

"Camilla?"

"Yes?"

"I really am sorry."

"Thanks, Darcy. Good night." In twenty-four hours, life had bounced her on her head, but she'd bounced back. Maybe she was as tough as her sister after all. Darcy had created the perfect opportunity for her to throw the firing back in Darcy's face. Instead, she'd handled the situation maturely. Evenly. Made it a win-win for all. Pride bloomed in her chest. She wasn't that same spiteful brat who'd left home.

When she returned to the table, Sean stood up. "Rodeo?" he asked.

"If you don't mind, we'll put that on next summer's agenda. I'm suddenly very tired. I've had a rather unusual day. Lots of unexpected things."

Sean nodded. "I understand."

After returning home, Sean left her at the stairs where their evening together had started. "Sleep well. I'll be around when you're ready to make the bus."

She bid him good night and climbed the stairs fully expecting to find Haley asleep on the bed. The hall light stretched across the room as she opened the door. The bed was tidy and Haley gone. A note waited on a pillow.

Camilla,

Jared has a job for you. Call him in the morning. Yay! This means you get to stay.

~H.

"Poor Boo," Camilla whispered. "Tomorrow already calls for different plans."

Camilla tugged on the Hello Kitty shirt for another night. She just might have to take it with her when she left. A reminder of Haley. Tired, she willed herself to sleep, but as quiet blanketed the room, her thoughts of Jared amped up as though someone cranked up the volume on a radio. What was he doing? Was he thinking of her? The temptation to call him was overpowering. She turned her phone off.

Flopping on her side, she pulled a pillow to her stomach, then allowed her mind to wonder through Jared memory land.

She closed her eyes and imagined his hands on her body. His lips against hers. The hardness of him. And the offering of love he gave freely.

It was true. She wouldn't have wanted to miss a moment of making love with Jared. It was better to have loved and lost, than never to have loved at all. Maybe she could risk seeing him just before she left, a final good-bye. At least, she'd have the memory of him riding away looking so fine in a saddle that her heart nearly burst with pride.

And if he protested her departure, she would explain her shame, the nature of her betrayal. Then, he would let her walk away.

But the memory of making love with him would linger forever.

Chapter 15

Early morning sunbeams streamed through the window. Camilla covered her eyes. She'd fallen asleep before drawing the drapes closed last night. No distracting streetlights or neighbor's porch lights, instead star gazing in Wyoming. Hopping up, she tugged on the drapery cord, obscuring brightness until darkness shrouded the room. Sleeping late two days in row wasn't a sign of slothfulness. After all, she deserved a treat now and again.

Crawling back into bed, she tried to keep her mind blank, or as far as possible in the opposite direction of Jared, making it easier to fall back asleep. Images flickered in her brain as though from an old-fashioned slide machine, and she couldn't pull the plug.

Fleur de Lis. The Old Aunts. Immediate family. Extended family on the steps for a group photo. Bayou waters. Cypress trees. Alligators. The roar of airboats on the river. Lacy Spanish moss hanging from ancient oak trees. Memories of scents floated to her. Gumbo. Stuffed mirlitons. Crawfish boils. *Cochon de lait*. Deep frying seafood.

She sighed. Her time away hadn't been like her college days when she returned home for holidays and for a few weeks in the summers, enjoying the barbecues, shrimp boils, and family football games. This absence had been an extended one counted almost in years. Her bedroom at home would feel grand compared to the barely five-hundred-square-foot apartments she'd rented since leaving home. Yet now her heart played tug of war between going and staying.

Did she really stand a chance with Jared? If he had a different life, one minus a betraying deceased wife, would his heart be open enough to forgive her past? And if that was a remote possibility, what real chance could a relationship have when she needed to replant her roots back in the south? A vacation in Wyoming every summer could be grand, but the long, cold, snowy winter would kill her. This place could never be home. And what would a Wyoming rancher do in Mississippi or Louisiana? The life Jared lived didn't exist in her southern world.

"No use in beating the dough to death," she muttered before drifting off to sleep.

Later she woke to the vibrations of her phone against the wooden dresser, initially mistaking it for an annoying insect buzzing. With barely one eye open, she grabbed the noisemaker.

"What?" she said without bothering to look at caller ID.

"Hello." Two voices blended into a cheery greeting.

"Branna, is Biloxi there with you?" she asked.

"Yes. How is it I can hear you so well now when most of the time talking with you is like deciphering Morse code?" Branna asked.

"Or like marbles in the mouth," Biloxi, her cousin, chimed in.

"I don't know. Technology isn't my thing. What's the urgency? I promised to be home at the end of summer, which isn't until late September. The calendar hasn't changed."

"Why so grumpy?" Branna asked.

Camilla clamped her lips tightly together. Her sister wouldn't annoy her this morning.

"Forget that," Biloxi interrupted. "Branna and I have talked it over. We're doing a double wedding."

"Okay," she said blandly. They woke her up for that? "Can't say I'm surprised. The two of you are peas in a pod. Always have been." She smoothed her hand over the duvet cover on the bed and mentally envisioned her sister and cousin in the sunroom giggling like schoolgirls. She missed family terribly in that moment.

"So you're going to be a maid of honor times two," Biloxi said in a rush.

"I can do that." Camilla rolled the idea around in her mind.

"I sold the Mercedes and donated half the money to the senior center," Branna added. "The other half will help pay for the wedding."

"Really? You sold the Mercedes?"

"It's been sitting in the garage for a year."

Biloxi interrupted, "There's only one catch about the wedding." Her tone sounded serious.

Camilla waited for further news.

"Yeesss?" she prompted when no additional tidbits were forthcoming from either of the two on the other end of the phone. A muted bickering of words she couldn't understand made an uneasiness bloom in her chest. The only reason Branna ever changed anything in her well-ordered life was to avoid some impending event of doom. Like when she canceled her wedding with Steven.

Was one of the Old Aunts sick? Had something happened to one of their grandmothers?

“What? Don’t keep me hanging,” Camilla insisted, grabbing up a fist full of sheet.

“Timing is a tad tricky,” Branna said. “We’re moving the wedding up to Labor Day. You have to come home now and help us get ready. Even though this wedding is family only, between ours, James’s, and Nick’s, people will be swarming Fleur de Lis like spectators to a Mardi Gras parade.”

Camilla waited. Branna had rushed to the punch line without delivering a joke. What made timing tricky?

“Is someone sick? It is one of the Old Aunts, isn’t it?” she whispered and clutched the phone tight in her hand. “Is Marie or Grace going to die?” She’d been gone for so long. She forgot things changed there, that they weren’t stuck in a time capsule…well, the house and the property were, but not the people she loved. The old matrons had been there all her life. She took for granted they’d live forever. They couldn’t leave this earth without knowing how much she loved Fleur de Lis. How much she loved and respected them. Or how much she’d changed.

“No.” Biloxi laughed nervously. “Why would you think that? They’re fine. But…”

“Camilla, you can’t tell a soul what we’re about to tell you,” Branna ordered. “Promise?”

“Yes, promise,” she said more than mildly annoyed at her sister’s secrecy.

“While you’ve always been pegged the wild child”—Biloxi’s hesitation provoked Camilla’s patience more—"it seems if Branna doesn't get married really soon, *she'll* be the disgrace of the family."

"What?"

"Camilla," Branna announced. "I'm in that family way." Branna's voice increased. "Preggo. Knocked up! I'll be the family slut if I don't marry quickly."

Laughter from Branna and Biloxi filtered through the phone's receiver. Camilla frowned. If there was something funny about Branna's situation, the irony had flown over her head. Once again, she was the outsider with her sister and cousin.

"But she's engaged. Got a ring on her finger. I saw pictures. Handsome dude. What's the big deal?" She paused. The pain her chest had lightened a little. She took a deep cleansing breath. No significant doom on the horizon. No one was dying. No funeral to plan. Beyond that, what mattered?

"Wait. Hold me down. *You're* going to be a mother? *And* you're not married." She didn't contain her glee. "I'm no longer the daily disappointment!"

"Gee, thanks," Branna said. "Yes, but that's our little secret, Camilla. I'm showing trust in you by sharing this information. Prove you're worthy. No one knows but the five of us. Biloxi. Nick. James, and me. I'm telling you, and you must keep the secret," Branna insisted.

"Nothing like putting me in a box with no windows or doors," Camilla said, sourly. "But the upside—I'm going to an aunt!"

"You've been gone way too long, little cousin," Biloxi teased. "If Branna starts showing before she walks down the aisle, there could be a funeral in the future. James's. The Old Aunts will kill him. Well, maybe try to beat him to death with their golf clubs. We have to save the groom-to-be. So cousin, get your butt home. Besides, you haven't met your future brother-in-law or cousin-in-law."

"I have to confess, the timing is pretty good," Camilla said, thinking aloud. "I just got fired from my job—"

"Oh, Camilla," Branna groaned.

"Wait just a minute, sister. Before you pass judgment on me, maybe you'd like to get the facts," she said hotly.

"She's right, Branna. Don't jump to conclusions. Let's hear her out."

"I'm in Cody, Wyoming—"

"Not Jackson?" Biloxi asked.

"It's a long story, but I had to help someone out. I helped a friend get home to her father. An abusive relationship that I worried would escalate if I didn't get her away from Jackson. Anyway, it cost me my job. Only, they called me yesterday and offered me my job back. I'll help them out for a week, until they can find a replacement—I can't leave them high and dry after I told them I'd show up tomorrow."

"You really lost your job to help someone else out?" Branna asked, her voice hushed. "That's really…I'm proud of you. Taking a stand and putting someone else before yourself. I couldn't be more impressed. Do you need money to get home?"

"No. I'll manage on my own. I'll go back to Jackson, clean out my apartment, and hope my car will hold together to get me south. I'll be there before your wedding." As she spoke, the plan had formed itself.

"It's Saturday, September third," Biloxi said.

"I'll work it out. Don't worry. I'll be there as soon as I can," Camilla said with conviction.

"I've made an itinerary."

"Of course you have, Biloxi." Camilla tried not to laugh. Her cousin was the queen of organization.

"The latest you can leave is Saturday, August twentieth. It's about an eighteen-hundred-mile drive home. Day one: Jackson Hole to Denver, day two: Denver to Salina. Day three will take you to Mt. Pleasant, Texas, then day four will have you driving through the gates of Fleur de Lis."

"Devil is in the details," Branna said in a sing-songy voice.

"That's a lot of driving. I don't know if I can keep that schedule. I might need a day or two more. But I'll figure it out."

"Perfect," Branna replied. "Can't wait to see you, Maid of Honor. And before I forget, Greta is making your dress. Are you still the same size?"

"You'll be surprised to see how toned I am, darlin' sister. What's the dress look like?"

"Well," Branna sighed, "Biloxi and I are still negotiating that."

"More details about the wedding party?" Camilla asked.

"Grooms, got them. Best man, choices still in the works." Branna spoke as though reading from a checklist. "Ushers are brothers and Lind cousins from Louisiana, daddy's side of the family. The flower girl, Ida, she's my little gardening friend in Florida. Biloxi and I decided to have only one. Bridesmaids are all cousins."

"Any chance you'll bring a date?" Biloxi asked.

"I'm hanging up now," Camilla said. A rattling unease settled in her chest. Never would she discuss any man in front of her sister. Not given their past. Branna had to have truly forgiven her, otherwise she wouldn't be maid of honor times two. And her sister trusted her with a secret that would put the family dead-center of local gossip if anyone found out.

Branna's trust in her buoyed her spirits, floating her above the treetops.

"I'll call you when I'm on the road home." Camilla clicked end, and the connection turned silent. The imminent need of her departure ensured she could leave with her dignity intact. Jared would accept the fact that family came first. She'd be on the road putting miles between her and Jared. But would those miles distance her feelings from the ache growing in her heart?

Chapter 16

Reluctant to rise, Camilla closed her eyes and hoped for a few more minutes of sleep, but her mind churned in rebellion. The trip home would be long and lonely. There wasn't time to sell her car and buy a plane ticket home. Besides, she'd need wheels when she finally arrived at Fleur de Lis. Shipping her car wouldn't work. That was far beyond her means, and if she could afford that, she had nothing left over to buy a plane ticket.

Over eighteen hundred miles of lonely highway with few radio stations between Jackson and Bayou Petite. Books on CD might keep the journey lively. Otherwise, she'd be riding in silence for hours at time making the trip even more arduous.

Camilla's phone dinged announcing an email.

Have a job offer for you. Can you meet me at Rock'n R about 1 p.m.? Sean and Haley know the way. ~Jared.

Sucking on her bottom lip, she considered the best response. It had to be short and rather vague. If she told him she'd be catching the bus back to Jackson, he might show up and complicate everything.

Can't accept any job, but will meet you.

Camilla quickly dressed in the clothes she'd worn on the trip to Cody. She folded the garments Haley had lent her for dinner last night and laid them on the dresser in a neat pile. She might never wear such expensive clothes again. The Haley that got on the bus with her and the Haley who lived in Cody were very different girls. At the ranch, she glowed in her element, calm, assertive, and relaxed, though without the benefit of peers her age, but it wasn't like Camilla had seen her hanging out with friends in Jackson. Only Mitch. Maybe a part-time job in Cody would fill her need for interaction with others her age. Or better yet, maybe she could teach riding lessons to children of tourists. Sean could work out the plans.

Gathering her few belongings, she discovered the box of pralines from Jared. She'd leave them in the kitchen for Haley and Sean to enjoy.

"Good morning," she called as she entered Sean's office with a ball of trepidation growing in her chest. The man could resent her suggestions.

The clock on the wall clicked to ten o'clock. She had a bit of time to spend with Haley before asking Sean to take her to Jared's to say good-bye. If Sean drove her over there, it assured a quick exit.

"Sleep well?" Sean asked. He rose from behind his desk. Curled up in a big recliner next to the fireplace, Haley looked up from reading a book.

"Yes, I slept very well." Turning to Haley, she said, "I put the pralines in the kitchen for you. Also, Darcy called me last night. She offered me my old job back. I'll be leaving this afternoon. Then, I'll be heading home as soon as Mountain View finds a replacement. My sister and cousin are having a double wedding at Labor Day."

"When will you come back?" Haley asked.

"Well…maybe next summer?"

"Can I come visit you?"

Camilla looked at Sean. He smiled and nodded.

"Sure, Boo. We'll plan on it."

"When?" Haley pushed.

"Gee. I don't know."

Sean rested his pen on his desk. "Haley, it's rude to push."

"Over my winter break," Haley insisted.

"It's certainly an option, but let me get home and figure out my life first." Camilla chuckled. "We'll get it settled soon."

"Haley, how about you make yourself useful. Go rustle up something for Camilla to eat. We'll join you in the kitchen in a minute."

"I know where I'm not wanted." Tossing a glare at her father, she rolled her eyes when she passed Camilla. "When will I finally be on the inside? The adult side of conversations? Waffles from the toaster in five minutes. Don't let them get cold." Haley stalked from the room.

"I wanted a private moment to thank you for dinner last night. I haven't enjoyed the company of a delightful lady in long time."

"I enjoyed hearing about the history of Cody," Camilla replied. "I wanted to mention something to you. A business proposition that might benefit Haley. She'll be starting college next month, so you'll have time to make the arrangements, but have you considered helping her open a riding school? Given all the tourists that come here, maybe she could start a small business. It would keep her focused and occupied."

"Not a bad idea. I'll talk to her about it. You've made a huge impact in a short time," Sean said.

Camilla shrugged. “It might seem like it’s been overnight, but I’ve been working on her all summer, since she started working at the diner. She’s a good girl.” Camilla paused. Sean had said he’d ferry her to the bus station, but how would he feel about a stop at Rock’n R beforehand? Given the exchange between him and Jared the other night, he might not be willing to accommodate her request. She clenched her hands together.

“What’s up, Camilla?”

“I have a favor to ask. I want to stop by the Richardson’s ranch before going to the bus station. I want to say good-by to Jared. He said you knew the way. I understand you have your differences with him…would it be too much of an imposition?”

“Only if you make me get out of the car and pretend to make small talk.”

“No.” Camilla laughed. “Just take me there, give me a few minutes, then drop me at the bus station.”

“Let’s get you some food. I’ll try my very best not to throw a punch at that skunk.” Sean smiled. “I’m not always so uncivilized.”

Walking down the hall to the kitchen, Camilla reveled in giddiness. Sean called her a delightful lady. Maybe she’d finally polished the rough edges off of her old party-girl image.

****

The morning dragged. Jared called friends for references in his search of a new assistant for his father. He also planned his speech to influence Camilla into taking the job. Gus might protest upon hearing her accent, sounding so similar to those in his mother’s family, but his father would get over it. Over the years

Jared had discovered how much his father had loved his mother, and anything connected to her caused him pain, except his youngest son. Gus-cuss, the nickname he and Ryan had hung on the old man as kids, covered up a big heart with all of his sputtering bluster.

Glancing up at the clock, Jared jumped up. Nicole would have his hide for being late. Running down the hall, he pushed hard on the front screen door. It flew back, smacked the side of the house, bouncing back, and missed hitting him by a paper-thin margin. He jumped aside and wobbled to keep from falling in an attempt to miss bumping headfirst into Nicole.

"You're late," she scolded. "You were supposed to meet me a half hour ago at the house. They're getting ready to pour concrete for the driveway. Lots of noise and commotion. I came down to round you up. I want another inspection of the progress on the inside of my house."

Nicole strode down the steps in worn, brown cowboy boots with heels clunking against the wooden steps, and she climbed behind the wheel of the four-wheeler, then turned the key and started the motor. Jared quickly climbed in beside her.

"How do you know Ryan is the one?" he asked, holding on when she jammed on the gas and the four-wheeler lurched forward like a sprinting jackrabbit. "Did you ever feel that way about me?"

"Ancient history, Jared. You broke my heart the summer you left after high school. You stomped on it when you stayed away even longer. We were both young and stupid then. It was puppy love."

He hadn't hurt her on purpose. He went south as usual that summer and fell in love with antebellum architecture. His grandfather put him to work on a crew handling a special refurbishing project of moving and refitting an old cistern before adding a modern amenity inside, an elevator.

"Do you think we only get one true love in a lifetime?" he asked.

"I don't know. I'm not that introspective. I'm a practical gal. Only need to focus on the here and now."

"You got the best man," Jared said. He caught Nicole's sideways glance and sarcastic grin.

"Are you trying to be funny?" she asked with a short snort.

"What?"

"You're Ryan's best man. And you're the best man at handling the construction of my new house. Beyond that, the thing you're best at is running away."

"Whoa. What happened to no introspection? I only meant between me and Ryan, you picked the better man."

"You bet," she said smugly. "I do still like you though." She patted his arm like a distracted parent might pat a kid on the head. "You'll make a fine brother-in-law despite your rambling ways."

"Just drive, Nicole."

Jared grabbed the overhead roll bar on the side-by-side ATV as Nicole hit the gas, and hoped time permitted him to show Camilla his latest project—Nicole and Ryan's cabin. A designer-perfect rendition with high-beamed ceilings, stone fireplaces—she insisted on one in the great room, TV room, and the master bedroom—and spectacular vistas of the ranch, the home contained every modern amenity from a sauna to lighted steps leading to a walkout basement. To catch

Camilla's expression when she first laid eyes on his work, to understand if she had a shared love of vistas, for some reason that mattered a great deal. His hunch said she had deep southern roots in all the ways that counted.

Nicole followed the long, worn packed-dirt path where trucks and tractor-trailers had traveled almost daily for the last six months delivering supplies and workers to Ryan and Nicole's new homestead. Jared mused. Every construction project experienced problems, and theirs was no different. Issues and cost overruns were an expectation of every foreman and the unwanted result of every homeowner or business owner he worked for. He fully expected Nicole to complain about the door from the family room to the deck. The wrong product had arrived. The correct one was on its way and would be installed upon arrival, but until then, given all the progress on the interior of the cabin, he chose not to leave the opening exposed to the elements and only covered with a flimsy tarp. He worked the finishing schedule down to the last hour. All would be completed a week before the wedding, but he hadn't shared that with Ryan or Nicole yet.

He'd made a promise to Nicole's mother, who planned to have the house cleaned top to bottom and decorated the way she and Nicole had designed. It was up to her to keep Nicole busy so the bride-to-be didn't wander over before the wedding. When the newlyweds returned from their honeymoon, they'd move into a fully furnished home rather than a mostly empty cabin.

"I was just thinking. Your southern grandfather," Nicole said, interrupting his thoughts. "I remember meeting him."

"Mr. Emery Duval. He sure commands attention and respect in his world. You had to be really young when you saw him." Jared thought back to the only time his grandfather had ever set foot on Richardson land. He didn't remember his grandfather at his mother's funeral, but the summer he was eight, his grandfather came to collect him and take him to New Orleans for the summer.

"I never gave it any thought until now, but why did Gus not insist your mother be buried here?"

"Angelique…Mother had a pretty name." Jared barely remembered her face, except that a portrait of her hung in his small hunting cabin. His first stepmother demanded its removal from his father's library. The competition of another woman in the house had been too much for her.

"I remember her singing." His mother had sung to soothe him. A sense of peacefulness came over him whenever he concentrated on the image of her in his mind's eye. She exuded grace and serenity.

"Grandfather insisted on taking her back to New Orleans to rest in the family crypt. There are generations of Duvals buried there…sort of creepy. The cemetery looks like those you see in photographs—classic New Orleans. Grandfather argued that Gus had her during all her adult life after snatching her away from her family. Grandfather wanted her resting place to be familiar."

"Crypt. Resting place. Too much voodoo-hoodoo for me."

Jared chuckled. "It's definitely a different way of life. It's got some great perks. Here, we represent the uncivilized Wild West to my southern family, with all their refinements steeped in traditions. My mother loved the wild outdoors. I don't think she fit in down south very well. From the photos I've seen, she loved hunting and fishing. But most of all she loved horses and wide open spaces."

Hmmpf. Nicole snorted. "Of course. Otherwise, she wouldn't have stayed at Rock'n R once your father brought her here, right?"

"You're asking *me* to explain a woman's prerogative?"

"I meant it more as a statement than a question."

The ATV hit a rut, and Jared bounced in his seat. "Whoa, woman. Slow down."

"Don't tell me how to drive," Nicole snapped, gripped the steering wheel tightly and sped up. The ATV hit another bump almost tossing Jared from the vehicle.

"Are you okay?" Jared asked.

Nicole slowed. "Yeah. Sorry. I just got carried away."

He stared at her. She frowned and shook her head, as though warning him away.

"What? Did I do something? The cabin will be finished exactly on time. Don't sweat it. I swear, I've been trying to follow all the wedding etiquette rules. I even decided to have the bachelor party the weekend before the wedding so Ryan won't be hung over." That had to buy him brownie points with his OCD, soon-to-be sister-in-law.

They drove the next hundred yards in silence. Nicole parked out of the way of the workers, but close to the garage. She cut the engine, then sat very still, looking straight ahead. Jared waited. He'd learned from living with Cheyenne that silence could be golden. Silence pushed her guilt button, and he always gained some new piece of information if he waited patiently.

After several moments, Nicole spoke. “I’ve known you and Ryan all my life,” she said. “I try to understand it all. You’re half-brothers. Different mothers. But, Ryan cared deeply for your mother, more than his own. He loved her.”

“Well,” Jared started. He could explain, but it didn’t guarantee Nicole or anyone could really understand. “He has no memory of his own mother. My dad married my mom less than a year after Ryan’s mother died. My mom raised Ryan. He actually had more time with my mother than I did.”

“I know all of that…but I can’t resign myself to the one thing Ryan has asked of me.”

Did he really want to know? She was behaving oddly. He chocked it up to bridal nerves, but the last thing he wanted was to be stuck in the middle of an argument between his brother and Nicole.

She turned and faced him. “If we have a girl, Ryan wants to name her after *your* mother.”

“I take it you find that objectionable. Does it make you uncomfortable?”

Nicole teared up. “I don’t believe in all that mystical superstitious stuff”—she sniffed—“but it just seems to me good old common sense says we shouldn’t name our daughter after a southern belle who broke her neck in a fall from a horse.

“You’re pregnant?” Jared asked, shocked.

“Huh? No! But you know Ryan, he plans everything.”

Jared coughed back a laugh. “Yep.”

"He's got the schedule already set. Any baby must be born during the winter of our second year of marriage, preferably when we're on vacation someplace warm, so as not to interfere with other ranching operations. And with you now announcing your leaving…I don't know if we'll get a vacation ever again or not. Ryan hates to leave details to anyone else. Only you."

Jared patted Nicole's hand. "If you manage to work my brother's schedule, let me know. I promise I'll be here, so Ryan can be with you when the baby is born…even if it happens in Hawaii."

"Oh, Jared"—Nicole leaned over and kissed his cheek—"you really are a good man. I love Ryan so much. I won't ever be able to say *no* to a girl named Angelique. Especially when I know he loved her namesake so much."

"Just don't name a boy after my father. One Gus-cuss is enough in any family."

Now, if only he could convince Camilla he was the best man for her. He, too, was a man of plans. He had one for her. A chuck-wagon date, a horseback ride on the ranch, a campfire beneath a blanket of twinkling stars would give him the time he needed to convince her of his love. In all his years of running wild, his heart had never experienced a completeness, a wholeness that came when he discovered he loved Camilla. It may have been from that very first kiss.

If his father could capture the heart of a southern belle and sway her thinking to move to Wyoming, how hard could it be to capture the heart of a belle already here and convince her to move back south?

Chapter 17

Camilla opened the front passenger door to Sean's car parked at the side the house while Haley waited in the back behind her dad. The scenery was another photo opportunity. Cloudless blue sky, craggy mountains, and green trees. Camilla stopped, scanned the view, and breathed in clean fresh air, then let out a long slow breath before ducking into the car and closing the door. It could be the last time she ever saw the place. A pang of regret stirred in her chest. Plans made for the future could change on a dime. But if she couldn't come to Haley next summer, she'd make sure the girl came to visit her down south.

"How far away is the Rock'n R?" Camilla asked, buckling her seatbelt.

"Five miles if you cut through pasture," Haley replied. "However, by highway miles, it's at least double that."

Sean drove past the stone gateposts of the ranch and pulled on to an empty blacktop road.

"Not much traffic here," Camilla commented. Now everywhere she looked reminded her of home. Unlike the interstate running through New Orleans to Picayune, Mississippi, no one living around Cody could complain about congestion at rush hour. However, this small town wasn't too dissimilar from laid-back Bayou Petite, but only in the number of cars. Here trees didn't know Spanish moss or liquid air. At home, traffic issues loomed only once year on Fat Tuesday when streets closed to make way for flambeaux carriers—people toting torches lighting the way for night parades—marching bands, dance troupes, and krewes tossing beads and other "throws."

Sean tapped his hand on the steering wheel to the rhythm of Sting singing a melodic melody. The rancher definitely walked a path to his own beat. He expanded her beliefs of the definition of Wyoming rancher to include a well-rounded man.

"Interesting song," Camilla said. "Don't hear much of that around here. Mostly just country twang."

"Oh, I like the Georges all right. Jones and Straight. I like George Dickel now and again. I'm considering investing in a Wyoming distillery. Not sure if we can ever reach the likes of Basil Haden or Four Roses, but don't know unless we try.

"The novelty alone will make it a hit."

"Dad, what's ranching got to do with distilling? You always said you could tell a good restaurant because it didn't serve fourteen different types of food, but specialized in one thing. Like steak, sushi, barbecue, or spaghetti. But not all of them at the same place," Haley piped in from the backseat.

"Quite the little business mind she's got." Camilla chuckled.

"Haley, I said I was thinking about investing, not owning or running the place."

"I can see it now. Tasting parties as part of the new lure for tourists to Cody. This isn't Kentucky, you know," Haley snorted.

When Sean stood his ground, the two tangled in a

verbal spar. Instead of taking sides, Camilla stared out the window, trying to memorize the color of the fields and the sky. Somehow, she had to capture the image and copy it to her brain for total recall after she left Wyoming. The best part, it kept her mind mostly occupied and off the topic of Jared. His kisses. How the heat of his touch branded not only her skin, but her soul. It was as though someone had tattooed *Jared* across her heart in bold letters. Memories were all she'd have of him when the craving for his closeness made her ache.

A few minutes later, Sean turned off the blacktop road. His fingers turned silent. He hit the button for the radio, and sound died. The car stopped after a few hundred feet, and Sean inched the nose of the car toward the closed gate, which then swung open. Tall stone pillars connected with an arched, carved sign that read, Rock'n R Ranch, greeted them.

"Richardsons and I have some unsettled issues," Sean said quietly. "None of your concern. Therefore, I'll wait in the car once we get to the house. You can go in and say your good-byes to Jared."

"I'll go in with you," Haley said.

"No. Camilla needs privacy. You stay with me. She can handle this on her own."

"Dad," Haley whined.

Sean glanced over his shoulder and gave Haley a look that silenced her.

"How far is it to the house?" Camilla asked once the car began to pick up speed again. Her gut knotted. She folded her hands together tightly. How could she say good-bye? But if she didn't walk away now, how could she live later on, once Jared discovered her shameful past? Betrayal was unforgivable.

"Not sure exactly, but at least three miles from what I remember."

A few minutes later, they pulled under a portico of a log home larger than Sean's with a covered porch spanning the entire front of the two-story house complete with dormers. On both sides of the porch, rocking chairs invited guests to take it easy and enjoy the views. The surrounding landscape appeared professionally done. Stunned by the grandeur of the place, Camilla hesitated to get out of the car.

"What's wrong?" Sean asked.

"I'm not quite sure." Camilla hedged her qualms and didn't dare utter her thoughts. If Jared came from such an established Western family, clearly a family of great means, what did he want with a southern girl like her? Did he say, "I love you," to every woman he rolled around with? Some men did. In that moment of euphoria after sex, some men would say anything, especially if they wanted the opportunity of a repeat performance. She'd said it before, too. Though usually she meant as "I love the feeling we just shared," rather than "I want to spend the rest of my life with you."

Her heart had latched onto Jared's confession of love and embedded it, believing with every ounce of blood it pumped that Jared meant exactly what he said. And her heart loved him in return just as strongly, if not more. His words ignited a radiating joy through her and made her believe a lifetime together could be possible. Yet leaving remained her only option, putting distance between them…for a lifetime.

Sean popped his seatbelt latch, then reached across her, opening the door. "You don't want to have this conversation with Jared in front of us. Go on, now. Get out. Talk with him in private."

Camilla climbed the handful of steps to the porch like she marched toward her own funeral. Glancing from side to side, she mentally calculated the porch's measurements, about the size of the front gallery at Fleur de Lis, which made the house less intimidating. She knocked on the wooden framed screened door, then stepped back. After a minute when no one answered, she knocked again, and harder. The door bounced against the doorframe.

As she peered through the screen, two men suddenly came into view, each stepping into a hallway beyond the large front room. One she recognized—Ryan. The other? She guessed he had to be the father. Ryan favored the older man.

"Camilla, how ya doin'?" Ryan greeted her warmly.

"She's Camilla?" the older man asked.

"Yes," she said, standing straighter and lifting her chin, hoping to create an air of confidence before the two tall men staring down at her from inside the house.

Ryan opened the door and motioned her inside. Camilla turned to catch him offering a friendly wave to Haley. The teen rested her arms and chin on the sill of the open car window, and she flicked one wrist in weak acknowledgment.

"Sean and Haley brought me over."

"Come on in, little lady," the older man said. He offered his large, calloused hand as though she might be royalty and escorted her inside. Ryan followed behind them. The screen door closed with a *whack.*

"I'm Gus Richardson," the older man said politely.

From his plaid, short sleeve, cotton shirt to his belt buckle and boots, he gave off an aura of a hard-working rancher.

"Camilla, this is our old man. Jared's and mine," Ryan said, before dropping into one of the leather chairs flanking each end of a couch in the large living room. She eyed the ranch's logo on his t-shirt. Clearly, the Richardson ranch was serious business.

Gus pointed for her to take a seat on the long couch facing a two story, stacked-stone fireplace. He sat in a chair closest to her. "Tell me about yourself."

"Pardon me?" Camilla asked. Was Jared going to join them soon, she wondered.

"You went to college?" Gus asked. His thick, full head of gray hair made her wonder if Jared would keep his looks like his father had.

"Yes. My bachelor's degree is in management. I started my MBA, but not sure if I'll finish it."

"Smart lady," Gus said, nodding to Ryan. "She got into graduate school."

"She's good with people," Ryan responded. "She keeps those old-timers at the diner in line. But does she have any actual business experience?" He carried on a one-way conversation with his father like she wasn't present.

"Do you?" Gus asked.

Camilla snuck a glance at Ryan, then turned back toward Gus. Had they been expecting her? Where was Jared? And why the inquisition? Still, she couldn't be impolite.

"I worked as a bookkeeper for one of my uncles during the summers I was in college. He owns a seafood business south of New Orleans. My family has a business, but I only fill in doing grunt jobs when I'm needed." They didn't need to hear about the drama of Branna and Biloxi and the job as Keeper at Fleur de Lis. In her world, originally Branna was the queen. Biloxi the lady in waiting, but the two of them twisted tradition and made the Keeper job fit them while she had no fixed role in the family business. However, she and Biloxi planned to alter that situation whenever she finally arrived home. She had that to look forward to.

"Did you hear the way she said, 'New Orleans'? Just like a native." Gus beamed.

"It's two words, not one," Ryan replied, dryly.

"Not down there," Gus insisted.

"Excuse me, gentlemen. I'm confused. I came over to talk with Jared. Is he here?"

"You're hired," Gus said.

Camilla furrowed her brow. "Hired?"

"You came to interview for the job, right? Jared convinced us you'd be perfect. At least until he leaves."

"Job? Leave?" Had she heard him right? And Jared was leaving? When? To go where? Back to Jackson?

"My assistant," Gus said. "Jared said you needed work, and I need someone to help me run the office. A man won't do."

"Ah. I see." But she didn't. "There's been a misunderstanding. I already told Jared I couldn't take the job. I came to say good-bye. I'm leaving town today."

"Today? No." Gus shook his head.

Ryan straightened in the chair and planted his feet squarely on the floor. He leaned toward her. "You can't." His words sounded like an order.

If Gus confused her, Ryan totally baffled her. "No.

I'm pretty sure I can."

"Camilla, reconsider. Jared said you got fired. Take this job."

"They rehired me at the diner."

"We'll pay you a signing bonus." Ryan stood up and paced. "How much do you need? Five thousand? If you leave, you'll wreck my life." There was a note of underlying desperation in his voice that worried her. What the heck was up with these Richardson men? Jared had said the "L" word and now they didn't want her to leave?

"You must go talk to Jared. He's up at my house, well, the one he's building for Nicole and me. My four-wheeler is out back. Take it. Follow the trail and go talk to Jared. We really need you to stay. At least stay until after my honeymoon. We need your help." The strong man who stood guard when she threatened Mitch had been reduced to begging?

"I'm only agreeing to talk to Jared. Nothing more," she said hesitantly. "I need to let Sean and Haley know—"

"I'll do that," Gus interrupted. "O'Connor and I have other business to discuss anyway. Now is as good a time as any." Gus rose and started for the front door.

"Let's go," Ryan said. He pointed beyond the living room to an opening to a dining room. "Kitchen's through there."

Beyond the back porch, a stone walkway took her through a raised-bed garden with planter boxes of herbs and colorful flowers to a patio and gazebo where a four-wheeler waited.

"Ever ridden one of these?" Ryan asked. He picked up a helmet from the seat of the all-terrain vehicle, larger and industrial-strength size compared to the pretty yellow ones they had at home.

"Sure. It's been a while, but I think it's like paddling a *pirogue*. You never forget."

Ryan pointed through a break in the evergreens marking the edge of the manicured backyard. "Go around there. Follow the tree line to the opening between the trees, then take the dirt path. Don't go too fast around the curves. My house is on the backside of that hill." He handed over the helmet.

"It's kind of nasty looking," she said easing back from the offered headgear. "I'll go real slow."

"Here." Ryan pulled a blue bandana from his pocket. "Cover your hair with this, but you've got to wear the helmet. Safety first."

Reluctantly, she obeyed. The unfamiliar twists and turns of the natural landscape could put her in a ditch. She straddled the hefty machine, turned the key, hit the start button, and the engine cranked.

"I'm going to tell Felicia to add another plate for lunch. Jared or I will run you back to Sean's later. I'm counting on my brother to convince you to stay."

Camilla shook her head. "No, I've got to go." He could do what he liked. She certainly wasn't going to waste time trying to convince him otherwise. Instead, she pointed out the path he'd shown moments ago. He nodded in agreement.

Taking off slowly to get the feel of the machine beneath her, she focused on the path ahead. No looking back. Just a final farewell to Jared. The sooner she left, the sooner the pit growing in her stomach would shrink.

Following the wide trail, dirt and gravel, she took in the sights of wild flowers and grasses. From every vantage point in Wyoming, mountains framed the view. She enjoyed the freedom of crossing the landscape on something other than a meandering horse. The farther she drove, the more comfortable the four-wheeler became, though she wished she hadn't agreed to wear the helmet, wanting to feel the breeze through her hair instead of the beads of sweat forming at her temples.

The trail rose deceptively slowly and at one point where it curved back on itself, she caught a glimpse of the tall evergreens blocking the view of Gus's house and surmised the trees provided privacy for both father and son.

Before long, the sound of workers shouting back and forth caught her attention over the grind of machinery. The path widened even more. Around the next curve, she spied a worksite. Forms and rebar and two concrete trucks. Beyond that, a house. Camilla parked the ATV well away from the worksite, removed the loaned helmet and bandana, then fluffed her hair while taking in the ongoing operations. A large driveway approached the side of the house, and a patio wrapped around the back. She moved in the opposite direction of the workers in search of Jared and Nicole. With no steps yet in place, she hopped up on the front porch spanning the front of the house, just like the one at Gus' cabin. Across the front casing of the hand-carved, double doors, an X of blue tape stopped anyone from entering there.

Peeking in the window, she noticed most of the interior of the home had been finished. Wooden floors glistened. Walls painted. Even an antler chandelier hung in the foyer. She guessed Ryan and Nicole would be moving in soon, maybe after their honeymoon.

Walking the rest of the length of the porch, she neared the last window. Peering inside, she spotted the two she sought standing with their backs to her while they gazed out a window that opened to the side of the house. She started to rap on the glass to get their attention, but stopped when Nicole turned and tucked a cell phone into her back pocket. Camilla caught her profile. A lovely face wearing a very pained expression.

Then Jared put his arms around Nicole, folding the woman into his arms. He kissed the top of her head as her shoulders began to shake. Her arms snaked around his waist. She grabbed hold of him as though he was her only lifeline. He rubbed her back and held her close. Pain etched his face. The pair stood like they were suspended in time and locked together in misery.

Rooted in place, Camilla tried to glance away, but the scene held her captive. Her breath hitched tight in her throat. Hurt pushed up from her gut to her chest.

Nicole appeared to say, "No. No. No." Jared lifted her chin, her face, blotchy from crying, scrunched into agony. He kissed her nose and said something, which made Nicole cry harder. She clung to him and again he wrapped her in a bear hug that looked way too intimate to be brother-in-law-like.

Camilla swallowed hard. The scene before her was a tender intimate one. Her heart cracked, oozing pain. Nausea rolled in her stomach.

She had been a fool in so many ways.

With fist clenched tightly, nails biting into the flesh of her palms, she shuffled out of sight of the window. Jared had told the truth when she was getting on the bus—he wasn't engaged, wasn't getting married. But was he fooling around with his soon-to-be sister-in-law? Surely, there wasn't something between Jared and Nicole. There had to be an explanation, one that wouldn't make her want to puke. Or kill him.

She sucked in a breath and let it go to quell rising panic. The moment she just witnessed had to be the ultimate karmic payback for what she'd done to her sister. Yet it had to have been even worse. Branna had been engaged to the most sought-after local man, an impending wedding-of-the-decade with the entire county invited.

Guilt welled in her gut. How could she have hurt her sister like that?

In a fast trot, Camilla headed to the opening where front steps would soon settle. Jumping off the porch, she raced to the ATV, and pulled on the helmet. After starting the machine, she revved the engine. Glancing over her shoulder, she caught sight of Jared in the window. His eyes widened. Surprised to see her? Or shocked at being caught? It didn't matter. Her heart still wanted him, and her head refused to condemn him. If there was a logical reason for his intimate embrace with Nicole, she didn't need to know. The only memory she needed to file away was their afternoon of lovemaking.

She raced off going as fast as she dared. With an ounce of luck, Sean and Haley would whisk her away quickly.

A few minutes later, she stopped the ATV where she'd first sighted it, climbed off, leaving behind both helmet and bandana. Before she could skirt the house, heading for the front drive, Ryan came roaring out the back door.

"Camilla, wait!"

She ran. Spotting Sean's car, she raced toward it.

In the backseat, Haley napped.

"Where's your dad?" Camilla called out as she opened the door.

Haley sat up and yawned. "Inside."

"Please, Haley. Go get him. We have to leave now." Camilla climbed into the car.

Haley rubbed her eyes. "Okay. What's the rush?"

"Now, please. Haley. I must get to the bus station."

Ryan, Gus, and Sean barreled out the front door before Haley had both feet on the ground.

"What happened?"

"What's going on?"

"Why didn't you talk to Jared?"

The three men spoke at once.

Camilla held her hands up, turned her face from the window, and stared straight ahead.

"Dad, come on. Camilla's ready to leave," Haley said.

Sean frowned. He shook hands with Gus, then Ryan, before getting in the car. He started the engine and pulled away. "Are you okay?" Sean asked as though he feared she'd lost her mind.

"Please, let's just go."

"Camilla, you're scaring me. What happened?" Haley asked.

"Nothing for you to worry about." Camilla tried to sound calm and soothing. "I want you to remember all we've talked about…decision making, integrity, and self-esteem."

"Okay," Haley replied hesitantly. "But what's that got to do with what's happening now?"

"There's an old expression about 'chickens coming home to roost.' Well, the boomerang just hit me squarely in the heart. I truly understand all the damage that I did to someone else."

As they reached the gates near the main road, a truck approached. Camilla sank down in the seat to avoid being noticed by Jared and Nicole turning onto the drive of Rock'n R Ranch.

"Jared called Ryan while I was still inside," Sean said. "Nicole's mother had called. Her grandmother on her father's side died suddenly. Nicole is flying out tomorrow to New York. I guess this might put a hitch in the wedding plans. Anyway, Jared said he saw you as you were leaving the construction site. He wanted to know what was going on and wanted to speak with you."

How could she have mistaken the moment for anything more than it actually was? Jared, the mere thought of him made her soul lift with deep satisfaction. His touches turned her loosey-goosey like silly putty. He was an upstanding man. Comforting a friend, a family member, over her sudden loss. He was all she'd thought he was and more.

"I'm so sorry for Nicole, but I really don't have anything to say to Jared." Camilla chewed her bottom lip. She should've stayed and faced him. But how? Confusion swirled, a centrifuge of turbulence. Someone as good as him would only shake their head with pity and disgust. He could never truly love someone who'd hurt a loved one as she had. When he learned what she'd done to her sister…he'd hate her. However, knowing Jared wasn't a snake slithering in the grass made the oozing pain in her heart clot. Her love wasn't wasted on him.

She'd follow her sister's lead and leave. Jared's

image of her need not be marred. If she never saw him again, he'd never know of her ugly past.

It would remain a painful secret.

She had to make everything right with Branna.

With determination riding shotgun and willpower at the wheel, she was going home.

Chapter 18

Jared slammed on the brakes bringing the truck to an abrupt halt in front of the big house. Every nerve in his body had urged him to chase down Sean's car. The man was taking his woman farther away. Camilla slinking down in the seat didn't hide her from view or lessen mind-twirling thoughts of her. Torn for the briefest of seconds, he made a decision based on the facts—Nicole's needs had to come first, not his own.

Ryan waited under the portico and opened the door like a man possessed. Nicole turned and stepped one foot on the running board when Ryan pulled her into his arms and set her on the ground. They melded together. Nicole began to cry again, soft whimpers and heaving shoulders. Ryan held her tight. Reassuringly, he told her all would be okay. Jared turned away from intruding on their intimate moment. Yet at the same time, his soul ached. He wanted that same loving closeness with Camilla.

After climbing down from the truck and heading in the direction of the front door, he spotted his father in one of the rocking chairs off to the right. Jared's boots thumped against the wooden log steps. He took the chair next to the old man, dropping into it and hoping Camilla's quick departure didn't mean the bottom was dropping out of his world. What was she doing at the house? Why had she taken off like a spooked filly?

"It's a pity," Gus said, quietly. "But these things happen. The cycle of life."

"I don't think she's ever lost anyone in her family before," Jared said, speaking of Nicole's loss. "I guess Ryan and I have more experience at death than I realized."

"Yes. I expect you and your brother could write a book. Now, I've made a decision." The old man sounded emphatic.

"Yes?" Jared wasn't sure he wanted to know. The old man could be planning his next marriage. People in town were placing bets on whether or not Gus would find his next bride at Ryan and Nicole's wedding.

"I'm going to tidy things up. Get all my legal paperwork in order. I'm going to order my headstone so I'll know I have one when I die. The two of you might take forever to put one up. Then, come fall, I'm gonna do some traveling. Leave things in Ryan's hands."

Jared raised an eyebrow. He wouldn't entertain the impact of father's maudlin thoughts. The old man could quite very well outlive all of them. "You? Travel?"

"Yep. Signing up for an over-sixty singles cruise. I won't need an office assistant, but Ryan's gonna need an office manager. I think that young lady of yours would work out real nice, if you can talk her into the job. But she says she's leaving."

"Leaving?" Jared cocked his head and focused on his father as Ryan escorted Nicole inside the house. "As in she's going back to Sean's house?"

"She came by to say good-bye. Ryan insisted she ride up to his house and talk with you. What did you say to her that had her trying to sneak away?"

"Say?" What was the old man talking about? She

wouldn't leave without speaking to him. Could she? No. No way. She cared way too much to just up and leave.

"Stop repeating me, boy. You sound like a damn parrot. What happened up at the job site?"

"Nicole and I were touring the house. She pointed out a few issues she has in a couple of rooms. Then she got the call from her mother about her grandmother dying. I caught sight of Camilla through the window as she was running flat out to the ATV. I never got a chance to talk with her. I don't understand what's going on." Camilla was leaving? His heart sank from his knees to his ankles. Why was this woman always on the move? First the bus to Cody, then the restaurant with Sean. Was Sean delivering her back to Cody? Had he developed an interest in Camilla?

"Excuse me." Jared rose from the rocker. "I'm going to call her now and get to the bottom of this." He trotted down the stairs. Before turning the corner and heading to the backyard, his father called out, "I'll find out Nicole's plan. Come see us before you leave."

Jared perched on the stone picnic table with his feet on the wooden bench and hit Camilla's number listed under Favorites. The phone rang and rang, then went to voice mail. He clicked to break the connection. He'd be damned if he'd leave a message. What he had to say could only be said face to face. He had to make the woman listen. Wherever she was running to, she was yanking on the tether to his heart. Each tug caused the tear to lengthen. However, he wouldn't allow the link between them to be broken. She might be fighting the attraction, but their hearts had completely joined when they made love. Not even distance could change that fact.

He sent her an email. *Where are you going? Why? Call me, please*. He'd added the "please" for politeness, but it had a ring of desperation to it. Maybe she'd take pity.

Tossing his phone back and forth between his hands as though it were a hot coal, he waited for it to ring. He decided he'd wait and answer on her third ring, to quell any notion she might have about his torment. He would be calm and cool.

Whom was he kidding? He'd answer on the first ring, couldn't wait to hear her voice.

After several minutes, he sent another message, just in case she hadn't received the first one. Then setting the timer for five minutes, he began to wait. She had to call.

When the timer beeped and he hadn't heard a peep from Camilla, he called Sean. When the man answered, Jared said, "Richardson here. Is she with you?"

"No."

Jared doubted the truth of those words.

"Look, I know we've had our differences in the past, but this is important."

"What is?"

"Camilla," he shouted. "Where is she? I need to talk with her now."

"Can't help you, man. She made me promise not to tell you anything. You're on your own."

Hating the smugness in Sean's voice, Jared raised his fist and slammed the picnic tabletop. The pain didn't stop anger rolling over him. "I hope I can return the favor sometime." Jared clicked off the connection. He flipped through his call list and found Haley's number. Hitting a button, he listened as the phone began to ring on the other end. “Come on, Haley, answer.” But he had no such luck.

“Jared,” Ryan called from the back door. “Come in? We’ve got to talk about what’s going on with Nicole.”

The urgency in his brother’s voice brought him out of his cloud of frustration. “Be right there.” He hopped off the table and crossed through the garden. His hand began to throb, and he tried shaking off the pain. When his phone rang, he grabbed for it quickly, his anticipation shooting to the mountaintops. A moment later, hope deflated in his chest like a rock disappearing into a lake. The construction foreman called, but Jared let it go to voice mail as he climbed the back steps to the house.

In the office, one of Nicole’s favorite rooms, Jared found her, Ryan and his father waiting. Nicole slumped in a chair while his father and Ryan sat on opposite ends of the couch. Jared parked in the rolling office chair and glided over to join the group.

“Jared, if you recall, Kurt is visiting his sick mother in hospital this week, so I don’t have my number one man as back up. Nicole and I are flying out this afternoon to New York. Her grandmother’s funeral date is yet undecided, but will be within a few days.”

“You need a ride to the airport?” Jared asked as the heel of his boot tapped out a continuous beat. He willed his shaking leg to stop the nervous habit.

“Dad will take us. What I need is for you to stay here. Run the ranch. Make sure the house is completed. Finish paying the monthly bills. Do all the stuff Kurt and I do, plus what you do. Until I get back.”

"I told you, Ryan, I can handle the office," their father said gruffly.

"Let's face facts, Dad. I'm going to be to-the-heart direct. You hate office work, and someone has to come behind you and clean up the mistakes. Better to get it done right the first time and save us all some headaches."

Jared paused and searched the faces of his family members. As always, Ryan remained deadly calm in a crisis. The only thing that gave away his tension was the flexing of his fist. His brother was a man's man, but when it came to handling a woman's tears, he always turned to silly putty. Nicole appeared lost in sadness. He ached to comfort her and lessen her pain. Was grief different for an adult than for a child? He'd had his fill of pain when his mother died. It bothered him a bit when he hadn't experienced much grief after burying Cheyenne. As for his father, the gruff old man had never let him down. He snorted a lot, pawed at the ground like a bull intent on a fight, but always supported Jared's life decisions, even if it meant Jared leaving.

His love for Camilla wasn't going to change. If she left Cody for parts unknown, he'd find her. He had a secret and would savor the moment when he shared it with her. He might have to pause in his pursuit of her, but only a momentarily; however, he would die a hundred deaths if anything happened to his woman.

"I'm your man," Jared finally replied. "I'm here to help."

"Yeah," Ryan said dryly. "Just don't go getting into any trouble while I'm gone."

"Let me start being useful right now. I'll help you

pack."

Nicole rose, walked toward him, and ruffled his hair. "You *are* the best man, but I've got this covered. Having something to occupy my hands will pause my tears." She left the room silently, floating on sadness. Ryan followed after her.

"I'm going to run over to Sean's for a minute," Jared told his dad.

"Wait until after we leave for the airport," Gus replied. "How about pulling the Caddy around? I haven't driven it much lately." Gus tossed him the keys.

Jared left the house out the back door. The garage and workshop sat between the big house and the bunkhouse. He hit the button on his phone and called Camilla again. No answer. Haley might be his best bet, and he tried her number again. He had to see Camilla, or at the very least speak with her.

"Hello, Jared," she said.

"Haley, I'm trying to locate Camilla."

"Okay."

Was the girl being purposefully obtuse? "Do you know where she is?"

"Yes."

He tried a different approach. "Haley, *where* will I find Camilla?" If he got beyond yes-or-no answers, he might actually uncover the information he sought.

"I can't say."

"Can't or won't."

"I made a promise. She's my friend, and I will keep my word to her."

Why would Camilla swear Sean and Haley to secrecy? No matter. He wouldn't be defeated by a teenager. "Are you going to Cody with her on the bus?"

"No, but I'm going to visit her over the Labor Day weekend," Haley said, excitement raising her voice higher.

"That's great! Will you be driving or flying?"

"Ha. Ha. I'm not as naive as you think. I won't tell you."

"Look Haley, I'm going to take you into my confidence. I love her. She left without saying good-bye to me. I know that's what she wants. That's why she came to Rock'n R, right? To say good-bye. She can't leave without knowing how I feel. I. Love. Her."

"Arg!" Haley groaned.

"Being an adult is tough. Sometimes you have to make hard decisions. Is keeping her secret more important than knowing someone loves her? Let me be that knight in shining armor on a white charging stallion. Let me go to her, Haley. But I need your help. Where is she?" Could he push the right buttons to make her teenaged heart override the logic of her brain?

"Haley?" he asked when no answer came.

"I'm here."

"Let's move it on, girl. I *need* to know where she is."

"All right! This is what I will tell you. She isn't in Cody anymore. In a week, she'll be leaving where she is and moving on."

Leaving? The woman was always leaving! "Good start. Thank you. Now where will she be going?"

"I'm not going to say. What I will tell you is that her sister and cousin are getting married. A double wedding. Labor Day weekend. And I'm going."

"Haley, if you were standing in front me of right now, I'd hug you and kiss you, girl."

Haley chuckled. “I seem to have that effect on men. But,” her voice grew softer and low, “you can’t let Camilla know I gave you any information.”

“It’ll be our little secret.”

“Bye, Jared,” Haley said before she ended the call.

“Hot damn!”

At the garage, he yanked on the roll up door to raise it, then he pulled the keys to the Cadillac from his pocket, jingling them in his hand. “I’m going to crash a wedding. I’m gonna be her plus-one.”

He turned the key in the ignition and the engine started. His brain followed suit, cranking through information. Mentally he scanned a calendar.

Damn! He couldn’t be in two places at once.

Ryan’s wedding was scheduled for the same day. He had to be there as best man. Camilla would be at Fleur de Lis. She’d never miss her sister and cousin’s wedding.

“Shit!” he slammed his palms on the steering wheel. “I’ve got to see her. How the hell can I work this out?”

Chapter 19

Camilla sniffed at the scent of bacon frying. The Tuesday morning breakfast crowd at the Mountain View would soon begin to appear. She craved eggs and cheese grits to go along with frying pork, but hadn't been able to convince Darcy to put the southern dish on the menu. When she'd returned to work, Darcy had said she'd serve them as a special today, Camilla's last day at work, *if* she managed to find a source for them, which was highly unlikely on such short notice. Darcy was still Darcy.

With Becky, the waitress-in-training, following her every move and taking copious notes, Camilla demonstrated the morning routine once again. Becky wasn't new to waitressing and caught on quick. The customers loved her bubbly personality and bright red lipstick.

Camilla poured cream into the ceramic cow creamers. "Becky, this is always the last thing I do when I work the morning shift before we unlock the front door and the Fivers arrive."

"They're such a cool group of oldies." Becky walked to the front door and unlocked it.

Camilla scooted over to the panel of switches. "Camera! Action!" All of the overhead lights flickered on. Camilla giggled. "I've wanted to do that every day since I started working here. Anyway, I've learned a lot from the Fivers." She'd miss them, but looked forward to opening Fleur de Lis Café and regulars of her own.

"They've been everywhere! I love to hear their stories. Someday, I'm going to travel like they have. Only in style. Not on a Navy ship or fishing vessel."

Camilla smiled. "You could come down south and try a day on a shrimp boat. I highly recommend traveling, but you'll never see a bluer sky than a Wyoming one." Every night for the last week, the color of the sky haunted her dreams, making sound sleep unattainable. Dark circles under her eyes were proof enough. Blue came to her in the form of Jared's eyes. Smiling. Loving. And just before she woke, those same eyes filled with confusion, then narrowed with harsh penetrating judgment.

She had refused to talk with him since she departed from Cody, though that hadn't deterred his calling and emailing. Multiple times a day his message was the same, over and over again. "I love you," as if he intended to subliminally tattoo the message in her brain. It already glowed like neon on her heart. He had no clue that his name was already emblazoned there. She wouldn't deny the thrill each and every message gave, running up her spine with a zing of excitement. No man ever pursued her like Jared. But she held her ground and refused to talk with him. In return, he'd taken to leaving longer and longer voice-mail messages detailing all the reasons a relationship between them would work.

She loved his wit and humor. Loved his mind and totally craved his body, but once he understood the truth about her, then in real life, just like in her dream, his eyes would cloud with confusion, then narrow with harsh judgment. The one thing he could never accept from her was betrayal.

"Coffee?" Becky asked. "Another jolt of java before the customers stream in."

Camilla nodded and Becky poured.

"Hard to believe this is my last day here. I can't wait to get home, but leaving is a little sad."

"I'll take very good care of your regulars," Becky promised.

"Oh, darlin'"—Camilla chuckled—"they're your regulars now."

While waiting for the Fivers to arrive, Camilla replayed voice-mail messages just to hear Jared's baritone voice. It blanketed warm fuzzies around her body.

I love your lips, skin, and loving.

You've lassoed my heart and a tether connects us. If you run too far or tug too hard, you'll rip my heart from my chest.

I love southern cooking.

Your accent is a sweet melody.

I won't stop until you agree to meet me. Any time. Any day. Anywhere.

She had to give him credit. He took persistence to new heights.

"Camilla, telephone," Darcy called through the pick-up window connecting the kitchen to the rest of the diner.

"For me?" she asked. "Who is it?" Who would call her at work?

"A man. Pick up or I'll hang up. I've got cooking to do," Darcy barked.

"Some things never change," Camilla muttered.

She picked up the phone by the cash register and heard a click in the background—Darcy hanging up.

"Good morning, Camilla."

She froze. Panic shot from her stomach to her throat. Jared's voice, live on the other end of the phone, caressed her name, and it struck a longing so strong in her core it could yank her all the way to Cody, back to him. She wanted to throw the phone down and throw herself into his arms. But couldn't.

"Good morning," she replied curtly.

"I want to see you. I'm giving you fair warning I'm headed your way."

"How do you know where I am?" she whispered. Duh! He'd called the diner. Did he have someone following her? Had Haley or Sean broken their promise of secrecy? Besides, she and Darcy hadn't discussed her harsh words about this certain cowboy after Darcy had first fired her. Now wasn't the time to bring it up. She wanted to leave on a peaceful note, just in case she ever wanted to come back.

"Let's just say technology has lots of perks."

"Please, I don't want to see you," she pleaded in earnest. Jared could *not* show up at the diner. Her mind raced. If he left Cody now, he wouldn't arrive until her shift had ended. Her body relaxed at that realization.

"You owe me dinner."

She gripped the phone tighter as Becky approached, concern written on her face.

"I'm sorry, sir, that's not on the menu." Camilla waved Becky off.

"You're just going to have to tell me that to my face." Jared's voice was calm and smooth as silk.

"When will you be coming in? We don't take

reservations."

"It's a surprise. But you can expect me before you leave for home."

Home? Someone had spilled *all* the beans. Who? "I beg your pardon. I think we have a bad connection. Can you still hear me?" She held the phone from her ear, looked at it, then hit the 'off' button.

"Cowboy really got to you, eh?" Darcy called out.

"What?" Camilla stormed to the window.

"You don't think I don't know the sound of Blond Honey's voice?" Darcy didn't look up, but remained focused on whatever she was working on in the kitchen. "Don't worry. I already hooked a different fish. A real, rodeo-riding cowboy."

The tinkling of the bell over the door drew Camilla's attention.

"Good morning, Camilla," a couple of the Fivers called out as they came through the door. She said a silent prayer of thanks for their interruption, then grabbed a coffee pot in each hand and began to pour for them. "Good morning, gentlemen. You remember Becky."

Becky came to her side and relieved her of the pots. Placing the carafes on their burners, Becky turned back to the group, flipped open an order pad and said, "Hey there! The diner appreciates your business. Camilla has told me each of your names and your usual. I'm going to read them off…just be to be sure I got my scribbles right, but I think I've got this down."

With Becky taking over, Camilla had nothing to do until other customers arrived. She picked up a cloth and began to wipe the individual buttons on the ornate, antique cash register. Something to do to keep her mind off Jared. Gazing out the window, she recalled the morning he jogged by the diner and the challenge she and Darcy started. That was old history now.

Her mind returned to thoughts of Jared. Exactly how long did it take to fall in love? An hour. A minute. A second.

Her heart had tripped and fallen in love the moment he first touched her at the Lucky Seven. Now the long trip home loomed and the idea of making it alone was bad enough, but each mile would take her farther from Jared. At that thought, her heart tripped into panic. A wave of anguish sloshed in her stomach. She had to be strong. Leaving was the right thing to do. She had a plan. Had saved money. Had the support of her cousin. For the first time in her life, she would be a contributing member of the Fleur de Lis estate doing something more than being *nice* and staying out of trouble. She had a dream, expectations and goals for herself, even if no one else did. However, to share a life with the man she loved was a new dream, one that could never come true.

She finished wiping down the register and tossed the cloth into the small sink beneath the counter.

In her pocket, her cell phone vibrated. She guessed Jared had started his daily messaging routine. What new way would he bring a smile to her lips? Her sadness lifted a bit when she read his name. Then she began to read.

One is the loneliest number.

Her phone vibrated again as the next email message popped up.

Don't go breaking my heart.

Saving all my love for you.

I'll stand by you.

"Oh, my goodness." She laughed and looked toward heaven for fortitude. "The man just doesn't quit."

"Something goin' on?" one of the Fivers asked.

"I've never met another man like this one." Holding up the phone, she walked to stand before the group seated at the counter. "Let me read you this list. Tell me what you think."

After she finished, she pointedly stared at the five older men seated before her.

"He's got it bad."

"Good taste in a woman, though."

"Interesting choice of song titles."

"Sounds like a keeper to me."

"Do you really want him to quit you, Camilla? Forever?"

Planting her fists on her hips, pursing her lips, she raised an eyebrow. "Well, when you put it like that..."

"Her face lights up whenever she gets a message from him," Becky eagerly interjected.

"Oh, she's got it bad," Darcy called out through the kitchen window. "Hook, line, and sinker."

A second later, the door to Mountain View Diner opened. The bell tinkled. Everyone turned toward the door. Camilla's eyes widened. Her jaw went slack. Her heart stopped, then slammed hard in her chest. She tried to swallow, but a lump caught in her throat.

"Good morning, Camilla," Jared said exactly as he had only minutes earlier over the phone, caressing her name as though it was exotic and special.

Stunned, she couldn't have spoken his name if she wanted to.

The Fivers rose and applauded.

Jared held out his hand. "Come with me."

Confused, she glanced at the regulars seated at the counter, who flicked their wrists, shooing her away.

Becky stepped closer and from behind whispered, "I've got this. Go. Just stop by later and say good-bye."

Camilla twisted to catch Darcy's eye. A half smile replaced the woman's regular scowl. "Gotcha. Now git. We've got this covered. You can pick up your final check in the morning before you head out. It's been a pleasure knowin' you, Camilla."

When she turned back to face Jared again, he remained rooted in the same spot, his hand still extended in offering to her. The man was steadfast and steady.

"I've got the whole day planned." Jared winked when she clasped his hand with hers.

Giddiness carried her out the door. Happiness gave her wings, and she floated down the street beside Jared.

Once they had walked out of view of the diner's large windows, Jared stopped. Tugging on her hand, he pulled her close. In front of the trees, the sun, and the empty side street, he kissed her like a man gone way too long without sustenance for the soul. The kiss curled her toes. Her heart lifted and sang "Halleluiah," though certainly off-key. Her hands sought his hair. Raking her fingers through the blond-streaked lengths fulfilled an itch she'd had since first setting eyes on him. Now he looked as though he was fresh-from-a bed, her fondest desire was to make the look happen for real—a second chance with Jared. Maybe her life had finally turned around. Delight hummed through all her veins.

Whatever happened tomorrow, it would have to wait for then. Now, she had Jared. Now her heart hammered with life, exuberance barely contained. Now she lived.

"What's the plan, Sam? We gonna have fun, Dunn?" she teased.

"Patience," Jared whispered in her ear. He draped an arm around her shoulder as they continued on the sidewalk leading to her apartment.

"You know where I live?"

Jared sighed. "Honey, I want to know everything about you. Discovering where you live—easy. Darcy helped with that, and she's the one who moved your car from the bus station. Learning more about you is proving harder."

"Haley or Darcy, I'm guessing, is the culprit."

Jared grinned and shrugged. When they reached the top of the stairs, he pulled out a key, opened the door and gestured for her to enter her own apartment.

Warily, she peeked inside. "What the..." Aromas of bacon wafted to her nose. Eggs in a bowl sat on the counter beside the two-burner stove where a frying pan rested. The second burner supported a pot, and unless her nose lied, the pot contained cooked grits.

She sniffed. "I smell cornbread in the oven."

"Wow. You're really good. Bacon and cornbread are cooked and warming." Jared chuckled.

Looking beyond the tiny efficiency kitchen to the living room, she spied flowers. Three big bouquets of lilies and roses. Rose petals created a trail leading past the bathroom to her bedroom. Picking up a petal with each step, she followed the path as anticipation bubbled up and loved bloomed like a fresh flower in her chest.

When she reached the threshold to the bedroom, she gasped. The floral scent of roses and lilies filled the room. Light streamed through windows that framed an unobstructed mountain view. Sunlight cast beams on a heart made from red and white rose petals covering the top of the double bed. A large bouquet of flowers tied with a wide pink, satin ribbon lay across her pillow.

"Oh…wow." She'd always been a party girl, liked comfortable and easy—jeans and a tee, skirt and tee, shorts and a tee. Not frou-frou or elegant like her sister. Yet the display before her brought every feminine cell in her body shimmering to life. Her fingers tingled. She shivered and reached for Jared's hand. He scooped her up, carried her across the threshold and delivered her gently to the bed.

"These are for you," he said, his voice low and sexy when he offered the bouquet. "All of this is for you." He spread his arms wide.

Her heart melted. She'd never expected to understand the feeling of being adored. She grasped the bouquet in front of her and sniffed. The image of a traditional bride and groom cake topper popped into her mind. She couldn't dare hope for a forever-after with this man, but she had today. Now. She laid the flowers on the small table beside the bed.

Kicking off her shoes and pulling off the white ankle socks, part of her waitress uniform, she kneeled on the bed, then tugged off the net covering her hair. While staring into Jared's blue eyes, she removed the white starched apron and tossed it. His grin grew wider when the fabric fluttered to the floor. She jerked on the V-neck opening of the button-down dress expecting the buttons to pop, magically revealing her lacy underwear.

Only the buttons didn't budge.

Jared chuckled softly.

Breaking her gaze from him, she looked down at the dress and yanked again. The buttons didn't give from the buttonholes. Nor did they tear from the fabric. So much for a dramatic reveal.

"Here, allow me," Jared said, climbing on the bed and facing her on his knees. The mattress shifted, and she reached for Jared's shoulders to keep from falling over.

Slowly, he unfastened each button on the uniform. When he reached the last one and the dress opened, he lifted her chin. Was it mischief and happiness that danced in his eyes?

He removed her dress as though used to undressing a woman every day, then tossed it in the corner.

"Wait there. Don't move," he told her.

Sitting on the corner of the mattress with his back to her, he tugged off worn, brown cowboy boots. She would never see a pair again and not think of him. He peeled away his clothing, dropping all into a pile on the floor. Her eyes feasted. She gulped. Just as she remembered. His body, lean and muscled, perfectly sculpted. She sucked in a breath when her feminine muscles contracted.

He stood next to the bed, pulled back the covers nearest him, and she scooted there. With a yank and a shake of the bedspread, Jared tossed the rose petals into the air, they took flight, then magically floated down around her.

"Scoot, woman," Jared said, and she did.

Stretching long, he settled next to her on his left side. She turned to face him. Warmth radiated from the palm of his hand as he cupped her cheek. He moved his hand to her shoulder and down her arm. Happiness bubbled inside her, a freshly opened bottle of champagne had nothing on her as joy zipped around like a pinball, taking her excitement higher.

She reached for him, placing her hand over his heart while his hand plucked at her lacy bra. Hot desire shot straight to her core. He massaged one breast, next attending to the other. She craved more and gently rocked her hips.

Jared moved closer, gently pushing her onto her back. On his knees, he removed her panties, then massaged her mound. The heel of his palm applied subtle pressure. She arched her back and pushed against his touch. When his finger stroked a path downward and touched her sensitive spot, she arched more, desire cranked up. When she reached for his hardness, wanting to guide him to her to ease the tension climbing in her body, he resisted. His mouth then captured one of her breasts while his hand massaged the other until both formed tightened peaks.

"Jared," she pleaded. "Let me touch you."

"Soon."

He rose to his knees again and offered his hand. Pulling her to sitting, he bent forward, wrapped his arms around her and freed her breasts from the lacey bra. The underwire couldn't be gone from her body too soon. She pulled at the straps and tossed it, not caring where it landed.

He cupped the fullness of her breasts. She covered his chest with her hands. When he stroked her nipples, she stroked his, then wet her lips with her tongue and rocked her pelvis.

Unable to resist the invitation of his hardened manhood, she smoothed the palms of her hands down his abs, and then lower, to grasp a treasure the most private part of her body craved.

His foreplay teased until her mind lost all thought. Emotion, deep, tight, and raw, drove her actions.

"Lie down," she instructed, unwilling to wait for him to offer what she wanted next.

Jared complied. A crooked smile tugged at one corner of his sexy mouth.

"I want you," she said, then straddled him, lowering herself on to his hardness, which only intensified her need. She tightened around him.

"Babe, that feels so good," he moaned.

Rising slightly, then sinking even lower, she gently rocked until they fit perfectly together. Jared's warm hands rested on her hips. Together they moved as one. He stroked her breasts again, the sensation shot to her core like hot lightning. She rocked harder and faster. He matched her pace, again holding her hips. As heated sensations grew and grew, she leaned forward, bracing her hands on his shoulders, which allowed her to ride higher and pound harder.

When Jared's finger slipped between her legs and rubbed her sensitive nub, she arched, threw back her head, and moaned, "Oh god!" Hot spasms raced through her body, and she quivered.

"Let it go, babe," Jared said hoarsely.

His movements quickened, the strength of his body slammed against her. Her racing need, stretched taut, reached a pinnacle. Jared's next thrust sent her higher than the Wyoming mountains, shooting her heaven bound. For a moment, she hung suspended in inky blackness as a luxuriant sensation washed through her body, smoother than silk and softer.

"Camilla," Jared hoarsely whispered. The sound drifted to her ears, but euphoric sensations now coming in waves captured all her attention and rendered her unable to speak.

His hands tightened over her hips. He thrust again and again. Like fireworks exploding and tiny fragments of light falling back to earth, behind her closed eyes, lights flashed like opening flower blossoms, then drifted into darkness only to be replaced by the next intense sensation.

"Oh, Jared, yes!"

Together they rode on waves of exhilaration.

Breathless, they panted in unison.

Slowly, moving back into real time, she collapsed on his chest and rested her head on his shoulder. The sound of his heartbeat pounded quickly in her ears. His arms encircled her, his hands clasping together behind her back. She savored the feel of their bodies still joined intimately. Never before had she experienced anything so wonderful or perfect.

"Camilla," Jared said, after a few minutes. "You know how I feel about you. What I don't know is your feelings for me."

"Can't you tell?" she whispered back.

A chuckle rose in his chest. "Yeah, but a man likes to hear the words."

Rising up, she gazed into his eyes. "I've never experienced such a profound intensity. I love you," she whispered, "but this can never happen again."

Chapter 20

"Are you crazy?" Jared sat up practically dumping her out of his lap and onto the bed. He had to get to the bottom of the barriers she kept throwing up. Giving her body to him apparently came with no reservations, but giving her heart freely was an entirely different matter.

"Nooo," she said slowly. "I'm completely serious."

"What we share is…is…there are barely words to describe it." His voice rose almost to a shout.

"In English," she snapped, flopping on the bed beside him, but not touching him. He immediately missed the warmth of their connection.

"I'm speaking English." Confusion clouded his brain. What was she talking about?

"You. Don't. Know. Me."

"You can't possibly be serious after all the places my body just touched yours. I'd even know your scent when blindfolded and pushed into a cave of women." His finger traced a line on the inside of her knee, but before he could reach the spot he sought, she turned on her side and crossed her legs.

"Okay, I'll agree you know my body, you make it feel delicious things, but Jared, you still don't really know *me*. The real me. With warts and sins and secrets."

"As if any of that matters," he scoffed. "I do know you, woman. And I love you. Why do you keep insisting I don't? You don't want to try to make this work?"

"What are we *trying* at?"

Had he been having conversations about a relationship in his head? Maybe he was the crazy one. "A bona fide relationship. You know, boy meets girl, falls for girl. Girl falls for him, too. Look, I have a rule—measure twice, cut once. I learned that after Cheyenne's betrayal."

Camilla flinched at the mention of Cheyenne.

"I can't blame her for the marriage. I allowed my ego to control my heart. Now, I've measured twice," he continued, "and I know you're the only woman for me. I have a motto—Move it along. Life needs to go in a forward direction. If we allow the past to haunt us, we'll be like ghosts who can't escape. Who wants to live in a haunted house?"

Camilla rose from the bed and quickly dressed in a stretchy cotton summer dress. "Get up." She tossed his pants at him. "You want to know the truth about me? I'm going to tell you. But I can't do it in here. Your naked self is too distracting. I'll be in the living room."

She stormed away.

"Wait!" he called out to her. "Let's talk in here. It's the best place to make up and plan the future," he muttered when she was out of sight.

Whatever she had to say couldn't be that bad. She wasn't like Cheyenne. Just the opposite. Caring. Compassionate. Creative in bed. Camilla was more than he ever dreamed. She treated others with respect. Always had a good word to say about everyone. Went out of her way for Haley, and look at the happy ending she created there! She cared about her family. And she loved him…she'd finally admitted it. What the hell was the problem?

He dressed, except for his boots, then scooped up a handful of rose petals and plucked a single red rose from the bouquet still resting on the side table. He had to convince her their love deserved a chance to bloom, just like the flowers.

When he turned the corner from the bedroom, Camilla pointed to the couch and motioned for him to sit. Back rigid, she sat in a wooden kitchen chair with her feet resting on the coffee table. On the floor beside her chair, he caught sight of a long neck bottle of beer. One also sat on the coffee table.

Glancing at the clock on the wall, he eyed the beer questioningly.

"Did you know in Louisiana, we pretty much drink twenty-four/seven?"

"As a matter of fact I do. But having the ability to do so doesn't mean you should."

"What? It's too early? Does it mar your image of me? Drinking before noon. Who does that?" She took a long draw of beer. "Me." She saluted him with the bottle. "I'm glad you brought your boots. You'll be leaving soon."

He dropped the boots beside the couch, they made a soft thud against the carpet. He walked to her and handed her the rose. He considered getting down on one knee, but given her mood, he feared she might hit him with the flower, or worse yet, knock him in the head with the bottle. He rained the rose petals down around her. Instead of the smile he hoped for, she ignored the gesture, took another swig of beer, and flicked off the petal resting on her shoulder.

Jared sighed. What was she so angry about?

Taking the seat she'd offered on the couch, he leaned over and scooted the beer bottle across the table closer to her feet. "I'm thinking you might need this, too. I've never seen you so riled." Could she be that burdened by her past? Had someone hurt her? Did her heart beat only behind a brick wall? Even pissed as a wet hen, she looked beautiful. She could holler and shout, as long as she kept talking. Together, they could find a way to navigate trouble.

"Exactly," she cried, slapping her feet to the floor. "You really don't know me."

Jared stretched out on the couch with his hands behind his head, his ankles resting on the armrest. "I'm comfortable now, doctor, please continue."

"Fine," she snapped. "Mock me." She took another sip of beer, pulled her feet onto the seat of the chair and covered her legs with the skirt of her dress.

Jared frowned. Camilla appeared as though she wanted to make herself invisible.

"In a place far away, and not so long ago," she began quietly, "a girl grew up on the Pearl River, the dividing line between two states. Her large family owned a grand antebellum home, but most of them didn't reside permanently in the house, except for the Old Aunts, widowed twins who inherited the home from their great-grandfather. And Greta, of course, their companion. The home is called Fleur de Lis."

"Got it. I'm tracking so far," Jared said.

Camilla scowled at him, and he refrained from making further comments. He wanted to tell her he was familiar with the river and the antebellum home of which she spoke. Once she got out her story, he would tell her his surprise. That soon, he'd join her down south.

"In this family," she continued, "the first-born in every generation becomes the Keeper—the person charged with the responsibility for making sure the property remains intact for the next generation. In this story, the current Keeper is the girl's older sister."

Camilla's voice softened. "The girl had a good life. Never wanted for anything, though she never had clothes or boots the likes of Haley O'Connor." A wisp of humor touched her voice.

"Given the largeness of the property and the family, if anything happened to the Keeper, family tradition dictated who would be the spare—the next in line to carry on family tradition. That would be the girl's cousin. Now the cousin and older sister were very close, often excluding the girl, though in fairness to the cousin, she did introduce the girl to dives and clubbing, taught her how to have a good time."

"May I say something now?" Jared asked, turning on his side to face Camilla.

"Shh. The story continues. The girl's mother, a true southern belle—beautiful, elegant, yet tough as nails, a get-the-job-done kind of woman, spent most of her time grooming the Keeper, or seeing to the youngest child, the only boy."

"So the girl had middle-child syndrome? It's not fatal."

Camilla popped out of the chair and paced the twelve-foot long apartment. "If you can't remain quiet, then leave now." She pointed to the door. "Don't let it hit you in the ass on the way out."

Jared drew back. "Potty mouth. Guess I hit a nerve.

Sorry. Please continue."

Camilla stood behind the chair, leaned over, resting her forearms on the top of the back of it. She didn't understand that position gave him an unobstructed view of her luscious cleavage in the deep v of the dress. Involuntarily, he hardened. What he wanted was to kiss away her anxiety and have her melt against his body, make love to her again. With her struggling to tell her tale, he wanted the angst to dissolve and to bask once again in her warm, radiant smile. Then take her back to bed. The woman was a southern witch, and his heart along with his body was under her spell.

"The girl liked to party. She liked to have a good time. The only thing ever expected of her was"—Camilla made quotations marks in the air with her fingers—"to be nice. And so she was…outwardly. She smiled at contributors at the fundraisers her mother held. She curtsied at the balls the family hosted. She poured tea for those customers who rented out the ballroom for ladies' afternoon teas, baby showers, or she poured champagne at bridal showers." She stopped pacing and swallowed hard. Pain etched her face, making him want to pull her to him on the couch, hold her tight and prove none of what'd she'd said made a difference.

"Sounds like a pretty good life," he said, hoping she saw him taking her words very seriously.

"See…" The word came out low and strangled, almost as though she was fighting tears. "People like to imagine living at Fleur de Lis, and they can for a little while if they pay the price."

"Camilla, if this is too painful—"

"I paid a price, too. Just not in dollars and cents."

"Babe, this can wait for another day." He sat up on the couch and patted the spot beside him. "Come here. I promise I'm not going anywhere…unless you want to take me back to bed." He wiggled his eyebrows as an invitation. "I think I've still got some moves you haven't seen."

She frowned. "Really? Just like a man with sex on the brain. I'm trying to be totally honest with you. Trying to get everything out. I'm trying to explain why *trying* at a relationship with me won't work!"

"I hate seeing the sadness in your eyes, Camilla. As I said, I have the whole day planned. You've shared enough. The rest can wait for later."

"Let me *try* to cut to the chase. I saw you with Nicole at the house."

"I know. Why did you leave?

"Because I *saw* you with Nicole."

"What does that mean? I'm not good at decoding women-speak."

"You had your arms around her. Hugged her. She was hanging on to you. You kissed the top of her head. She's. Your. Brother's. Fiancée."

Angry, Jared stood, planting his feet on the floor as he faced her across the coffee table. "I was *comforting* Nicole, not putting moves on her. She'd just gotten news of her grandmother's passing." His tone came out sharper than he wanted. "I would never, never, betray my brother."

Camilla stood up straighter and held up one finger high. "That's exactly right," she said emphatically. "Betrayal is the one thing you absolutely can't abide. It's a total deal-breaker."

"Yes, if someone would betray a loved one at that

deep a level… it's a big deal. But that's not an issue for you and me," he protested.

She narrowed her eyes at him. "Have you ever lived with a secret only one other person in the whole world knew? What if the person had been betrayed and was so upstanding and so loyal to their family, they'd face personal shame rather than bring shame on the whole family?"

Confused, Jared shook his head. "It wasn't a matter of me *not* keeping Cheyenne's betrayal a secret. I don't get the comparison. You've got a secret?"

Camilla strode toward him and sank down on the floor on her knees between the couch and the coffee table. He sat.

She took his hands in trembling ones. "The reason I left home was because I couldn't live with myself. I betrayed my sister. I slept with her fiancé."

Jared jerked his hands from hers. He scrubbed his face, unable to process the information. "You slept…" he started, "with…with the man your sister was engaged to marry?"

Camilla lowered her gaze. He stared at the top of her head.

"Somehow Branna found out about what I did. How, she's never said. Then, she called off the wedding…*the wedding of the decade*. It was a really big deal in Bayou Petite. To this day, she's not told a soul the reason why."

Stunned, Jared stared at her bowed head. Coldness slithered around his chest. Shocked, he blinked to keep his focus.

After a minute, Camilla reached for the untouched beer on the coffee table and gulped down half the bottle. "Yep," she said, wiping her mouth with the back of her hand. "Men were only ever a competition for me. If my sister had a boyfriend, I always tried to steal him. She had the adoration of the entire family. Saint Branna. So I tried to compete with her."

"Why would you do that?" He searched his mind for understanding. The woman before him had just admitted to intentionally manipulating men to hurt her sister? Why?

Camilla rose. She picked up Jared's boots and carried them to the door. "I don't expect you to understand," she said, quietly. "In fact, I don't *want* you to understand. If you did, then you wouldn't be the wonderful man I know." She opened the door and dropped the boots on the landing outside the threshold. "Jared, please leave."

Stunned into silence, he continued staring at her, unable to believe the words she'd uttered. "You're lying right? This is a test…of my sticking power, or something? To see if I really love you."

"No test. If we have a relationship, it would need to be cemented in the truth. Sooner or later you'd learn about my behavior. And later, if you discovered the truth and looked at me with the same expression of disgust as you're wearing now, it would absolutely kill me dead."

"Then why tell me? If it's a secret between you and your sister…"

"Because when I go home, I have to atone for my past sin. Please leave, Jared. I have nothing else to say, and your expression tells me all." She hung her head.

Jared rose from the couch.

"Jared, go now. I need to be alone."

Numbness wrapped his heart and his mind. Had he slipped into some alternative reality where everyone looked the same, but acted differently? "I'll go for now," he said, a solemnness holding him tightly. "I need some time to process what you just told me. But, I assure you, this conversation isn't over."

When he reached the door, he tried to take her in his arms. All she shared had to be a lie.

She scooted away, then stood on her tiptoes and kissed his cheek. "Jared, this is our good-bye."

Chapter 21

The next morning, Camilla turned and took one last look at the Mountain View Diner. She waved at Darcy, Becky, the Fivers, and other customers standing near the widows.

"Bye! Maybe I'll see you next summer." She wiped tears from her face before hopping into the car. She tucked a bag containing a BLT sandwich and chips, Darcy's parting gift, along with her paycheck and a small bonus in the seat beside her. The engine roared to life when she turned the key. Pulling away from the curb, she waved again, barely able to see through watery eyes.

Several blocks past the Lucky Seven, she stopped. Everyone she'd left behind in Jackson and Cody would continue with their comfortable lives and everyday routine. After nearly two years, her world looked new and unknown. She was heading home, yet the long drive stretching before her brought fear rushing to her like the rising waters of a flooding river. Grabbing a tissue, she mopped up tears and blew her nose.

"Buck up, girl."

She sighed deeply to beat back anxiety. Yesterday, she'd packed all her clothes, boots, books, and other gear and loaded it into the car. She'd slept on the couch last night, unable to face the bed and tender memories of making love with Jared. No matter how hard she tried, she couldn't wipe from her mind Jared's expression of shocked disdain when she revealed her darkest sin. Her secret had cost her the only man she'd ever loved.

Guilt thrummed in her conscience. Jared's disgust was fitting punishment given how much she'd hurt her sister and her family. Maybe not having a life with him equaled karmic payback for her bad party-girl behavior.

Pulling her cell phone from her purse, she hit the button to call Fleur de Lis.

"Hello?" Greta, the Old Aunt's companion, answered the phone.

"Greta, darlin', how are you?" She tried to sound bright and cheery.

"I'm excited for your arrival. We're having breakfast right now. But I'll be making all your favorites for the party. Pickled okra salad with cukes and tomatoes fresh from the garden. Shrimp and grits with andouille sausage. And peach bread pudding for dessert with that bourbon sauce you love."

"You always know how to spoil us," Camilla said, forcing a chuckle as her mouth watered. Greta's cooking was legendary in and around Bayou Petite. Rumors from home hinted that Biloxi landed her fiancé, the local veterinarian with the help of Greta's meals.

"Say now, your sister and cousin are here doing wedding stuff. Your great-grandmother Marie is standing right here and wants a word with you. I'm handing over the phone to her."

"Camilla? Camilla? Is that you, darlin'?"

Camilla's breath hitched. G.G. Marie's voice sounded breathy and more feeble than when they spoke a month ago.

"Yes, ma'am, it's me. I'm coming home."

"Oh my, that's music to these old ears."

"You know the saying, 'leave the porch light on,' because I'll be there by the end of the week. God willing."

"It will be so good to see you. Pictures just aren't the same. Grace sends her love. Now, your sister wants a word with you."

"I love you, Great-Grandmother. Please send my love to Aunt Grace."

"Hello? Camilla?" Branna's voice lilted through the phone.

"Yep, it's me."

"We're all so excited. We're having a big welcome-home party on Saturday to celebrate your return."

A lump formed in Camilla's throat. She ached with homesickness. Her sister had to be the strongest and most loyal woman in the world.

"Camilla? Are you there?"

"Yes," she squeaked.

"Drive safely. Take pictures, but not while you're driving, and send them to me. I want to be sure you're really headed southbound. I can't wait to see you." The genuine excitement in Branna's voice touched her.

"Branna…"

"Yes?"

"I'm…a little scared."

"Scared? Do you want me to fly up and drive back with you? I might be able to manage that…maybe tomorrow."

"Thank you, but no. I made the drive here. I can make it home. I'm scared…to see you again. Talking on the phone is easier. Seeing you after what I…did? How can you ever forgive me? I'm so sorry, Branna, for being so shameful. I'm sorry." Her voice broke and tears followed, dribbling down her cheeks.

"Shhh. I have forgiven you," Branna said softly. "Moved on. I'm in love with James. We're perfect together. He's not every woman's cup of tea, thank God, but he's smart, interested in so many things, and he loves me. In a strange way, I thank you. I would've been miserable married to Steven. And if I'd married him…I'm sure we'd be divorced by now."

"Really?"

"Sister, I see good changes in you. Maturity. Even all these hundreds of miles away. How you live your life now…I'm really proud of you. So get your butt back home!"

"Thank you." Camilla's eyes misted again. "I love you. See you soon. It feels really good to say those words. It's been sooo long." The weight of guilt lifted some, but it would take more time before the pain and regret became a mere shadow.

"I'm just glad some cowboy didn't lasso you and keep you there."

Branna's words pricked her conscience. For a few moments, Jared had slipped to the back of her mind, but the mere mention of a cowboy sent thoughts of him careening through her brain.

"No," she said, trying to sound strong. "No cowboy in my life. I'm waiting for a solid southern man." It was a lie, but Branna would never know it. "I'm going to hang up. I'm leaving right this minute."

Camilla tucked her phone in her purse and snapped it closed. That lessened any temptation to call Jared.

While technology had been banished from sight, it failed to stop her thoughts from spinning round and round like a hamster powering a wheel.

Jared's face had made a permanent imprint in her mind. His touch left an invisible tattoo on her skin. Her heart sang with joy from his words whispered with love. Yet heartache overshadowed all. Late yesterday afternoon, he'd called and left a message. She didn't dare talk to him then. Returning the call was out of the question. Later, he emailed and invited her to dinner. Again, she didn't respond. She had zero appetite. Instead, she quickly packed her car, then cleaned the apartment, dumping food from the fridge. Around ten p.m., he knocked on her door. Wanted to be sure she was okay and wanted to talk things out. She couldn't bear to see anything but happiness in his eyes, and her secret had stripped that from them. Like a bell that couldn't be unrung, she couldn't erase her ugly past, nor the memory of his shock. After fifteen minutes of knocking, he gave up and left. Exhaustion claimed her after his departure, and she'd slept fitfully, waking up often.

Passing a strip mall, she spied a guy strongly resembling Mitch. She took a second look. Whatever hold the man had over Haley disappeared once she'd gotten the teenager home. For that, she was grateful. Maybe there was something to the idea that the energy of a place had influences over a person. Like Sedona being soulfully beautiful and Las Vegas being a black hole of addictions. Jackson, Wyoming, was bad news for Haley O'Connor.

Buzz. Buzz.

Camilla grabbed for her purse and wrestled with it

while keeping one hand on the steering wheel. She pulled out her phone, her heart pounding so hard her chest hurt in anticipation of Jared's call. Her fortitude crumbled. She wanted so much to talk to him.

When she saw caller ID, her heartbeat slowed and she answered the phone. "Haley, girl, how are you?"

"I'm sad because I know you're on the road, but I've got some good news!"

"Tell me quick."

"I got a job. A real job. Not at a burger joint, but one with real responsibilities."

"Awesome! Tell me more," Camilla said.

"Jared got me a job."

"Jared?" She could not escape the man.

"Yes! He said something about how I could never be number six—whatever that means—and I know about ranching. My dad and Gus talked it out. They've come to a peaceful truce of sorts." Haley laughed. "We'll see how long it lasts. But I'll work full time until school starts, then part time. Dad agreed I could take a year off before going away to college, but I have to take some courses online as part of the deal."

"Aww, Boo, I'm so proud of you!" Sadness punched a hole in her heart. Haley would see Jared every day. She would be there when he fell in love with someone else…maybe even got married. She might even be a bridesmaid in his wedding.

"Since I'm making my own money, I want to fly down and visit you, as soon as you think it's a good time."

"I miss you already! Yes, once I get situated, we'll plan a time." That was a better idea than her returning to Wyoming and risk running into Jared.

"How far are you driving today?"

"Hopefully Denver. Five-hundred-plus miles." Would Haley appreciate the irony of the mapping directions taking her through Cheyenne, Wyoming?

"I'm here if you need anything," Haley said. "And Camilla?"

"Yes."

"I didn't properly thank you, so I'm doing it now. Thank you very much."

"You're welcome." The teen would grow into a fine young woman. Haley made her proud.

"I love you," Haley said in a rush then ended the connection.

"I love you, too, darlin' girl," Camilla whispered, her heart savoring the bond between them.

Haley had changed overnight since returning home. Jared had added the icing to the transformation. A good man. Solid. Strong. He brought Gus and Sean into talking distance about water rights and hopefully sealed the truce between the two families, especially since Haley now worked for the Richardsons. Jared's philosophy of measuring twice and cutting once proved to be a good one. It kept him from making foolish decisions…well, except when it came to her. She told him, even argued with him, that he didn't know her. The stubborn man had refused to listen.

Turns out, she was right.

And now she had to find a way to survive a broken heart.

Trying to memorize the scenery, she scanned the vistas and named everything, adding color, shape, texture. The game occupied her mind. She welcomed the silence around her. The drive to Denver would take more than eight hours given her plans to stop for fuel and take a break in Rock Springs, and then Cheyenne. She'd planned the trip and selected motels in advance. The overnight stop in the Mile-High City was actually at an I-70 exit east of town, a good way to avoid morning rush hour traffic, Denver-style.

When she hit Rock Springs, she stopped for gas. She took a selfie with a sign and emailed it to Branna as proof of her journey, then walked around to stretch her legs. Prior internet research provided information. The small town had established itself around a spring that dried up long ago. Mining became big business. Trona. She'd never heard of it, but through further investigation, she learned it was a rare sodium-rich mineral, which when processed, turned into soda ash, an ingredient in baking soda and detergents. Her mother would be proud she'd made her traveling adventure into an educational one. Would the trivia ever be useful? She had no plans to appear on a game show. But it would help if she ever got the chance to match wits again with Jared. Would he be happy to learn how much she loved his home state?

Hitting the road again, she focused on the scenery once more. Her fingers gripped the steering wheel, though they itched to check for messages from Jared. If he hadn't called, maybe she could risk calling him and listen to his voice-mail message. Hearing his voice would soothe some of the ache inching up with every mile farther away from him she drove. If the tear in her heart leaked blood, one drop at a time, before long it might drain all the life from her.

Rather than giving in to the ache, she turned to food. Hunger made her light headed. She hadn't eaten in quite a while.

She opened the white paper bag. Darcy had wrapped the BLT in wax paper. Besides the sandwich and chips, a sweet treat rested in the bottom of the bag with a note.

My first try at pralines. I'll practice making them and add them to the menu in your honor. They'll go great with ice cream. Have a safe trip home ~ D.

Camilla sighed. Darcy had never accused her of being something she wasn't, had accepted her just as she was. Their friendship might not extend beyond the diner, but worked just fine. Yet, she couldn't help but wonder if, now that she was gone, Darcy might just try to win Jared over…would he ever return to the diner?

After munching down a few bites of a sugary treat sans nuts, she sipped cold coffee. "Yuk." She slowed the car, opened the window, tossed the brown liquid out, then pitched the empty paper cup on the floorboard on the passenger's side. No one would accuse her of littering the beautiful scenery of Wyoming. Thankfully, she'd picked up a bottle of water back in Rock Springs and washed the cold coffee from her palate.

A while later, signs for Cheyenne appeared. Keeping her stop short, she fueled up and after a quick walk around the parking lot, she pointed the car south again. Denver was another ninety miles, and the hotel another ten or so beyond the city center. Maybe a swim would exhaust her body and allow sleep to claim her. However, she fretted. Darkness left her alone with her thoughts and the ache in her soul. In the deep of night, Jared danced in her dreams. Only there would she ever share a life with him.

****

Jared raked his hands through his hair, then pushed open the front screen door heading for a rocking chair on the porch. Twilight surrounded him. Coolness was a welcome change from the afternoon heat. Only a faint light from the bunkhouse, yards away, hinted at any other life nearby. Never before had loneliness settled around him like an old scratchy blanket.

He missed Camilla. Where was she now? Driving alone, somewhere he couldn't get to if she needed him.

Damn her!

Her words still burned like a branding iron in his gut. She'd betrayed her sister. Her story caught him completely off guard. Then she threw him out! Out of the apartment. Out of her life. Now he was out of sync in his own life. The woman left Wyoming, taking his heart with her, and making him a crazy man.

"That little Haley is a firecracker," Gus said, banging open the screen door.

Jared groaned inwardly. He didn't welcome company, especially his old man. Loneliness was a state better wallowed in alone.

Gus carried a bottle of something under his arm and two glasses in his hands. Setting the items on a small wooden table between them, he opened the top on the bottle and splashed liquid in each glass. He gestured his offering and Jared picked a glass, squinting at the bottle in the dim light spilling through the front window. Kentucky bourbon. The good stuff.

Gus knocked back half the liquid in his glass, then wiped his mouth on his sleeve. "Son," he said, "you refused to listen to me when you were chasing after that first piece of ass."

"Old man," Jared growled, "be careful where you

tread with words."

"Truth is truth, no matter how you sugar coat it. Cheyenne was bad news from the get go. You were thinkin' with the wrong head." Gus sipped, then cradled the glass in his hands. "This one, Camilla, she's a whole different story. I can't figure out why you're still sitting around here."

"What?"

"Go after her."

"I'm not a buck in heat. I take responsibilities seriously. I told Ryan I'd be here until he got back. He and Nicole come home tomorrow. I promised to have the house ready for her mother's arrival. At least that's done. But I can't go running off over a woman."

"It's exactly what you need to do. We can handle things here."

"What makes you think that?"

"Who, not what. Haley."

Jared snorted. "Haley?"

"She sang Camilla's praises all day. How the woman never gave up on her, even after Camilla repeatedly told Haley to stay away from that dirt-wad who hit her. Haley said she didn't listen, and yet, when she needed Camilla most, the woman didn't turn her away. Didn't say, 'I told you so.' No, the woman risked her job to get the girl to a safe place and initially, she lost her job over doing what's right."

Jared knocked back the contents of his glass. "Didn't realize what a chatterbox the girl had grown into." He clunked the glass on the wooden table before pouring himself another two-fingers worth of bourbon. "The truth?" Jared said.

"Always helps."

"She threw me out. Camilla doesn't want me. Okay, I admit her confession about her…choice of behavior…stunned me, but she didn't give me time to recover or think it through. I've had time to process what she said. What she did." Jared took another big swig from the glass and took a sideways glance at his father. "Do you even know what she did?"

"Nope. Doesn't matter."

"If you knew, you might think differently."

"Everyone deserves second chances, Jared. Even you."

"Exactly!" A slow warming moved through him, the effects of the bourbon. A few more shots and he might be able to sleep—through the night for a change.

"In this case, I'm thinkin' you need to beg that woman. Get her to forgive you, whatever it was you did. Haley says Camilla loves you. I met the woman. She's a good one. Don't know about her past—that's done and over, but now…be sure you want this woman to slip away. Don't measure too long."

"Oh shit," Jared muttered. "The picture becomes crystal clear." He held up the glass and looked through it toward the faraway light as though looking into a crystal ball. "She needs to believe she deserves a second chance…for what she did. Only she can give that to herself. *But* she needs to give *me* a second chance for being such an ass."

Gus rose, poured a splash more in Jared's glass, then tucked the bottle under his arm. "I raised smart boys."

"You could leave the bottle, old man," Jared said, before Gus opened the door.

"Nope. Like I said, I raised smart boys. Alcohol

won't heal the pain. 'Night, son."

Jared flexed fists. He should have handled the whole situation with Camilla differently. She was right, they really didn't know each other. Not the minuscule details of the past. Hell, Haley was the one who told him Camilla was allergic to pecans and couldn't eat the pralines he'd given her.

Regardless of Camilla's past, what mattered was who she was now. Excitement thrummed in his chest, creating a growing urge. He had to fight for her. How could he possibly have a life without her?

"What about getting to know someone?" she'd said in rebuttal when they'd argued.

"That's what dating and lovemaking are for," he muttered to himself. Hell, to really know someone requires a lifetime commitment. Like a journey, a relationship, even marriage unfolded adventurously, one day at a time. He wanted all of that: a journey, commitment, lovemaking—only with Camilla.

"Done measuring?" he muttered. "Yep," he answered himself quickly.

Tomorrow, he'd leave at dawn. Camilla was in for a surprise.

Chapter 22

Camilla yawned.

"Sorry," she said to the clerk at the gas station. "Not enough sleep last night. Moonlight horse ride." She failed to mention the horse and ride were with a man, but only in her dreams. Unlike when Haley had put her on a horse, during dreamtime she rode fearlessly, one with the animal…until she and Jared engaged in some horseplay of their own leading to joyous lovemaking. The intensity of those sensations seemed so real, as though she existed with the man she loved in an alternate universe where clouds were beds and stars lit the night like candles' soft light flickering all around. Breathless, she had woken, drifting back to earth, immersed in the sensation of having just made love. She fanned herself at the thought. Jared might not appear in her day-to-day life, but in her dreams…they shared *everything*.

After purchasing a co-cola fountain soda, preferring syrup and carbonation not from an aluminum can of Coke, she checked the oil in her car and topped off the gas before leaving the outer edge of Denver. The most boring part of the trek home lay ahead of her that day. Denver to Salina, Kansas, about four hundred and eighty miles. However, CDs would occupy her mind and solve the problem of spotty radio coverage—songs that would *not* remind her of *him*. She wouldn't even think his name again. Something had to lessen the pain of missing him. Everyone said time was the best healer, but how much time? A lifetime?

With the volume cranked, it didn't matter she sounded like a screech owl when she sang, something her brother Carson teased her about, him with his Michael Bublé voice.

The first planned stop of the day, two hours away, was in Goodland, Kansas. There a giant reproduction, twenty-four by thirty-two feet, of Van Gogh's *Three Sunflowers in a Vase* perched on a neck-stretching eighty-foot steel easel erected in 2001.

Never planning to make the same drive again—that's why airplanes had been invented, plus her brother and cousin were pilots, along with her soon-to-be cousin by marriage, Nick Trahan—she intended to catch the most unusual attractions on the plains during the trip home. However, one place she planned to pass up—Cawker City, Kansas, which claimed to house the World's Largest Twine Ball.

Traveling I-70, she settled in and started the first song. Judy Garland singing "Over the Rainbow." She giggled. There couldn't be a more perfect tune to carry her across the Sunflower State of Kansas.

Buzz. Buzz.

Camilla stopped the music and answered the phone. "Good morning, sister."

"Camilla," Branna said, "We're watching the news this morning and this is probably nothing to worry about, but we'll have to watch it."

"Is this a guessing game? Do I get twenty questions?"

"No," Branna said. "I'd call you"—her voice

lowered to a whisper—"the backside of a mule in urban terms, but the Old Aunts are within earshot, and they *do* have selective hearing."

"What, pray tell, is the problem?"

"It's that time of year."

"Oh. How could I have forgotten?"

"You know how weather is dramatized here. It gathers the same notoriety as Mardi Gras. The weatherman just announced Tropical Depression Twelve has been upgraded to Tropical Storm Katrina. She's sitting in the Atlantic. We're counting on her quiet death, but…"

"Thanks for the update. Keep me posted. I will check the weather when I get to the hotel tonight. Big times in Salina, Kansas, watching the weather." She chuckled.

"Be safe," Branna said. "The Old Aunts send their love."

Camilla clicked back to music, beginning "Over the Rainbow" again. Belting out the lyrics, she tried her best to hit the notes with Judy Garland, but her ears caught the cracking pitchiness even over the cranked-up volume.

A while later, the fields turned from green to mostly yellow. Sunflower fields replaced corn and soybeans as the crop of choice. Large faces of bright yellow with dark centers lifted, gazing at the sun. How could anyone be sad when surrounded by them? Camilla approached the exit for Goodland and slowed for the ramp leading toward town. The painting she sought rose high above the flat terrain like a lighthouse perched on rocky cliffs to warn ships off the coastline. With the colorful artwork in sight, she made turns until she drove up to a vacant lot and stared at the long legs of the easel, like something from a sci-fi movie. Suddenly, a bus of tourists pulled up beside her. A horde of older, white-haired people with cameras hanging around their necks filed out of the vehicle casting a shadow over hers. She exited the car and paused. With efficiency, the group clicked pictures, then returned to the bus like ants lining up at a picnic. Unless one of them were to lie on the ground and focus the camera upward, there was no way to capture a photo with anyone in the shot with the painting as the background.

Within minutes, the mammoth carrier left her alone in the lot.

It was as though she'd blinked the other tourists away.

Crossing the street, she stood back and craned her neck for a good look at three sunflowers high in the sky. She snapped a photo like a good tourist and emailed it to her sister. She'd read about the Canadian artist from Manitoba who'd pitched the art project to the town, which hosted an annual sunflower festival and laid claim as the undisputed sunflower capital of the United States.

After taking a few other photos from different angles, she headed toward the car. Her phoned dinged in her back pocket. She fully expected her sister to show Biloxi the photo, and in response, her cousin would offer tips about the best angle to capture the sky-high painting. Pulling out the phone, she clutched it tighter when she read the email message.

I want to see you. ~Jared

Jared? Her heartbeat bumped up her blood

pressure. He had no clue where she was or where she was headed. She never shared an address for Fleur de Lis, but he could have researched it. The man had some savvy. A knot of anxiety in her chest loosened and partially melted into anticipation. Would he actually come to her? No man would unless…

No. To dream of a future with him would be foolish.

But her heart hung by a thread of hope. Maybe someday he could look at her like he had when they made love.

Jared was a cautious man. What promoted his decision to meet up with her? The memory of his shocked expression flashed in her mind like an interstate billboard lit up at night. Had he had a change of heart? Could she be cautiously optimistic? Who would travel so many miles just to tell someone off?

Leaving Goodland behind, she drove and relived every moment with Jared since their very first introduction. The bar, the diner, the bus station. Their time in Cody. A lovely daydream. Memories to last forever.

Soon, the landscape became a green blur. After hours of driving, she planned for her second pit stop before arriving in Salina. The monotony of green fields, blue sky, and a few white clouds, along with the greasy burger and fries she'd eaten, dragged her into sleepiness. She batted her eyes a few times to moisten them and reached for a water bottle for more hydration.

When her phone rang, she clicked to talk without looking at caller ID. No matter who it might be, the Devil himself, conversation would help keep her awake.

"Camilla?" Branna's voice floated through the phone's speaker.

"What's Greta cooking for dinner?" she asked. In two more days, she'd make it home and looked forward to once again sitting at the dining room table with the family to enjoy Cajun cooking.

"I don't know. That's not why I called."

Her sister, always the serious one, weighed down with responsibility, didn't fit in the "funny" category. Thankfully, with James, her sense of humor had rallied.

"I'm all ears," Camilla said.

"That storm is now Hurricane Katrina, and it's projected to hit Florida around six thirty this evening. That's five thirty our time. There's all sorts of speculation about what might happen once it enters the warm waters of the Gulf in just a few hours. It's like Mother Nature suddenly blew life into it."

"But after it hits land, it will deflate. They usually do."

"Yes, but the hurricane season has been so crazy this year. Just want to keep you updated. I've got the Old Aunts to think about, along with Fleur de Lis. Hurricane prep isn't an easy task for me. Biloxi's here to help, thank goodness."

"I'll be there day after tomorrow. I'll be able to help if things get serious."

"I appreciate your willingness. We'll just both hope Katrina is a non-event."

Later that evening, after checking into a budget motel, Camilla hit the pool for several laps to stretch her cramped muscles, then crossed the parking lot to the burger joint for take-out. After showering and dressing in a t-shirt, she plopped on the bed, and opened the paper bag to eat. Switching on the TV, she searched for the Weather Channel.

"Hurricane Katrina made landfall about six thirty p.m. Eastern daylight savings time in Florida between Hallandale Beach and Aventura with sustained winds of eighty miles per hour. The well-defined eye of the storm remained intact during its path across Florida. Parts of the Florida Keys are experiencing tropical-force winds."

"In the world of hurricanes, that's not too bad," Camilla said aloud.

Halfway through her burger, her cell phone rang. She closed her eyes and wished for Jared's voice to come through when she answered.

"Camilla," Haley said excitedly.

"Hey there? How's my favorite cowgirl?"

"Jared left today."

Camilla paused. Her pulse quickened. She looked around and listened. Could a knock come at her door and it be him? Taking a deep breath, she let it go. Silly girl with silly thoughts. The man had to be miles from Salina.

"He caught a plane out of Billings. Oh, and Ryan and Nicole got home. Nicole's mother came with them. Interesting folks—"

"Haley," Camilla interrupted. "Back to Jared. Tell me more. Details."

"I don't have any. He wouldn't tell me. Gus wouldn't tell me, even when I begged. I put on my best pouty face, the one that makes my dad cave, but it didn't work. I watched him and Gus drive away. Jared had a leather tote bag, that's all. Gus returned with Ryan and Nicole, but no Jared. Gus said it was none of my business. But, later I managed to overhear he'll be back for the wedding."

Uncertainty started as a small dot and grew larger in her gut. Was Jared okay?

"Sorry, I'm not a good spy."

"Oh, girl. You're not there to spy," Camilla chuckled. "They're your employers. You need to keep your nose clean."

"Yeah, but Gus keeps asking me questions as if I don't know he's trying to pump me for information about you."

"What kind of questions?"

"About if you drink a lot, or have any addictions. He asked about your family. Asked if you wanted kids. Odd sorts of questions, but that's just Gus."

"What did you tell him?" Camilla asked, her brow knitting together.

"The truth, of course."

Camilla waited a beat to determine if Haley would spill more information. She sipped her drink to avoid coming across over-anxious.

"Okay, I told him as far as I know, you're not a drinker. Nor do you have any addictions…You don't, do you?" The teen sounded suddenly concerned.

"No," Camilla said. *Not unless you consider Jared one.*

"I said you had a solid family. Parents' still married to each other. That really surprised him. But about the kids part—I didn't have any idea, except that you're a traditional woman and probably would want kids *after* you got married."

Camilla's breath caught. She coughed. "I'm traditional?" No. That described her sister, not her. Fun.

Party-girl. Love ’em and leave ’em gal. Maybe she’d finally earned the right to claim the title of “woman,” but traditional woman? A shocking thought.

“Yeah,” Haley said, defensively. “Look at all the stuff you taught me. My mom could give a sh—”

“Crap,” Camilla interjected.

“See what I mean. You correct me. Want me to be a better person. My mom thinks it’s cool when I swear. Loves it when people ask if we’re sisters. Only men do that. The kind looking at her boobs and not her eyes.” Haley’s voice lowered. “You helped me see the light about Mitch. I don’t know what was wrong with me. It was like he had me under a spell. Anyway, you’re mom-like, but really more of a big sister. Someone who has my best interest in mind.”

A pang of guilt hit Camilla hard. She could never live up to the pedestal Haley put her on. “You make me sound old and boring,” she joked.

“No at all! I had the best time with you. You believe in me.”

Camilla swallowed the lump in her throat. All that she’d done for Haley, she’d learned from her sister. Branna deserved the credit. And how had she repaid her sister? With a life-altering dose of betrayal. Camilla grimaced. What if Haley were older and did to her with Jared what she’d done to her sister? Could she forgive Haley the way Branna had forgiven her? Had the shoe been on the other foot, she would’ve told the whole world the awfulness of Branna’s actions, and banished her from her life. Shame burned like a red-hot poker in Camilla’s gut. How could she ever make complete amends with her sister?

“Camilla?”

"Yes, Boo. I'm here. Just thinking. Is Nicole doing okay?" She had to change the subject. Guilt and shame ate at her insides. She wadded up the rest of the burger and fries, then pitched them in the garbage can. "What about Nicole's mother? How's she doing? Let me know if the wedding date changes. I'm going to send them a gift." *Jared will look so handsome in his tux. I'm sorry to miss that.*

"They arrived when it was time for me to go home. I don't know anything, but I'll call you tomorrow if I learn anymore."

"Focus on doing a good job," Camilla encouraged. "I'm always happy to hear your voice. Night, night."

After she signed off, silence engulfed her. Shame sprouted deep inside from a dark recess still unhealed. One single error in judgment had cost her happiness for a lifetime.

"Shit. Shit. Shit," Camilla yelled and punched the pillow beside her. Jared could never forgive her. Whenever the pain of the past lessened some, it came storming back, just like the hurricane growing in the Gulf. Could she and Branna successfully rebuild a bond after the destruction she'd caused? Could Jared ever forgive her?

Chapter 23

"Jared?" Camilla called out, the sound of her voice penetrated her sleep. Disoriented, she woke. Blinked. Sat up. Scanning the unfamiliar room, she grimaced at the small and dingy space, but then nothing compared to her room at home, which is where she'd been in her dream—with Jared. She reached for the spot on the bed next to her. No body impression in the covers. Cool to the touch. No lingering body heat from the man who'd just rocked her dreams.

Yesterday it had been a fight to keep him from her mind. Last night, she'd welcomed him willingly and wantonly, eager for the feel of his hands on her body, and his lips.

In her dreaming interlude, she'd started with a tour of Fleur de Lis at the *garçonnière*, the bachelor's quarters above the garage where her brother and cousin lived whenever they were home from college, and also the place that housed single, male guests. Fleur de Lis still upheld very old southern traditions.

Jared had been impressed with the architecture, furnishings, and the multi-car garage below. In its original form, the building had been the carriage house. While the exterior kept its antique charm, the renovated interior showed well with modern amenities, including running water and air conditioning.

They wandered hand-in-hand through the formal

gardens toward the house and its majesty. Some of the rooms at Fleur de Lis had changed little over the years. Hundred-year-old Aubusson carpets, imported marble fireplace mantels, along with mahogany furniture collected through the generations.

In her dream, the house was unusually silent, unsettling. No family in residence. It was like they'd all left for a party and forgotten to invite her. Yet, she brushed off the unease, taking full advantage to show Jared the private residence part of the house usually off-limits to anyone but family members.

"And this is my room," she whispered, then flung open the door. To her knowledge, no single woman at Fleur de Lis had ever allowed a man through her doors. The thought of being caught with a man in her room titillated her sense of naughty adventure, and her desire to make love to Jared pulled so strong it would take a natural disaster to change her from her intended course of action.

White plantation shutters covered the tall windows. Soft, peach-colored silk drapes embroidered with a lace pattern stood out against cream-colored walls.

"Because my sister is the heir, the Keeper of Fleur de Lis, and my cousin is the spare should anything happen to Branna, I received the special privilege of the antique bed my great-great grandfather made for his bride when they married." She sat on the bed and patted the spot beside her.

When the mattress moved as he sat, Jared turned to her. Gazing into her eyes, he lowered his lips to capture hers. A deep, long kiss. Breathless, she broke their lip lock and pushed him backward onto the bed. In an urgent rush, she tugged at his shirt. He raised up enough for her to rid him of it.

"Woman, you know what I want." His voice was husky.

Tingles raced through her. Desire ran hot through her veins. She swallowed and licked her lips. "And darlin', I'm going to give you all you want and more."

She kneeled on the bed and drew the pink cotton dress over her head, revealing a lacy, barely pink bra and matching panties. Reaching behind, she undid the bra, but captured it with one arm across her breasts.

Jared's lips parted. His eyelids lowered. He wet his lips and swallowed hard.

Tossing the bra aside, she freed her breasts and her remaining inhibitions. As she stood, her panties slid to her ankles with Jared's help.

He made a move toward her, but she moved out of his grasp and stepped off the bed. Reaching for him, she unbuttoned his jeans, exposing his body. His clothes heaped on the floor. His lean muscled form sent tingling sparks through her veins, and she stroked his hardness.

"You're killing me." Jared moaned softly and arched his back.

"Let me soothe your pain," she whispered, and lay on the bed beside him.

In a quick move, she was on her back. Jared's warm hands swept over her breasts and down her body, then massaged the inside of her thighs.

He raised a questioning eyebrow, and she nodded. She was ready. She arched upward to offer herself. Closing her eyes, she breathed in deep when he joined their bodies. Want and need melded. Intense joy shot through her. The strength of him, his hardness, his tenderness captured her mind and heart. Her body reacted to the thrill of joining with his.

They rocked together, pelvises undulating. Sexual tension tickled with delight, then heightened the growing pressure so large and tight it cried for release. When his mouth captured the tip of her breast, the sensation shot her higher.

"Oh," she groaned.

He pumped faster and harder.

"Jared! Yes!"

"I got you, baby." Jared slid in and out quicker.

When his body grew taut, she rocked against him, holding tightly to him. Tension exploded as though the roof of the house had opened to the inky night sky and stars raced across the heavens. A celestial display settled over her just as Jared's heated body covered her waning warmth.

Their breath finally evened. Camilla started to move, but Jared held her in place.

"I want a life with you, if you'll have me."

With watery eyes she smiled at him. "The future will be wonderful."

Cuddled next to Jared, she drifted back to sleep wrapped in love and contentment.

But it was all only a dream.

"Girl, get a grip," she mumbled, then rubbed her eyes and took another look around. The clock beside the bed glowed red numbers. 7:10 a.m. She flopped back on the pillows and pulled the sheet up to her neck. Barely five hours of sleep. She was tired before she started.

"Get up! Get up, now," the voice in her head shouted urgently.

"All right," she groaned and pulled on her jeans and shirt. She hit a button on the remote, the TV flickered to life, and she turned up the volume on the Weather Channel before heading to the bathroom to brush her teeth.

"She's growing slowly in speed, but the diameter of the storm is widening nearly by the minute. Its projected path is hard to determine. Could go as far west as Texas. Could hit Louisiana and Mississippi. Or swing around and blast Florida again. Hurricane Katrina has increased from a category one to a category three."

Camilla finished packing her toiletries in the black tote bag and stood in front of the TV. "Wow! She's huge. Wind and rain. Deadly combination. Thank goodness, Fleur de Lis is raised."

The video shot by the Hurricane Fighters, meteorologists who flew into the storm, stopped her cold.

"We are urging people to take all precautions. Have food and water on hand. Batteries for a radio and flashlights. Gas up vehicles. Be prepared for possible power outages."

With trembling fingers, Camilla clicked off the television and called her sister. "Branna, I'm coming home."

"I know."

"No, I mean, I'm not stopping tonight. I'm driving straight through. I'll nap when I get tired, but I'll be home before the storm hits, wherever it's going."

"Just be safe," Branna cautioned. "Falling asleep at the wheel can be worse than riding out a hurricane. I need you home in one piece. Healthy and happy."

After ending the call, Camilla tossed her bag and purse in the car and headed south. If she pumped enough caffeine into her system, power napped for twenty minutes at a time, she might, fingers crossed, crawl into her bed during the wee hours of Saturday morning.

The wide-open Kansas terrain with gentle swells for hills gave way to flat, broad scenery of Oklahoma. She imagined Haley galloping across the vista at full speed. In Tulsa, she stopped for gas. The city on a river appealed to her; she might like to visit again. She only caught a short span of scenery in Texas. Crossing into Louisiana, she waved and yelled, "It's great to be home," and blew the car's horn in celebration. At the Welcome Center, she stopped for a short break and a nap. First, she emailed her sister.

Just entered LA. Stopping for a break. Any news?

Butterflies posing as ballerinas danced a ballet in her stomach. Excitement bubbled up into her chest, filling her with joy. Smiling wide, she entered the Welcome Center.

"Hey, there. Hope you're having a good day," she said to each person she passed. A woman approached her and asked for directions to a restaurant in Shreveport. "Sorry, ma'am. I don't know. Let's go to the information center."

"You don't work here?"

"No, ma'am, but I'm a native, and I'm always happy to help out."

She made a quick trip to the facilities, then headed back to her car, sipping co-cola and checking to see if her feet actually touched the ground. Or did she glide on giddiness at being so close to home?

After leaning the driver's seat back, she pulled her pillow from the top of the pile of things in the back seat, punched it twice, then snuggled in to catch forty winks.

Her eyes closed. The temperature in the car began to rise. She cracked the windows for cross ventilation hoping mosquitos were on vacation.

The ding from her cell phone woke her. She checked it. The nap had been close to four minutes. Branna's email read:

Change of plans. Don't come home. Go to Memphis instead.

"What the hell?"

WHY!?! She shot back her reply.

Hurricane Katrina.

Hurricane? Camilla punched the message into her phone. *Rude of her to try to run me off. Some sort diva, is she? Since when do we abandon Fleur de Lis?*

When it's a cat three storm and the size of Texas. I'm responsible for everyone's safety. I'm evacuating the Old Aunts.

Frustrated by the snippets of information, Camilla selected her sister's cell phone number. "Branna," she said when her sister answered, "what's going on?"

"The storm is huge. Growing faster. Feeder bands are dumping water by the bucket loads. Dutreys are going west from New Orleans. The boys are still in Florida. The rest of the family is going north to Memphis. Meet us there."

Camilla paused for only a second. "Sure. I'll meet you there. Bye."

She ended the call before Branna could ask any questions. She hadn't exactly spoken a lie. She would go to Memphis, but not before setting eyes on Fleur de Lis. If the incoming storm forced the family to flee, it had to be significant in size and wind speed…Branna had said the size of Texas. Surely that detail was the product of Branna's overdeveloped sense of responsibility and an extreme exaggeration.

Pushing south, Camilla focused on the road. Gripping the steering wheel tighter, as though somehow it would make the car reach Fleur de Lis faster, Camilla barely noticed the landscape as tracts of pine trees grew thicker.

Drops of rain hit the windshield. She ignored them, allowing them to dry in the wind. She refused to turn on windshield wipers until a downpour obstructed her vision. An irrational response, but glued with her resolve, it had to keep the storm away. At least until she could set foot on Fleur de Lis land again.

Her cell phoned dinged. She ignored it.

It dinged again. Still she ignored it, then sat up straighter in the seat and gripped the steering wheel in the ten-two position. The radio, cranked loud enough, would drown out any further contact from the world. No amount of cajoling from her sister would make her deviate from her plan. Not even some bitch of a storm named Katrina.

Ding.

Ding.

Ding.

Ding.

"Ding it to hell! What is it?" Camilla reached for her cellphone. Emails from Haley, not Branna, hit one after another.

Are you okay?

Where are you?

I'm worried.

I'll cuss if you don't answer.

Camilla checked the gas gauge. It registered almost empty. The car wouldn't run on fumes. She caught sight of a sign for the approaching exit, one with multiple pit-stop opportunities and the break she needed to respond to Haley.

After filling the tank, Camilla headed inside to the ladies' room, and then to grab orange juice and several bottles of water. She perused the snack aisle. Clapping like a little girl, she grabbed up several bags of Zapp's potato chips to munch along the way.

Climbing back into her car with junk food and two sausage and egg biscuits from the diner next to the gas station, she opened a bottle of orange juice, gulping down half. Taking a bite of a biscuit, she punched speed dial for Haley.

"Took you long enough," Haley snapped. "I was worried."

Camilla chuckled. "Now you know what it feels like to be a parent."

"Yeah, anyway, where are you? When will you be reaching Fleur de Lis? What about the storm? Is it safe to go home?"

"Slow down, Boo." Camilla took another small bite of food. She chewed, then replied, "I don't care what the weather is. I'm going home. If the storm is as kick-ass as they say, depending on where it actually makes landfall, this might be my only chance. I have a box with some special mementos I need to retrieve."

"Nothing could be so important as your life," Haley cried.

"Look, Haley, you have to trust me on this. I'm going home. I'll get out before the storm hits."

"But the storm is moving so slow. It's ginormous! Roads will be flooded."

"Look, Mom," Camilla teased, "I promise, I'll be safe. I'm driving through the night to get there ahead of the storm."

"You have to call me before you get there. Like…like when you get to Hammond."

"What do you know about Hammond?"

"Duh! I can read a map. I've been tracing your route. Just in case something happens. I have to know where to find you."

The wail in Haley's voice caused a coil of pressure in Camilla's gut. Who knew the teen had such mothering instincts? "I appreciate your concern. I'll call you when I'm passing Hammond. That will put me about an hour out."

"Not if traffic is bad because people are evacuating."

"Okay. Okay." Haley's worry plucked a cord of concern. "I'll be cautious. Now, I have to get going. I will catnap at rest stops. My plan is to be at the house tomorrow at nine a.m. Get what I need. Then, join my family in Memphis."

She ended the call with Haley and checked the time. If no problems crept up, she could keep her schedule on track.

"Lord," she said looking heaven bound. "Help me make it."

But as she looked toward the darkening sky and raindrops began to fall, doubt filled her mind and fluttered her heart with trepidation. Heading into a category three hurricane that still had time to ramp up in speed and size could be foolish. Deadly even. Fast moving floodwaters could float her car off the road and into a ditch where she'd become alligator bait.

At least with Haley tracking her progress, if disaster struck, someone would find her…hopefully.

Chapter 24

Near midnight, Camilla pulled into a truck stop in Lafayette, Louisiana. Rubbing her cheeks, she groaned with fatigue. She scrunched her shoulders and released them. But that did little to coax the ache and knots in her muscles into releasing.

"I need a massage," she grumbled and headed into the travel center just to hear the sound of a human voice and to make sure her legs still worked.

She crossed a parking lot with big rigs lined up one after another. Inside the store, only a few people mingled in the aisles. Scanning for signs, she sought one for the ladies' room. An arrow pointed to a hallway. Purposefully placing one foot in front of the other, she plodded zombie-like in that direction. Just before the opening to the hallway, near the cashier station for the truckers, a large television blared with news.

New Orleans is in danger. In 2001, a newspaper predicted a storm of this magnitude would produce a disaster. The prognostication is of 250,000 people stranded and deaths for one-in-ten from drowning. Katrina is a category three hurricane with 115 miles per hour winds and south-southeast of the mouth of the Mississippi River.

If the storm reaches a cat five, most of the area will be uninhabitable for weeks. Expect homes to have roof and wall failures. Destruction of wood-framed, low-rise apartments is certain. Even concrete block structures will sustain significant damage. High-rise office buildings may collapse. Expect widespread flying debris. Light vehicles are at risk. Pets and livestock exposed to forces of these winds will face death. Trees will be uprooted. Expect power outages for weeks. Frequent gusts at or above hurricane-force winds will be certain over the next twelve to twenty-four hours.

Weak-kneed, Camilla slumped against the wall. Katrina would be a killer. Devastation, the likes of which hadn't been seen on the Gulf Coast since Hurricane Camille struck ten years before she was born People still reminisced about that disaster. Branna had the right idea to move everyone out of Fleur de Lis, especially the Old Aunts. What treasures did the family save? Though the house stood high above the ground, the chances of the roof holding were slim. Everything inside would be drenched and ruined, including antiques their family treasured for six generations or more.

The white lie to her sister weighed heavy on her mind. She'd told the same one to her parents when they called insisting she join the family in Memphis, out of the direct line of the storm. She would, but only after first setting eyes on Fleur de Lis. The place was family. And now a bitch of a storm might beat the house until it gave up. Hopefully, the bones would remain standing. After which, the family could rebuild.

A few minutes later, back in her car, she levered the seat back as far as it would go. Grabbing her pillow, she fluffed it. Sleep. It would keep her mentally sharp. She needed a clear head to navigate the traffic and

Katrina. In the morning. When it was day. No matter how much the storm blacked out the sun.

****

Camilla's heart pounded. Her clammy hands gripped the steering wheel as she rounded the corner onto Loblolly Lane. Small waves of nausea rolled in her stomach. How had she ever left this place? Racing down the long drive, she hit the gas and the speedometer reached eighty. She slammed on her brakes, just missing the fountain in the circle driveway. No one was there to hear the screech of her tires.

Jumping out of the car, she ran up the front steps. Feeder bands of the storm tortured everything in its wake. Tears mixed with rain and washed her face. Fleur de Lis rose from the landscape like a large treasure chest brimming with memories. Scanning the house, she tried to memorize every detail. She whispered, "You're anchored in the bedrock of all our lives. Hold strong." Then she wiped wetness away from her face.

Home. She was finally home.

Fleur de Lis was coded in her DNA. She would do anything to save her. She lifted her open arms as though cradling the house. Her chest ached as though a load of bricks rested there. The storm would offer no mercy. Not for the land, the home, or her. An errant thought of leaving was snuffed out by solid determination. Branna might abandon their home. Biloxi, too, but she refused. Now that she had arrived, she had to stay.

A muffled cry reached her ears.

"Camilla!"

Someone yelled her name? She turned. Jared appeared from around the corner of the house wearing a dark blue windbreaker as he ran toward her, his hair soaked. “I thought you’d never get here.”

“Jared?” Couldn’t be.

“We can’t stay!” he shouted over the winds and pelting rain. “Come with me.”

“Jared?” She blinked. Exhaustion didn’t cause hallucinations, did it?

He ran up the steps and scooped her up into a bear hug. “I was worried about you.” When he set her down, his warm lips found hers. Urgently, she kissed him, wrapping her arms around his neck. No delusion ever warmed her like this one. She raked her fingers through his wet hair. His strong hands cupped her jaw and drew her in for another soul-searing kiss.

“How did you find me?” she whispered and kissed him again.

“One guess.”

“Haley?”

Jared smiled. For a brief moment, the world stood still. Captivated, she clung to him. He’d come for her. It could only mean one thing. He cared. Tremors of happiness vibrated through her body,

“We have to go,” he said, holding tight to her hand when he stepped back.

“What?” She blinked, then reached for his other hand for reassurance he was real, not a delusion from lack of sleep. Heat met her hand. Solid strength radiated to through her sending shivers zipping through her veins.

“It’s not safe.”

“No.” She shook her head.

“Let’s go.”

“I can’t. Everyone has abandoned her”—she pointed to the house—“I can’t leave her. I just got here.

Someone has to stay. I'll show them."

"Them?"

"My family. I'm not a frivolous piece of fluff. Not the party girl. I've changed. I'll make them proud."

Jared's palm cradled her cheek. The tenderness of his gesture softened all resistance. The heat of his hand empowered her will. If he could see good in her, then maybe her family could, too.

"If you don't leave, you might make them grievingly sad."

"I haven't seen my home in nearly two years. I won't go." She pulled away and sat on the porch with her back against the double front doors.

He reached for her, but when she balked, he scooped her up into his arms. "Woman, you don't get any choice in this matter." He held her tighter when she began to flail her arms and legs.

"Wait!" She pushed against him. He staggered and set her down.

"There's something I need," she shouted over the whipping wind and the thunderous downpour. "Come on."

Pulling a key from her pocket, she opened the lock to the front door. It barely moved. She shoved harder. Rocking chairs that used to sit on the front porch blocked the doorway. Reaching around the door, she grabbed a chair and slid it away, enough to gain entry.

"One sec." Camilla raced upstairs dripping water as she climbed. The Old Aunts would have a fit and Greta would skin her alive, but only if they knew.

Reaching her room, she flung the door open and stopped. Everything remained exactly as she'd left it. A time capsule of her life down to the quilt at the foot of the bed and framed photos of family members.

"Camilla, let's go," Jared shouted.

She quickly crossed the room to the armoire. Carefully opening the antique, she grabbed a box with her diaries, cards she'd saved from family members, and the precious gift of a pearl necklace nestled in a velvet box handed down from her great-great grandmother. They meant more to her in that moment than ever before in her life. Regret and anguish wrapped her heart. She had no way to protect Fleur de Lis from whatever possible doom Hurricane Katrina brought.

She raced to the bathroom, grabbed some towels, then reached the top of the stairs. Below, Jared paced. His mouth set in a firm frown. He checked his watch.

"I'm here," she called out, running down the steps.

An expression of relief washed over Jared's face. He reached for the box she carried before she made it to the bottom step.

"Do you need anything from your car? We're taking my Jeep."

"I've got two bags."

"I'll bring the Jeep from around back," Jared said.

"Go this way." She led him through the house to the kitchen, the closest exit for him to reach his vehicle. "I'll meet you around front," she told him as she unlocked the back door.

A few minutes later, they loaded her bags into his Jeep.

"My family is in Memphis," she said climbing into the passenger's front seat. She shoved a towel in his direction after he removed his wet coat. "What a way to baptize a new vehicle." She rubbed the towel over herself to capture the dripping water.

"That's the least of my problems." Jared made the turn around the fountain, the centerpiece of the front drive, and raced down the long driveway to the main road. "We're going to Jackson."

"No. Memphis. My family's waiting there."

"Let's head to Jackson first. My grandparents are staying with friends. We'll see how the storm is moving. I promise, you'll see your family."

Camilla climbed into the backseat. "I've got to get out of these wet clothes. Then I'm going to sleep."

"Do you need to call your family?"

"Not now. They know I'm heading their way." She opened her duffel bag and pulled out clothes. "Keep your eyes on the road," she insisted as she began to strip wet clothes from her body.

Finally changed, she climbed back into the front seat and buckled herself in place. The rain had stopped, though the sky remained dark. The lull of the Jeep and soft music settled her nerves a bit. "I've got to sleep," she whispered, closing her eyes.

As she drifted off, Jared slid his hand to her and laced his fingers with hers. "Sleep. I'll take care of you."

A while later, Camilla woke when the Jeep stopped. The sky remained overcast, however, no rain or thunder or lightning. "Where are we?"

Jared had parked in the driveway of a house. She took in the white Creole cottage with black shutters and floor-to-ceiling windows. Several rocking chairs adorned a wide front porch supported by four pillars. A homey and welcoming place. A tall woman, smartly dressed with silver hair, exited the front door and walked quickly toward them.

“Jared!” she said. “I was so worried.”

“Grandmother!” Jared exited the Jeep. He rounded the front of the car and hugged the woman. She kissed his cheek, then wiped lipstick away. Stepping close to the passenger’s door, he opened it. “Grandmother, this is Camilla Lind.”

Camilla pushed her damp hair behind her ears and swung her legs around to get out. “Hi,” she said hesitantly. Her mother would be appalled that she was meeting Jared’s family looking like a drowned scarecrow. Only one chance to make a first impression, her grandmother always said.

“I apologize for my appearance.” Camilla accepted a hug from the woman.

“Nonsense. You’re safe. That’s all we care about. Let’s go inside and get you something to eat. We’re all watching the weather, and the exploits happening in New Orleans.”

“Camilla, this is my Grandmother Dupuis.”

“Thank you for allowing me to take refuge with your family.”

“Come this way.” Mrs. Dupuis motioned, then turned and led the way. “The Harrisons are putting us all up.”

Camilla narrowed her eyes at Jared. “Dupuis. As in from New Orleans. The accent gives her away. No wonder you know about pralines.”

After meeting the hosts, other friends, and family members, then having a bite to eat to satisfy Mrs. Harrison, Camilla excused herself and took a seat in one of the rocking chairs on the front porch. She called her mother’s cell phone.

"Camilla, I've been waiting to hear from you." Her mother's voice rang out strong and clear, though tinged with concern and worry. Momma was so close, closer than she'd been in almost two years. Only mere miles separated them, rather than hundreds.

"Momma, I'm nearby, in Jackson, Mississippi, with a friend."

"Oh? I didn't know you had anyone with you."

"Well, I'm actually with him. At the house of some of their family friends."

"Him?"

"Jared Richardson."

"I see." She rolled her eyes at her mother's knowing tone. "And when will we be seeing you and this Mr. Richardson?"

"Tomorrow. Jared said he would bring me to Memphis."

"I could have your father come and get you. I don't know if I can wait till tomorrow to see you knowing you're so close and yet still so far."

"Aww, Momma…" Camilla's eyes swam with tears. She pinched the bridge of her nose to stop from crying. With the bottom of the t-shirt, she wiped her eyes. "But I want everyone to meet Jared…"

"I see."

"Yes, he's special." There was no sense in delaying the announcement.

"Then, we'll be waiting tomorrow. Can you make it for brunch?"

"If we can't, I'll call you back. Otherwise, yes. What hotel?"

"The Peabody, of course."

"Yes." Camilla chuckled. "Of course."

As she ended the call with her mother, Jared opened the front door. “If you’d like to shower, I’ll show you the way to your room. Dinner will be at six. I think more people will be arriving.”

“I wouldn’t doubt it.” Camilla sighed. “A hurricane is just another reason for a party.”

****

A hot shower eased the tension in Camilla’s shoulders. She toweled dry and slipped into a thick, white terry robe her hostess had provided. When she entered the bedroom, on the floor by the dresser, her two bags waited. Jared must have brought them inside for her. She folded the towel and laid it over the pillow on the bed, then reclined. A short power nap would help her stay vigilant through the night watching the path of the hurricane while praying it would diminish before making landfall.

Closing her eyes, she slept.

A warm hand stroked her leg and brought her partially awake. She shivered and snuggled against the warmth behind her. When warmth traced a line from her throat to her stomach, her eyes popped open.

“Hey there, sleepyhead,” Jared whispered.

“Are you supposed to be in here with me?” she asked, turning around to face him. The last thing she wanted was to offend her gracious hostess.

“No worries. The house is buzzing with people. The hurricane party has commenced, no different from a sporting event. No one will miss us.”

“If you’re sure…”

Jared leaned in and captured her lips. She stretched out, molding her body next to his, and wrapping her arms around his neck. He kissed her deeply. She nipped at his bottom lip.

"Camilla," Jared whispered. "I have a confession."

"I don't want to hear any bad news."

"Well, I'm hoping you might think this is good."

She sat up and clutched a pillow to her. Depending on what he had to say, she'd use it to snuff out her tears or hit him.

"I've been to Fleur de Lis before," Jared said, sitting up and facing her.

Her eyes widened. "When?" She didn't believe him.

"My grandfather's company created the architectural design for the remodel, and I worked on the crew that did the work. A hot-as-hell summer job. My grandparents do live in New Orleans. I've met your mother Macy."

"W-w-what?" she stuttered.

"I've met—"

"I heard you. Why didn't you tell me this before?"

"Well, it took me a while. I didn't put it together until our picnic. Afterward, you were busy trying to avoid me. There's more.

"You know my sister, too?"

Jared shook his head. "Never met her. No, I planned to move down here before I met you. I plan to split my time between here and Wyoming, being there only when Ryan needs me to manage things, like when he and Nicole take a vacation."

"And you never thought those to be important facts to share?" Her surprise grew to irritation.

"I was waiting for that dinner…anyway, I want you to forgive me. I'm sorry about the way I acted when you trusted me enough to share the truth about your past. If you forgive me, kiss me."

First, she teased his lips with her tongue, then pressed hers against his. Firm and warm. Heaven.

"Camilla, I love you." His gaze softened. The corners of his mouth lifted to a sweet smile.

The look of love.

Surprise struck her like a brick, shattering the glass wall protecting her heart. Her breath caught in her throat. Hope flowed like running water.

He loves me. Truly loves me.

She tossed the pillow aside and leaned forward to press her lips against his again. Excitement bloomed in her chest and heat radiated over her body. Love matched no other wonderful feeling. The man who held her love had offered his.

"I think we're meant to be," Jared said.

If Jared lived in New Orleans, then they stood a chance at a future.

"Everyone deserves second chances," he said. "We have to move it along. Keep this relationship going forward. Please tell me how you feel, Camilla."

"I love you, too, Jared Richardson," she said, then snuggled closer.

They'd weathered their own storm.

The one battering the landscape might bring devastation, however, they would ride the storm and forge a bond protecting them from any blows life sent their way. Love was a solid bond.

Epilogue

Around her, people hurried inside to catch their flights. Overhead the roar of a plane distracted Camilla. She looked up into a blue sky. Hard to imagine, only days ago, darkness, rain, wind, and destruction hit the Gulf coast given the sunshine now. Camilla glanced in the direction of Jared and her father deep in a private conversation. Whatever they discussed, she imagined it included plans for repairs to Fleur de Lis, yet their intense expressions worried her a bit. Once on the plane, she'd make Jared tell her what they were saying.

"I hate that you're leaving so soon," Macy, Camilla's mother said, hugging her once again.

"Momma"—Camilla took her mother's hand—"it's only for a few days. We'll be back after Ryan and Nicole's wedding. We'll pitch in and help with the repairs to Fleur de Lis when we return. Branna and Biloxi will have it under control until then."

"Roof half gone. Most of the windows broken. Drapes ruined. Furniture damaged. The Old Aunts have never lived anyplace else in their life. It breaks my heart to watch them fret in a hotel room in Memphis…"

"You're doing what's best for them."

"I'm looking for an independent living community to get them out of the hotel after you catch your flight."

"Make them focus on the weddings," Camilla encouraged.

"I can't understand why Branna insists on getting married so soon. Two weeks. I'm not pleased your sister won't wait until she can be married inside Fleur de Lis. It could be the wedding of the decade."

Camilla grinned. "It will still be the wedding of the decade. Branna always does the right thing."

Branna's pregnancy remained a secret, one her sister would have to announce…or not, but she would never tell. Her sister trusted her. With the rebuilding of Fleur de Lis, they would rebuild their relationship, too.

"Momma, white tents decorated with lights and dripping with flowers. Everyone's spirits will soar. We'll be celebrating the joining of Branna and James…and also celebrating Fleur de Lis' survival, just as all of us did. Damaged, but repairable. Time will heal it all."

Her mother's nod was filled with resignation.

As Jared and her father walked toward her and her mother, Camilla's gaze locked on Jared's. His eyes danced with mischief.

"We're off, Mrs. Lind. I promise to bring her back in a few days. I appreciate your understanding about my only brother getting married," Jared said, shaking Macy's hand. He kissed the air beside her cheek.

Camilla kissed her mother's cheek first, then her father. He grabbed her into a bear hug. "See you soon."

"Weddings don't bring out the best in me," Camilla said, taking a step back from her parents. Their forlorn expressions made her want to stay, but the need to be with Jared was greater.

Jared grasped her hand, hooked their arms together, and led her through the automatic opening doors of the airport terminal.

The zing of heated attraction remained the same as their first encounter in Jackson, Wyoming.

As though hypnotized, she followed his lead.

He had her on an imaginary tether.

And soon it would return them to Fleur de Lis.

A word about the author...

Award-winning author Linda Joyce has deep southern roots. In New Orleans, you'll find several cemeteries with graves bearing the names of her ancestors. She's lived coast to coast in the United States and in Japan. Now she lives in Atlanta with her husband and three dogs: Beau, Jack, and Reni.

Linda loves boiled peanuts, sushi, and grits. She and her husband share a passion for college football. She's also a foodie, music fan, and traveler.

Linda serves on the board for Southeastern Writers Association. She's a member of Romance Writers of America, Georgia Romance Writers, and Georgia Writers Association.

Linda invites you to join her at:

http://www.linda-joyce.com

https://www.facebook.com/LindaJoyceAuthor

Twitter: @LJWriter

http://www.goodreads.com/author/show/6950241.Linda_Joyce

https://www.pinterest.com/LindaJoyceWorld/

~*~

Other Linda Joyce titles
available from The Wild Rose Press, Inc.:
BAYOU BORN Fleur de Lis Book 1
BAYOU BOUND Fleur de Lis Book 2

~*~

Book four of the Fleur de Lis series, *BAYOU BRIDES*, will be coming soon!